Meditation
on
Space-Time
A Novel

LEONARD SEET

Excelsior Publishing

Published in the United States by Excelsior Publishing

ISBN-10: 0-967-49372-2
ISBN-13: 978-0-967-49372-5

Seet, Leonard

Meditation on Space-Time / Leonard Seet.

p. cm

1.   Meditation

2.   Space-Time

3.   Leonard Seet

Second Edition

2012946156

CONTENTS

CHAPTER 1

WHEN THE STRANGER STEPPED INTO THE CONFESSIONAL to narrate his crimes, which my vow had forbidden me from disclosing, I was meditating on space-time to recuperate from the ten-hour drive to Gilead, Tennessee.

Dark night the boundary between reality and dream somewhere at a memory's frontier fading near a singularity's ledge surfing upon a probability wave across the space-time fabric through a neutrino sea skirting the edges of black holes searching for dark matter searching for the Higgs Boson. Photon gluon graviton clusters criss-crossing tangling and weaving a unified fabric symmetric space-time hydrogen atoms merging and emerging a helium atom along with neutrinos and photons annihilation and creation interaction and transformation the brightest night the loudest silence the fullest void the darkest knowledge…

"Father, I sinned."

The confessor's rasp stirred me from my meditation, my dream, and I yawned and inhaled the stale air in the confessional. A strip of light slid through the door crack and cut across my left hand as I turned my head and my hair dusted the screen separating me from the stranger. I wiped the sweat from my forehead and shifted to a more comfortable position on the hardwood seat. I stretched my leg and kicked the confessional's wall. The newspaper flew from my knee and rattled toward the floor as the article about genocide in Rwanda flickered between light and shade.

"Father, I sinned."

The sound of sandpaper against steel sounded again beyond the screen. I twisted my body and my elbow knocked against the wall. I squinted but only saw a shadow distorted under the slanting light beyond the partition. Probably an insomniac who couldn't afford to go to the bar.

Two days ago, I was chopping wood in the forest beside the monastery, and had looked forward to enjoying *The Four Seasons* in Boston's Symphony Hall with my friends Camellia and Ichiro. I didn't plan on visiting St. Barnabas Church in Gilead but this stranger, from some hallucination, had foreseen my arrival and booked me for *therapy*.

The penitent knocked twice on the other side of the partition. "Hey, dude, wake up from your wet dream, you're supposed to say 'when was your last confession' or some crap like that. You hear me?" His breath was contaminating the air.

Perhaps I should grunt a mantra. But I was only a monk contemplating the meaning of death, the mystery of alternative universes and other such nonsense. What could I know about confessions? When a man in a Mission Hill soup kitchen confessed to using heroin and stealing his mother's funeral dollars to keep the habit, I listened like a Buddha, not because my wisdom had transcended words and even sounds but because all replies, no matter how concise, how insightful, how articulate, appeared as frivolous as a gilded coffin. In the end, my friend Ichiro bailed me out by impersonating a priest.

Now, this insomniac beyond the partition, from some itch or pang, insisted on harassing a confession-phobic monk, who had evaded the parish, a.k.a. purgatory, by pretending to suffer from attention-deficit disorder. Had I wanted to hear about adultery, thievery, murder, or insider trading, I would've become a bartender or, unable to concoct spirituous potions, a pseudo-Freudian psychotherapist. Even now, twenty-three years later, after having one too many drinks, I would still dream of my former high school classmate Daphne, as she sobbed out her pain in a March evening. Her blue eyes, her blond hair, her smiles fleeing into the mist. In those dreams, unlike this reality, I actually pulled her out of the abyss.

"You should talk to Father Jones." I offered my wisdom. "He'd be glad to hear your confession. Why don't I ask him to come over? I'm sure he's not yet asleep. And even if he is, he'd delay his dreams and hear your confession in his pajamas." Father Jones, the tongue-flapping priest who had begun substituting for this church's parish priest five days ago, would savor this soul's secrets as a thief would Queen Victoria's crown. After delivering this stranger's message but before allowing me to read it, the priest had already complained about not having heard any confessions in a week. He probably envied me for hearing one the first night here. Amid babbles about apple pie recipes, all-meat diets, school shootings and movie-star divorces, his eyes betrayed the lust for confessions—pyramid schemes, clandestine liaisons, corporate double-dealings or plain old government conspiracies. I wouldn't be surprised if at this moment his ear was kissing the other side of the confessional's door and itching for some tale, some yarn, some anecdote of unadulterated sin. I wouldn't be surprised if he was a reformed con man who had sold aphrodisiacs or perpetual motion machines. Or a repentant banker who had bundled junk bonds, sub-prime mortgages and high-risk insurance policies into kosher derivatives. But he better not be taping with a recorder.

"You know, buddy, never confessed before so you can imagine I got lots to say, but of course ain't got much time. So here we go if you don't mind. Well, of course, even if you do, what can you do about it? To start with something simple, I've embezzled money. Oh, not from a bank or a high-tech company, no sir. That'd be dull and cliched as heck, not worth your time. Nope, I stole from a church and a nice one at that too. Well, ain't nothing new, but the amount is something, you know?"

"You should return the money."

"Hey, what's this bullshit? You're supposed to say 'I absolve you in the name of the Father, and of the Son, and of the Holy Spirit' or some crap like that. If I wanted to return the money, what the hell am I doing here confessing? Right? What kind of a priest are you anyway? Don't you know your only job's to listen and to absolve sins? What else are you good for? Anyway, why'd I return the money? Ha, ha, we're not talking about chicken feed, if you know what I mean. You have any stinking idea how much I took? Take a stupid guess. Oh forget it, with your petty allowances, you'd never seen that much money in your life. What'd priests know about money anyway? Hell, man, I bought a mansion with a marble hall, a wine cellar, an outdoor pool and complete automation, you know, with the latest hi-tech gizmos. I also bought a Lamborghini Gallardo even though I ain't into racing. But hey, makes me look macho. Well, you know, helps to pick up chicks, I mean nice ones. Hell, I enjoyed every penny of it, as I'm sure you'd if you got the money. Not that you'll ever see so much money, you poor pitiful man. But you probably understand indulgence, right?"

"If you're trying to make me jealous, you've failed. Come, face me and we'll talk, man to man. I want to know why you chose me for your hide-and-seek." I peeked through the screen but the shadow doubled over with laughter and began choking before calming down.

"Father, I sinned. I got two mistresses and enjoy every minute with them. I made love to a minor—"

I opened the confessional's half-hinged door and slipped out of the seat. I stepped on an insect and tiptoed into the hallway, where the statuettes of Peter, Paul and John guarded the Creation fresco in which a chip on the wall removed the serpent's head. I wanted to open the confessional's other door, mark out the fangs and two-prong tongue and squeeze the serpent-neck.

A door slammed. Footsteps echoed throughout the sanctuary. I scared away a rat and dashed down the hallway, past frescos of the Passover, the Passion, the Resurrection, and the Pentecost. I stepped into the sanctuary, where on the left wall a crucified-Jesus statuette stared down at the altar. I bypassed the altar and skipped down the marble steps. I sprinted down the aisle between the pews, while beyond the benches, under candlelight, the mosaic windows flaunted Crucifix-ion, Resurrection, and Ascension scenes. Claw-like shadows darkened the multicolored windowpanes to overlay a second scene and cast phantoms onto the aisle and pews.

A draft wafted through the aisle. A screech, a thump and several clangs echoed through the sanctuary.

"Damn it," Father Jones said. "Someone poked your eyes out, you clumsy fool? Get a new pair of eyes, man. Don't you know it's against the law to walk without eyes? Ouch, oh my poor and innocent back."

When I reached the entrance, Father Jones was moaning on the floor beside a golden chalice while, near the door, holy water dripped from the baptized donation box. The priest rubbed his back and took out a flask of whiskey. He gulped down a mouthful and winked as if a mosquito had stung his eyelid. "Didn't like your advice, did he? Well, don't worry, the important thing is you heard his story. Oh, by the way, Father Lawrence, just between you and me, one priest to another, was it interesting? Visiting a prostitute? Cheating the IRS? Stealing intellec-tual property? Oh, come on, you can tell me."

I helped Father Jones get up and sidestepped his whiskey breath. I ran through the candlelit foyer past the Madonna's icons and exited the main entrance. The humid night air slammed into my face while a fly landed on the back of my hand. I flung it away, stepped out of the archway, and skipped down the steps into the graveyard. No footsteps, no shadows, only a cow cawing on a branch above the headstone.

I took out the flashlight and highlighted several headstones. The raven shrieked and flew into the fog. I stepped onto the earth searching for life among the dead, but only found faded letters among the epitaphs.

The most generous person… Worked the hardest in the office… An inspiration for others… A pious man… Beloved son… Born April 1, 1979… September 2, 2007…

I felt I had stepped into the wrong city and the wrong dream. If I hadn't heard the confession, I would've been more peaceful, ignorant of theft, fraud and statutory rape. Blessed be the ignorant.

Past the headstones, a fence stood at the ledge. Beyond the fence, below the hill, Gilead's houses slumbered in the evening, while the town hall's Tower of Babel pierced heavenward through the fog.

I came to Gilead only wishing to find Camellia, to know that she was safe, that she was well. I wanted her to break free from her nameless lover's pull but would rather she orbit around the married man than enter the black hole of her father Donald Larsen, that fugitive on the run from one Ponzi scheme to another. Under her father, Camellia had tasted enough pain and shouldn't have to help him escape to Mexico or some Caribbean island, where on his beachfront mansion's porch he would enjoy coladas and massages while his victims must dine in soup kitchens.

In the distance, above Memphis, neon lights against the fog hinted at the bankruptcies, the foreclosures, the layoffs, and the Pyramid schemes powering the land. But in front of me, a piece of paper taped to a cracked headstone was fluttering in the wind as if thumbing its nose at the heavenly shimmer. I stepped over the decomposing rat and scattered the flies. I grabbed the note, on which a smiley face was drawn above Camellia's name.

While I glanced beyond the graveyard and pondered on the connection between the *penitent* and Camilla, Father Jones called from the entrance, "Someone has left you this memory stick."

CHAPTER 2

I COULDN'T SLEEP DURING THE FIRST NIGHT at my friend Jim Whit-field's mansion, his odor having awakened high school memories. Last night, after returning from St. Barnabas Church, I phoned Camellia's mom, Mrs. Larsen, whom I had met for the first time yesterday. For two hours I rehashed the same dozen consolations, not knowing where to find her daughter or her husband, not knowing whether their disappearances were related. Between sobs, she repeated her desire to apologize to her husband Donald for a transgression, which praise to God she didn't divulge to this confession-phobic monk.

After the phone call, I examined the password-protected memory stick Father Jones had given me before I left the church. He had found it three days ago in the donation box, with an anonymous note addressing me and hinting the files might explain Jim's disappearance, which had coincided with that of Donald Larsen after the FBI had exposed the Ponzi scheme. I was surprised Jim had also disappeared but was glad to avoid his face, even if just for a few days. When I requested a list of the passwords he had tried so I could save time, Father Jones just snickered and patted me on the shoulder.

Early next morning, I entered Jim's bedroom and, suspecting he had left the files, paced from bed to desk to shelf to window searching for the password. Outside, a fog had blanketed the lawn and was hiding the heads of three marble statues guarding the garden. On the wall hung a debate team award from Jim's high school junior year. On the desk the best salesman of the year award next to a book: *Ten Easy Steps to Master Persuasion.* On the bookshelf: *The Super Salesman*, *Effective Communication in a Nutshell*, *Negotiate to Win, Win & Win Again*. I entered "salesman," "win-win," "winner" and "money" but none unlocked the memory stick. I searched through the books only to find dust and a few naked women's pictures.

While flipping through Jim's NIV Bible, I discovered around 1 Corinthian Chapter 13, an old photo of Charlotte, my best friend in high school. She was about seventeen at that time, about the time Jim had asked me to help arrange a date with her. Her simple smile and warm gaze, which had comforted me, stirred ripples in my bosom.

***

After finding out about my calling, she had divulged her love for me. She shed tears on my shoulder and at that moment time stood still as if waiting for our pain to seep into the marrow or perhaps for me to reconsider my choice. I had contemplated forsaking my vocation but we agreed that choice would stifle my journey and our love, which we treasured more than any smile, any embrace or any kiss. But she suffered and I felt it. She would be jealous as when I told her about helping my classmate Daphne. More than once, I would stand on the cliff facing Great Falls and ponder: am I selfish to maintain my journey, to realize my vocation? But had I forsaken it, I would've lost my bearing and drifted among strangers and through alien soils even while she accompanied me. Though the tension had threatened to tear us apart, we continued to be best friends. We would confide secrets, desires and aspiration to each other, not having to guard against the dagger that one day would thrust through my back into my heart. And Jim Whitfield's pursuing her, like billows refusing to retreat even after confronting the levee, helped secure our bond, as we mimicked two tribal leaders who joined forces against a Genghis Khan.

Then came Charlotte's letter, a dynamite stick severing our bond and shoving us one to the North Pole and the other to the South. To this day, I didn't know why she had written the letter and must speculate among betrayal's ashes. Though, despite the slander, I entered the monastery, the letter had shredded our friendship and left a scar to remind me of lost love in this desert we called earth.

***

Perhaps Jim's files, drenched in his life's daily laundries and possibly nightly scum, could provide clues to Donald's and Camellia's whereabouts. Through ignorance, my friend might've introduced the Ponzi schemer to the congregation and exhorted most, if not all, members to dump their savings into the con. At least, those files might clarify Jim's disappearance.

While putting the NIV Bible back on the shelf, I discovered another picture, of a young rosy-cheeked girl in a morning-glory-blue dress, at Chapter 1 of Song of Songs. The childlike face against the rustic lake reflected a joy unadulterated by greed or lust. I entered "apple-of-my-eyes" and "lily-of-the-valley" but they also failed to access the files. After trying several other passwords, including "Camellia," without success, I decided to take a break and examine the handwriting of the graveyard note. As I was pondering on the penitent's role in Camellia's disappearance, the maid informed me a man was asking for me in the living room.

CHAPTER 3

Before leaving Boston, I had sent an email to my friend Ichiro, telling him I would be going to Gilead to search for Camilla. I left Jim's address, knowing he would come to look for her.

After the maid had left the room, I put on my habit while the tune of "Amazing Grace" drifted out of the wall speakers. I walked down the winding marble staircase to greet Ichiro, who was sitting cross-legged in the velvet armchair I had enjoyed earlier in the morning. Under Jim's pumpkin-headed portraits, which decorated the living room walls, Ichiro's cheek, as if sculptured by Michelangelo's hands, presented a crease from cheekbone to chin.

"Where is Camellia?" Ichiro got up from the armchair and smoothed his trouser legs. He walked around the coffee table and faced me with hands behind his back.

"Are you alright?" I could feel the damp seeping through the front door as I studied the shadow under Ichiro's chin. He had aged since I last saw him.

When I first met Ichiro more than two years ago at the lecture *Zen and the Cloud of Unknowing* in Harvard University, death had smeared a cloud of resignation in his eyes and painted a scar across his cheek. After the lecture, he walked up to the speaker and asked him how to attain satori or enter the cloud of unknowing without abandoning a beloved's memories. Now, next to Jim's statue, its arms raised as if parting the Red Sea, I confronted the familiar cloud but a less jagged scar, a resignation close to detachment and a suffering almost serene.

"Is she alright?" With his hand, he combed aside the hair covering his right eye.

"Do you love her?"

"I love Sonya."

"One day, you would have to let go of Sonya."

"Maybe I don't want to lose my eyesight, my hearing, my mobility, my reasoning." He paced to the bay window and glanced at the fog in the garden. "Maybe I don't have a choice."

"But you must choose whether you have a choice or not." I walked to the mantel and from the vase pulled out a withered rose. I walked up to him and showed him the flower but he only stared beyond the fog as if searching for a rainbow among the gray landscape.

After his fiancée Sonya had died on that Christmas Eve, Ichiro drank sake for one week to numb the pain in his brain, his heart, and his abdomen. But the stupor only delayed his suffering until New Year's Eve when firework showered the globe and an electronic apple descended upon Times Square where millions sing, dance, hug and kiss to usher in another four seasons, another twelve months, another three-hundred sixty-five days. On the snowy ledges of Mount Lafayette, under the starlight, he had contemplated seppuku, a determined lunge against chaos, random events and stochastic processes, to join Sonya in eternal glory. Her death seemed to have refuted her aspiration to join Doctors Without Borders and sneered at their love, which had blossomed in spite of sand and gust.

But he had told me he wasn't a coward and that he still had some unfinished business. "For her sake, I must finish it. Anyway, I would like to see the cherry blossoms in Washington at least once more."

He didn't divulged the unfinished business but showed me his symphony in A minor, The Sonya Symphony, where in the second movement a lone flute moans a melody more desolate than that in Dvorak's Symphony No 9 and the accompaniment evokes the steppes of Siberia. I rejoiced in his delaying the lethal thrust and, though believed no heart should infect another with hope, wanted to vanquish that conviction and preach the gospel according to Lawrence, a gospel of sunshine and beaches. But I also questioned my attachment to life, to its beauty, to its possibilities, to its fulfillment. Perhaps a sign of spiritual immaturity, the inability to contemplate and appreciate the mystery of death. And yet, I couldn't forsake the sacred breath, the temple of God, not only the genius of Leonardo daVinci, the love of Mother Theresa, the vision of Martin Luther King, Jr. and the magnanimity of Nelson Mandela, but life itself, in its nakedness.

"I must find Camellia." Ichiro now grabbed my sleeve and shook my arm. I imitated a puppet and waved my hand in the air while the maid, after entering the living room, frowned and put two cups of tea on the coffee table.

I described Donald Larsen's multi-billion-dollar scam, its collapse and in its wake the trail of tears and blood. "Mr. Walker and Mrs. Chandler—"

"I know, but what do I care about Donald Larsen and his scam? I want to find Camellia before it's too late." He let go of my sleeve and again held his hands behind him. He scrutinized a Ming vase on a side table as if he had discovered the secret behind its floral patterns. "Ah, you don't think... but can it be..."

"Doesn't matter what I think... reality—"

"No, no, it's not possible." He tumbled onto the armchair, grasped his head and panted like a hound sulking after an unsuccessful foxhunt.

"Okay, it's not possible. Now, tell me what's not possible." I rotated Jim's statue, which was beginning to annoy me.

"Random events shouldn't have an evil purpose." Ichiro swigged the Earl Grey and, after finishing the tea, was about to throw the cup into the fireplace when he gazed at the carpet. He studied its twirls as if the interlocking patterns might reveal the key to life's meaning. "I hacked into Donald Larsen's corporate computer system and got the evidence to nab him. I knew about the scam all along."

"Good job. Not bad at all." I raised my right eyebrow and rubbed my chin, but before the handsome face and proud nose, said, "Is that your *unfinished business*?" I didn't know whether, after the *unfinished business*, he had hidden in his knapsack a blade for his *final business*.

"Remember, your memory of Sonya." I reminded him of my insight on that June day when we volunteered in Mission Hill to renovate an elementary school's classrooms. I had said, as long as he lives, Sonya would live in his memory, which would display the most vivid picture of her. So for her sake he should keep that brain pulsating as long as possible. At that instant, while I held a plank for the bookshelf, he missed the nail and almost hammered his thumb. He threw down the hammer and stopped working. Ignoring the beams, nails and pails on the floor, he paced around the scaffold and retraced his path until the sun began to set. Since that day, he had been more cheerful, sometimes even humming a tune from "Winter" in Vivaldi's *The Four Seasons*, and hadn't discussed his *final business*, which continued to haunt me. I sensed suffering had planted pain deep in his heart to sprout a lily, which would fling away the surrounding dirt to display its nobility.

But now, he seemed indifferent to the same words. "If I depart from you," he said, "you'll find someone else to harass you. I am sure."

"But you would grieve Camellia."

"Camellia, Camellia, it's not possible. How could she have anything to do with crooked Larsen?"

"But she is a Larsen." I wanted to ask God permission to curse at greed, selfishness, and causality. "The sin of the father—"

He charged at me but on touching my habit, only adjusted the collar and smoothed out the wrinkles.

"You do love her." I wished he had thrown me across the living room onto the carpet next to the bay window instead of swallowing his frustration and mimicking a stoic.

"I'm sorry. I was only angry with myself. What have I done?" He marched across the living room and through the hallway until he reached the study. "I have to find Camellia before it's too late."

"Don't blame yourself. I'm sure she wouldn't." I followed him into the study, where the scent of cologne attacked my nostrils and Jim beamed at me through his portrait.

"There's not much time." He walked around the desk, lifted the portrait to reveal a safe and examined the keypad.

"You're right. There won't be enough time to pick Jim's safe." I opened the window to diffuse the stench.

"Camellia told me to be careful about Jim Whitfield."

"How does she know Jim? How do you know Jim?"

He turned around and examined the computer keyboard. After about a minute, he ruffled his hair and left the study.

"Before you leave, tell me one thing." I lifted my habit and ran after him. At the foyer, he almost crashed into the vase and knocked the New York cheesecakes from the maid's hands.

"I have colon cancer." He swung open the door and leaped onto the marble pathway.

***

Ever since Sonya had passed away, Ichiro would go to the Tidal Basin every year for the cherry blossom festival—the blossoms, shed in the hour of their greatest beauty, youth and happiness and immortalized, never to wither, never to shrivel and never to crumble into ashes.

This year, before taking his annual pilgrimage, this time with Camellia, he treated me to lunch in Lexington where the colonial buildings reminded me of the Founding Fathers' independent spirits. As we walked along the cobblestone sidewalk, he revealed a deeper appreciation of his suffering, which was chiseling away the scraps. I didn't inquire about his unfinished business that had taunted me during sleepless nights, but rejoiced in a new Ichiro, fashioned by the chisel's precise blows. Perhaps his unfinished business was just to bring down Donald Larsen.

I knew intimacies would distort my views and attachments would stifle my journey. I knew no one could or should replace Sonya. But I had hoped our friendship—Camellia's and mine—would irrigate Ichiro's heart, that desert once a meadow of orioles and swallowtails among rhododendrons and a turquoise stream but now parched through Sonya's death. I knew there's a time to be born and a time to die, a time to plant and a time to uproot, a season for everything under the sun, but I dreamed of a land, of a dawn, of a dimension...

I trotted through the desert of knowledge to search for an oasis, where understanding no longer would stifle learning and where my potential could gush out, only to confront another sea of sand beyond the dunes, another sandstorm beyond the gusts. Yes, I knew, I knew, but... When would I discover the oasis in the grain of sand?

Meanwhile, the melody of a shriveled leaf and the fragrance of a decaying worm attracted death, which had lifted its head to point its two-pronged tongue at the ticking hand and to bequeath the wisdom of life. That I was squandering my hours and days contemplating the foliage on Mt. Lafayette and having cappuccino with Camellia and Ichiro in Harvard Square. Yet, my mind reflected on these moments, precious against eternity.

***

I charged through the front door onto the wet pathway, only to encounter Jim's wife Sylvia under the drizzle. This morning, she was sporting a tight black dress, a crocodile-skin handbag, crimson lips and in-your-face perfume, when she grabbed a low-fat yogurt, kissed her poodle and left for a double funeral. Two casualties of Donald Larsen's Ponzi scheme—a woman who had suffered a heart attack and a man who had committed suicide, both members of the Church of Jim Whitfield. Now, across the front lawn, she was leading a crowd of black suits and dresses, faces from cheerful to blank to solemn. Behind them, the caterers were carrying bottles of champagne and Chardonnay and trays of smoked salmon, ham rolls, chicken nuggets and sirloin strips for the funeral reception.

CHAPTER 4

I WANTED TO RETURN TO MY ROOM and continued to search for the password, but Sylvia insisted I join the reception and enjoy the food and drink. So I took a cup of hot chocolate and watched the others eat ham rolls, drink champagne and chat about Sunday night football, all the while scanning the room for clues to the password.

After avoiding a boy running toward the table, I walked over to the armchair and offered the old lady in black dress a cup of hot chocolate. "I'm sorry for your loss, Mrs. Walker."

"Well, the Lord giveth and the Lord taketh, blessed be the name of the Lord." Mrs. Walker scratched her face and accepted the cup with both hands. "Me and Daisy ain't worry of tomorrow on account of the Lord always taken care of us." She sipped the hot chocolate and with her nose pointed at the young lady next to the Ming vase, whose eyes locked onto the carpet and whose rosy chin rested on her collarbone—the young girl in the morning-glory-blue dress. "Take this here." Mrs. Walker thrust me a tract with the words "Jesus saves" on the cover.

A middle-aged woman in purple silk dress, whose pale skin revealed veins in her arms, wobbled across the living room scraping her heels on the carpet as if trying to remove chewing gum from her sole. She put the pumpkin pie on the table and said, "Poor Mr. Walker, a right pious man, come to church ever Sunday, prayed the longest, and given according to Pastor Jim's requirement. Pastor Jim even given him the

Monthly Pious Award for five months straight last year. Never could of allow…" She took out a tissue and tapped her eyes.

From the kitchen, Sylvia thumped across the living room in her high-heels and grabbed the tract before I could accept it. "He won't need no tract, Mrs. Walker. And don't forget the barbecue here this coming Saturday." She pulled me to the corner near the bay window, glanced around and whispered, "She don't know she lost every penny and got to sell her house too. That's why old Walker jumped ship. Smart of him. But Mrs. Walker will be alright because that slut there sure know how to sell herself for some quick cash." She pointed her lips at Daisy, who without lifting her eyes from the carpet had walked in front of Jim's statue between his arms.

I had a headache and wanted to leave the house for air, for silence, and for solitude. Voices rose and fell, and crashed against my eardrums. Outside the bay window, the drizzle looked refreshing and the sound—I could imagine the sound of rain against the trees, roofs and pavements relieving my headache.

"How you enjoying the party, Father?" Before I could escape from the inferno, a middle-aged man in an Armani suit, eyes beaming, lips twisting and hair greased, slapped me on the back, almost dislodging the hot chocolate from my mouth and my lungs from my chest. "Like the smoked salmon? The Chardonnay? Compliments of Gilead Funeral Homes. Edgar, Edgar Cunningham at your service." From his shirt pocket he pulled out a business card and thrust it into my face. "We provide one stop shopping for all funeral needs, from building the coffin to polishing the tombstone to designing the epitaph to selecting a priest to catering for the reception to selling your house to finding a retirement home. Our subcontractors are first-rate, selected them myself. And right now, we have a Labor Day special, buy our basic buffet service and get the second for half the price. Damn good deal if I do say so myself."

"I don't think I need a funeral yet. Unless you know something I don't." I took the neon business card, his name glistening in silvery Gothic letters.

"Ha, ha, didn't mean to imply… oho, you certainly look healthy and with your vegetarian diet and meditation and without much worries or work… Ahem, Father, I was referring to your work, you know … in your business you must come across, oh shall we say, sad occasions. You must perform a dozen prayers at funerals every month. Why, if you refer your flock to my funeral home, I can give, well why not, five percent discount. And on top of that, I'm feeling generous, I'll donate five percent to your church. What do you say, father? It's a damn good deal." He coughed twice and rubbed his nose.

"I don't preside over funerals. You should speak to Father Jones instead." I could imagine this man and Father Jones vying for talk-time and in the end either parallel-talking or wrestling on the floor and pulling each other's hair. I could also imagine them as two New York subway commuters who wanted the same seat, but pretended not to notice the other, backing into the same empty seat and banging heads.

"Oh, I'll talk to him yet, the good Father. But you have your parish too, I presume. What's a priest without a parish, his own dominion, his own kingdom, his own fiefdom?" He took a ham roll, removed the toothpick, unrolled it, took the ham, thrust it into his mouth and savored the meat while rolling his eyes. "Just doing some quality assurance, making sure these caterers aren't cheating my clients with fake ham."

"I'm a monk, not a parish priest."

"Well, monks die too, right? I know, I know, you believe in eternal life, but of the soul or the spirit or whatever, just not of the body, right? So might as well have a decent burial, nothing wrong with a humble monk being buried in a gilded coffin."

"We bury our dead in a plot of land nearby."

"Well then, you need coffins too, right."

"We make our own coffins, nothing fancy, just the bare essentials."

"Well, well, that's quite entrepreneurial. I'm actually looking to source low-cost coffins. You know, with the economy and all that, people are more and more interested in low-cost coffins, though I believe the deluxe combo is our best offer. And between you and me, mortician to monk, this is imitation salmon, to cut cost you know, but taste damn real if I do say so myself. And the Chardonnay... Well, anyway, I know you monks sell milk and bread, so why not coffins. In fact, the margins are much higher. A single coffin can cover hundreds of gallons of milk and I don't know how many loaves of bread. And to let you in on a secret, this is a great time to sell coffins. Whenever I hear about a Ponzi scheme, or a bank going under, or... What do you say? It's a damn good business proposition. No need to ask your superiors, just do it on the side. I'll take care of the paper work." He rubbed his teeth and wiggled his brows.

"Our Pastor Jim a right godly man, yessir, most godly man but ever seen, is what I am saying. He blessed us lots. I declare you got to help us find him." The lady in purple offered me a piece of homemade pumpkin pie and raised her hand toward the portrait of Jim posing as Napoleon. "He always blessing our barbecues and picnics, teaching us being pious, devout, and reverent, not like them godless lawyers and scientists." She thrust a smoked salmon into her mouth and slurped the champagne.

I took the pie as the headache worsened and imagined mopping the mortician's face with the dessert, but couldn't squeeze enough venom out of my soul's alcoves. I only wanted to find Camellia and leave town. Enough of the stench, the clamor, the phantasms...

"Damn him Canes, can't he throw no football? What the hell that last night anyway? Throwing five yard short, that there sissy. A lousy day don't even say it." A bulky man, leathery face, dull eyes and a naked lady tattooed on his right arm, charged into the living room, picking his nose. He gulped down the champagne and was about to smash the glass against the table but the woman in purple frowned and wagged her index finger to stop him.

"Yes, you please find him, won't you?" Daisy walked over and raised her eyes for a second, her voice barely reaching my ears. "Without him... without him... we... we worry lots..." She hung her head and locked her eyes onto my loafers.

"God damn—" Sylvia's eyes rolled and her lips curled but my gaze lassoed her tongue. The maid approached and whispered into her ear and she grinned and hurried into the kitchen.

"Well, Pastor Jim right good, good man. He sure preach long sermons and teach us the truth. Bless him." Mrs. Walker tapped her face with a handkerchief and raised her eyes to the portrait of Jim posing as Genghis Khan on a mustang.

"That God damn whore monger Yankee banker." The bulgy man cursed Donald Larsen for several minutes and walked toward the other end of the table eyeing the sirloin strips. But before he could reach the food, he tripped over Edgar's extended leg and fell onto Mrs. Walker. She shrieked, spilled hot chocolate over his right cheek and shoved him from the sofa onto the floor. His body almost squashed the poodle sniffing for food on the carpet.

"Wow, nice move, very memorable. Did anyone videotape that?" Edgar the mortician raised his champagne glass and toasted the man's fall.

"Hey, Chandler. Quit assing around and hold your dirty, ungodly tongue. Don't want none of that language in my house. Of respect for Barbara, oh bless her deceased soul, I invite you and Johnny. But you gonna foul mouth, then you buzz off." Sylvia dashed out of the kitchen in her high-heels and watched him cover his face, roll over and stagger onto his feet. "And you stop dripping that brown stuff on my Persian carpet."

His face flush and his hair dripping hot chocolate, Mr. Chandler almost cursed again, but after the initial "shhhh," he only grumbled and hissed. He wiped his face with the back of his hand like a cat with its paw. He handed Sylvia a slip of paper but she sneered at him before taking it. After reading the note, she scratched her face and drank a glass of champagne. She handed the note to me and hurried back into the kitchen.

"Now, now, Mr. Chandler." The lady in purple cut a slice of cheesecake and wagged her index finger. "God blessed us with Donald. Now He done taken him away. So we just prays for someone to replace him, that's all. God'll answer our prayers and send someone. Don't you never worry. And you clean yourself up good, you hear?"

Before I could read the note, Edgar said, "Well, your prayer's answered. I'm here, aren't I? People always think bankers are God's answer to their prayers, but you know, a mortician can be a greater blessing. Think about it. Death's such a nuisance. Wouldn't it be a blessing to whiz through mourning and burial and get back to our lives? Well, I'm here to help. One-stop shopping funeral service. No muss, no fuss, no tossing on your mattress." He winked at me, thrust a piece of smoked salmon into the mouth and gulped down some Chardonnay. But before he could open his mouth again, his phone rang. At this cue, I walked toward the kitchen and tried to escape his odor but I could only set one foot into the Promise Land before he, eyes sparkling and lips dancing, overtook me.

"Wow, Father, this is big. Can you guess what it is? Well, anyway, got to go. Can't lose time. You know, competition is fierce, especially during these hard times. It's great news... ahem, ah bad news. Aren't you curious? Oh, you look pale. Don't feel well? Did you know about it, too? No, how could you? It just happened. Wow, it's something." The mortician slapped his cheek and charged across the living room toward the door.

"You fixing to share?" The woman in purple rubbed her nose. "And tomorrow, we going to that there new restaurant, grand opening, for barbecue ribs buffet. You come with us, but don't you bring no funeral smell, you hear me?"

"Somebody killed three guys in the post office. They think it's a disgruntled ex-coworker. Well, got to run. Time is money." He grabbed the leather long coat on the statue's right hand, opened the front door and charged onto the walkway.

I glanced around the living room, as a medieval peasant would the New York skyscrapers, wondering whether I had awakened into the wrong dream, stepped into the wrong era, tunneled into the wrong universe. A stranger passing through a foreign land searching for an acquainted tree, a familiar cloud or a recognizable star.

I went into the kitchen, away from the mouths, and took some painkillers for my headache. I read the note: *Don't call those donut-eating cops or your beloved Jim will be dead meat.* Glancing at Mr. Chandler, I wondered whether he was a clown or a mastermind trying to eke out a few million dollars during this recession. But I preferred to believe Donald Larsen was growing his retirement fund while escaping from the police. Was Jim's kidnapping related to Camellia's disappearance? Was she helping her father?

Beyond the backdoor, near the trashcans, Sylvia was embracing and kissing a broad-faced man in beige shirt and striped tie. But, as if a guest was playing a trick on them, a clang came from the living room, followed by clatters of broken glasses. The screams interrupted their romance.

***

Earlier this morning, after kissing the poodle, Sylvia had apologized for the *Charlotte incident.* "Oh, dear, imagine, how shocking, and how could she thought... just because of a tiny kiss, well, just a peck. Of course, it ain't impossible. Flatter though. But had my eyes on Jim." She rubbed her forehead and downed half a cup of coffee. "But how could she wrote that. One thing for sure, she had a thing for you, slick man, you. Anyway, didn't know how that letter... ah, must been careless, left it on the desk, must be some prankster took it to the seminary."

I told her I had never blamed her. Through the years, I would wonder why she had kissed me that night at the party but this morning couldn't bring myself to ask her. Perhaps she wanted to stir Jim's jealousy but he only considered her one among scores of girls clutching at his sleeve. The prank provoked Charlotte, who as if on cue had entered the ballroom with Jim and witnessed the performance. Her features haunted me till this day. I had never seen such a twist on her cheeks as if her heart's creases surfaced onto her face. The music's tempo seemed to shift with her anguish but the chill slithering through my back prevented me from tracking the rhythm. The chandeliers seemed to twirl while time halted. Sylvia giggled. Jim frowned. Charlotte stormed out of the ballroom and that image burned into my memory, resurfacing during the still hours.

"Good thing it turned out fine. With you going to the seminary and becoming a priest, else my poor suffering heart... Of course, don't know why you'd want to live without TV, restaurants, cinemas and shopping malls. And goodness, I heard from Jim, that place of yours..."

***

On that July afternoon before Independence Day twenty-three years ago, while helping Jim get a date with her, I discovered Charlotte had been fond of me since freshman year but didn't have the courage to approach me. At first I thought she was joking but her eyes confirmed her words. When we went on a date to the local ice-cream parlor for mango sherbet, she told me how she despised Jim Whitfield. Shallow, arrogant and insensitive, as she said. She made a list of his girlfriends and arranged them in the order of their getting pregnant by him. We were so engrossed in the list that the sherbet melted onto our hands.

When I told Jim she didn't want a date with him, he accused me of stealing her. He grabbed the bat in his bedroom and smashed the clock and desk lamp. He took the rifle and shot the pair of squirrels playing on the branches. While he cussed and destroyed his room, I went to Charlotte to confide in her, and she held my hand and said, we'd protect each other.

Some mornings, when I woke up in my cell and prepared for laud, I still could hear her voice, as a distant solace on my monastic journey.

Though sure of my calling, I had thought of marrying Charlotte. She was kind, gentle and thoughtful and would've been a supportive companion on life's journey. I loved her and even lusted after her but probably wouldn't have married her even if she hadn't written that letter. Once in a while, I would imagine the life I might've had with her. Probably happy and memorable, but she couldn't fill that void inside me, perhaps tiny but crucial, and it wouldn't be her role or responsibility. But we would've been the best of friends and I would probably make her husband jealous. If it weren't for that letter... if only... Why? Why had she written that letter? I regretted being so unforgiving in those days.

CHAPTER 5

Dₑₐᵣ Sʏʟᴠɪᴀ,

I don't wish to be blunt but must discuss with you a most importance matter, at least for me, which has weighed on me since last night and deprived me of sleep. And yet, precisely because of its magnitude, I couldn't bring myself to speak in person with you. As I write this letter, my heart is throbbing and my hands are trembling under the burden of love and pain and jealousy. As the matter concerns me as well as someone most dear to me, with the weight of my anxiety and worry and pain I etch every letter and every word.

Even though we were never close, I have always liked your easy manner and friendly smiles. Unlike me, you get along with our classmates as if you have known them since childhood, as if you have played with them as toddlers. And though many boys were drawn to you, I knew that ever since freshman year you had your eyes on Jim Whitfield and thus admire your tenacity and perseverance. Now, to your credit, most of us regard you as a couple and I wish you the best.

Last night, during the annual dance, when I entered the ballroom, I saw you kissing Lawrence and was shocked. I have never seen you two chat for more than a few minutes or heard Lawrence mentioned you, except in connection with Jim. You are naturally friendly and might not have thought much of the kiss but Lawrence, sensitive and reserved, might think otherwise and could mistaken it for something else. I don't mean to reproach you for it, but as Lawrence's intimate friend, actually lover, naturally wouldn't want another woman to tempt him and take him away. I'm selfish and don't apologize for it because I love him with all my heart and have joined with him as one flesh. Lawrence means everything to me and though he told me more than once that the greatest love is selfless, I have not reached that level, on the heights of saints and immortals, the beacons guiding him through his adolescence.

I do not want you to complicate our relationship just as you probably would not want anyone else yours. I believe you are good-hearted and would not want to destroy my relationship with Lawrence. I still remember two years ago when you found the rabbit on the heated school playground, you took it to the nurse to treat for heat exhaustion. At every encounter with you, I would recall that incident, reminding me of your generosity and kindheartedness, which shall be your trademark. I sincerely believe you will always be such a person to me.

I wish you and Jim the best.

Charlotte Gibson

CHAPTER 6

THE SEMINARY'S ADMISSIONS COMMITTEE, after receiving Charlotte's letter, reconsidered accepting me, citing my attachment to the world and specifically to Charlotte. Though not convinced of the relationship, the members still questioned our attachment to each other and the resulting love-hate-jealousy. I took the bus from Washington, D.C. to Boston to meet the members and tried to convince them of my dedication to God. I fasted and prayed for a week to examine my heart for attachments and I found only my feelings toward Charlotte, which had turned from love to hate. In the next two months, I tried to eliminate this last attachment while Father Theodore from the seminary intervened and convinced the committee to accept me on a six-month probation. I thanked the theologian. I vowed to relinquish the world and focus on study, prayer and meditation. That summer, I mimicked the seminary's daily activities, from rising at two o'clock for laud, to prayers before dawn, to chores in the morning, to studying in the afternoon, to sleeping at seven o'clock after mass. For two months, I practiced the routine.

Three weeks after the seminary had informed me about this letter, Charlotte came to see me, but to stress my resolve to relinquish the world, I refused to see her and focused on Thomas Aquinas's *Summa Theologica*. I heard her crying and apologizing but wouldn't open the door. After sobbing on the steps for two hours, she staggered down the sidewalk while her head drooped and her back bent. When I saw her profile through the bedroom window, I wanted to rush through the front door and embrace her, but kept my vow to forsake the world and devote my life to study, prayer and meditation. My aunt told me Charlotte had come by another time when I had gone to the library to study St. Augustine's *City of God*. At summer's end, I left for Boston to study in the seminary and, returning for Thanksgiving, found out she had moved away. I cried through the night and repented of my callousness, but the pain, like herbal medicine's aftertaste, lingered through the years to remind me of the day when drizzle splattered on Charlotte's dress. Looking back, I shuddered at my insensitivity toward her. I trembled at my determination, without which the discipline life would gurgle down the toilet.

Since then, I had been searching for her, from Cape Cod to Staten Island to Denver to Silicon Valley. Her profile on the porch, its image dangling at the edge of consciousness but refusing to drop into unconsciousness, haunted me through the years, and its edge deepened the wound and lacerated my prayers and meditations. I kept a copy of her letter to remind me that through a storm, doubt and confusion would refine the soul, peace beyond calmness, peace toward steadfastness. The storm might rage; the bearings might shift; but I would persist toward the goal.

The night before coming to Gilead, I had dreamed of meeting Charlotte again under an overcast sky. Her eyes oozed tears and her lips tightened into a trembling line. In front of a colonial, I rushed toward her and studied her profile until a nimbus darkened the sky. She moved her lips but only silence wafted through the air. A transparent wall blocked our path and isolated us into our own hell. Before I could stretch my hand to reach her, she disappeared along with the colonial and the suburban street. The cloud descended and engulfed me, but I raced toward where Charlotte had stood and emerged from the darkness into a plain of sand dunes. My feet sank into the sand, up to my ankles, but I continued to run toward the horizon as an athlete would toward the unseen goalpost. I called to Charlotte but the emptiness consumed the sound. I fell and woke up, sweat on my forehead and down my back, and darkness again surrounded me.

***

Now, a familiar overcast sky beyond Jim's bedroom window and in front of me Charlotte's picture. I entered "Charlotte" as the password and opened Jim's files. Should've guessed it from the start. He, like I, couldn't forget her face even after all these moons. Those memories— picnic at Bull Run, protest at the National Mall and research in Arlington Central Library—deposited between the mind's crevices and solidified over the seasons, not even storms and floods could dislodge. The clouds outside the window reminded me of another day lost, another twenty-four hours deposited into memory, another dawn and evening immortalized in mortal minds. I yearned to reenter the nightmare and hold her hands. But I must sift through Jim's files and search for clues to Camellia's whereabouts. Yet, I feared ruffling his skeletons.

To dispel the nausea and fever from the reminiscence and to prepare my mind to survey Jim's cesspool, I read Thomas Kuhn's *The Structure of Scientific Revolutions*, which I'd brought to treat insomnia. While comparing the deterministic and probabilistic views between Newtonian and quantum physics, my eyes kept scanning the smiley face on the paper scrap from the graveyard. I realized it was the lower right corner of Daphne's letter, which I had lost last summer. Who was this *penitent* who had stolen the letter and taunted me with the confession? I tried to link the letter to Camilla, but they related to two different segments of my life, as distant in time as in location.

During sleepless nights after volunteering at the airport or the soup kitchen, I would read Daphne's words against the lamplight and recall her tears and sobs. I would wonder whether visiting her again would've created an alternate future, where she would marry and have children. More than once, my guts would churn and my mind would swirl, while in silence and darkness, I prayed and listened for wisdom and guidance. More than once, the broken moon would cast through the window a silver light and remind me of independent events yielding to their own momentum and interacting under natural laws while my mind would impose happiness, grief, beauty, ruin, justice and chaos. Even now, without the letter, I could recite in my dreams its content and search for answers in another world, another reality.

***

On a snowy March evening twenty-three years ago, Daphne had called me and wept out incoherent syllables through the phone speaker. Sensing some calamity had tumbled onto her shoulders, I offered a few placebo-words and, though not knowing how to counsel, drove to her place intending to rescue her from the affliction. I cared about her but, by impersonating a knight, I wanted more to fulfill my Camelot dream. While driving down Route 50 through the snowflakes, I couldn't contain my excitement for the chance to help Daphne as if her suffering had fulfilled my lust to become a savior. Whenever I recalled that feeling, the delight welling up from the heart, I would baptize myself in a shower to cleanse my soul's blemishes.

When I arrived at her house, her blue eyes gushed out tears, her blond hair wiped her cheeks, and her lips curved down a horseshoe. In the living room, where mildew must've been blooming, she muttered half-words among sobs and her tears flowed down her cheeks and dripped onto her shaking laps. I turned on the heater and cleared the table, the counter and the floor. I made her a chamomile and tried to listen to her mangled words and twisted phrases. But consolations surfaced upon my mind and distracted my attention. Only through my willpower could I lasso those words and focus on her voice, her sobs and her pain but the cushion beneath me began to hurt my backsides.

After two hours, I assembled the words into the puzzle's upper right corner: she was pregnant. She was only sixteen and I could imagine her fear and confusion and, without asking, guessed the scoundrel had abandoned mother and child.

"I loved him. I'd given him everything, but..." Grief twisted her cheek to the left. The trill of "but" ricocheted from the wall to the coffee table to the TV, a lost soul lamenting in the inferno. I turned to watch a ladybug crawl across the wall above the TV, not to admire its polka dot beauty but to avoid her eyes, which without looking, seemed to pierce into my heart. Before I could turn my eyes toward the spider, she tumbled forward and her chin landed on my shoulder and through her eyelids, torrents. I patted her on the back and, feeling helpless, muttered more placebo-words.

"I'll talk to the scoundrel. I'll convince him to marry you." Whenever I reflected on those words, I would scold myself, pray for forgiveness, and promise never to counsel another victim. Had I been able to persuade him to marry her and thus thrown her into hell, I would've taken on a different vocation and a different vow. But before her watery eyes and down-turned lips, though for only a few moments, my reason faltered under the onrush undulating from my guts toward my chest and threatening to engulf my brain.

"Oh, will you? Will you please? You're a savior. I knew you'd help me. I'd always known, even back in seventh grade when I first met you. I'd even thought you'd be the boy. But then Jim came along. And he was, oh gosh, so charming. He has a way with words and..." She wiped her tears and her cold wet fingers, one of which wore a ring with a carved carnation, seized my arms as a drowning man a floating plank from a sinking ship's fractured hull. Under the lamplight, her watery-blue eyes frightened me, then as it would in those dreams where I saved her more than once from Jim Whitfield's talons. I wanted to save her as a savior should, and feel the joy of my omnipotence and of her salvation according to Lawrence, as a thousand angels in heaven dance and sing hallelujah.

She wanted to marry the playboy before her parents could discover the fruit of love inside her, so a week later I talked to my friend while sleet, then drizzle obscured the contours of the trees, the cars, the buildings and the faceless figures. But Jim, shirt opened and sleeves rolled-up, leaped out of the chair and patted my face. He showed me a picture of a Marilyn Monroe lookalike in bikini and said, wiggling his brows, "Hey, would you choose Daphne or her? Now, tell me the truth." An epicure, for sure. But the joy in his eyes frightened me more than the appetites epitomizing his words, actions and decisions since our first acquaintance.

"Look, you like her, don't you? Well, that's alright, since we're buddies, you can have her if you want. And here, I'll pay for the abortion. Don't say I'm heartless. But get lost. My new chick's coming over." After handing me two hundred dollars, he walked over to the mirror, adjusted his hair, opened a little more his shirt, and sprayed on some cologne. Though aware the scorpion's nature is to sting, I still left in disgust.

On learning that Jim was dedicated to upgrading to a new lover, Daphne thanked me and said, "If you'd seduced me, I might've had a happy life." After the tingle squirmed down my spine, I volunteered to accompany her to the abortion clinic but she only said, "Why didn't you seduce me?" and hung up the phone before I could answer.

I received her letter two days after her Easter suicide and had kept it until losing it last June. No, until some itchy fingers stole it from me.

CHAPTER 7

MY DEAR LAWRENCE,

Jim and I were so happy, like in a fairy tale. I thought I'd met my Prince Charming and we'd live happily ever after. Everything was going so great. What went wrong? Why, oh why, has this happened? What did I do to botch the whole thing?

I'm not blaming you. You're so kind. You comforted me so much. I thank you, I really do. And I wish it'd been with you, instead of him. I know you'd marry me. You would, wouldn't you? Yes, you would, even if it'd make you unhappy. But love's blind, we can't control it, we're controlled by it, swept away by the flood of emotions. Oh, that feeling, I still remember that feeling, like flying to heaven, leaving all the pain, all the tears and all the burdens of this silly world. Why couldn't it last? Why'd it have to end? Wouldn't it be wonderful if we could feel that way all our life? Is that too much to ask?

I'd noticed Jim since sophomore year in English class. He sat in the next row and during class would pass notes to me to tell me how pretty I was. Oh, I was so happy when the teacher called on me. I just stared at her thinking she'd selected me to kiss Jim. During class, I'd daydream that Jim would ask me out but soon found out he was with another girl. I became ill for a week and couldn't attend school. Oh, I was really ill, not trying to avoid classes. I had a fever and was delirious and in my dreams he would ask me for a date. When I recovered and returned to class, I saw that girl, so fat, so ugly, so cheap and wondered what Jim liked about her. But whenever I had a chance, I'd follow them to see where they'd go. One time, I saw them kissing behind the school building and became so upset I started weeping but they didn't notice me. Didn't Jim know those tears were for him?

Jim began to talk to me and, can you believe it, even asked me out. I knew he was seeing that other girl but was so happy he'd asked me out that I didn't care how many other girls he was seeing. When Jim kissed me on the first date, my body burned with an enjoyable fire and I lost all strength. But after the first date, he didn't ask me for another and when Christmas came I was totally upset. Later, I found out Jim had dumped that girl and was with another one. At first, I thought it was that Sylvia girl with the protruding lips because she was always hanging around him. How I hated her like a pest. But then I found out it was another girl, with a body much better than Sylvia's. During that time, I felt so, so miserable, a gnawing ache always at the pit of my stomach and fever always hanging over my head. Oh, how I suffered. I know you wouldn't torture me like that, but he would. The thing is, I couldn't resist. It's not in my power. Jim has total control over me.

One day during recess, your good friend Charlotte showed me a list of Jim's previous and current girls with a check next to those he'd slept with and a star next to those that got pregnant. I became so angry I almost hit her. She told me to dump him before I regret it. But how could I? How could any girl? None of his girls ever dumped him. Jim always dumped them. How can I fight against absolute truth? I was so scared Jim would dump me but I thought I was different, better than the other girls.

Starting last September, we had been dating regularly. And of course, we did that, you know. How could I resist Jim? But I was so happy to know I was *the girl*. Even Sylvia, he'd see her only once a month or so. I knew she was so jealous of me and I was so happy just because of that. I was so, so happy. Just sitting next to Jim and watching his handsome face made me so happy. I'd do anything for him. And I didn't think about what'd happen next because I was so happy. I just wanted the feeling and the moment to never go away—never, ever go away. Yes, I was scared everything would fall apart, like now—the nightmare has arrived.

I thought I'd found true love, you know, like in the fairy tales my mom used to read to me. They always ended up happily ever after, so why couldn't I? Oh, Jim's everything any girl could ever want: handsome, charming, witty, humorous, self-confident and more. Lawrence, you're a good man, and I would say, a better man than Jim, but it's just that I love him. Oh, how I wish it was you, sometimes I do wish it, but it couldn't be because this is the way of love. Ever since I was a little girl, I knew one day I'd fall head over heel for my Prince Charming because that's the normal way. How else could it be?

That's why I don't understand you. Do you know there are some girls interested in you? Oh, you probably don't care. What do you care about? Why do you let love go away? What else could you want from life? Of course, it's not for me to say. I've nothing now, not a thing, except for this baby I don't want.

Oh, you're such a good man. Don't you care about what your friends would say if they find out you went to an abortion clinic with a girl? But anyway, I thank you; you're sweet. I thank you for listening to me. I thank you for trying to convince Jim to marry me, but deep down inside, I knew he wouldn't. He's not the marrying type. Oh, how I knew it, but I still couldn't let him go. How could anyone? How could anyone let go of love? No, only love can let go of us, release us from happiness and pain.

I'm very scared. I'm scared of dying but I'm even more scared of living, without Jim, without love, without anything but pain and sadness. Oh, how could this be? I was so happy. Now, the pain is eating me away. I could feel my stomach and belly twisting in pain. I could feel myself choking with a slow dull ache. Oh, I don't want this. I can't stand this. I just wanted love. I just wanted happiness. I don't understand this. I just know I have to escape from this pain, from this fever, from this suffocation.

Do you think Jim will be sad after I'm dead? Maybe he will. Tell him "don't be sad" because I won't feel anymore pain. No, but I want him to feel sad for me, forever. And remember me, forever. I'm so scared no one would remember me after I'm gone. Will you remember me? Yes, I believe you will. Jim might not, but you will. Oh, please, please, remember me.

Oh, goodbye my sweet Lawrence. Say goodbye for me to my beloved Jim. Tell him how much I love him and would've loved him all my life. It's getting late. I must go. I've prepared the sleeping pills, but I'm scared of taking them. I won't be able to turn back. I wish I had another choice. I wish life could be happy. But no, ah no, it's not. Farewell and all the best.

Your dearest,
Daphne

CHAPTER 8

AFTER PUTTING AWAY THE CORNER of Daphne's letter, I went to get a cup of tea before reading Jim's diary. When I opened the study door, I saw across the marble hallway the broad-faced man, in a white silk shirt, probably Jim's, walking out of Sylvia's bedroom, whistling and adjusting his tie. He had started down the stairs and didn't see me, so I continued to walk along the colonnade toward the stairs. Before I reached the stairs, Sylvia swung open the door, brushing several locks of hair and pressing her wrinkled dress, and noticing me, switched the upturned lips into an open mouth but greeted me and commented on the weather. After complaining about Mr. Chandler's falling over and smashing the Ming vase, she wanted to introduce me to Agent Peter.

In the marble hall, next to the pool table, the broad-faced man shook my hands and offered me a glass of whiskey but I declined. He said, twisting a ring with a carved carnation on his index finger, "Well, well, Father, Sylvia said you knew Jim well from way back in your youth and may be able to help us locate him. Though we've got people working on this case, even profilers, we're always glad to get more information and insight."

"I don't presume to reveal anything the FBI hasn't found."

"But you'd be amazed at how helpful citizens can be." He grabbed the cue and downed the eight-ball into the corner pocket while Jim, as if blessing each game, beamed at the pool table from his portrait on the wall. "In one case, we were looking for a serial killer. The bastard killed six women. Well, the mom told us that when he was five, he killed his cat and went to the lake to bathe once a day for seven days. So we searched the lakes closest to the latest victim's body and found the bastard bathing peacefully just two miles away. Well, I gave him a thrashing, just what a serial killer needs after a refreshing bath."

"So you believe Jim might want some ice-cream after Donald Larsen kidnapped him and locked him in a cell, just because as a child, he cried for some after his father had locked him in a closet?"

"You sure it wasn't a prostitute he wanted after he got locked up?" He winked and glanced into the hallway where Sylvia had gone to order the maid to prepare lunch. "My dear Father, it's victimology, the more we know about the preacher, the more we understand the kidnapper and the easier it is for us to nab the financier."

"What if you find out Jim's a sociopath with a Napoleon complex?"

Agent Peter just smiled at my remark and pointed the cue at Jim's marble statue, which jabbed its right index finger forward as if ordering his followers to march into enemy camp and only return with the leader's head. "That's easy. In that case, since we have both profiles, we just switch criminal and victim, and focus on nabbing the preacher. Not much more work. You see why we want the profile, just in case the victim decides to become the criminal. Either way, I'll nab a fiend, unless of course they kill each other." He took out pen and pad and continued, "So, let's have all the damning evidences."

***

Every time we played basketball, Jim would always be a captain and choose Dwayne the Bulldozer or Andy the Bullet or Jeff the Elbow, leaving me and Tom the Midget and Ed the Flagpole wondering whether some potion had turned us transparent. He could always persuade the other boys, even the Bulldozer, to follow him into some adventure, including stealing a license plate from an out-of-state car, writing fake parking tickets, breaking into the football team captain's locker, and sneaking into a strip bar. Once, he rallied the troop to kidnap his neighbor's dog and, as an underling, I followed his order and would've fed my leg to the bulldog, had Charlotte not risked her life to save me. While making a bomb, he burned the instructions Tom the Midget had copied from a bomb-making manual. Instead, he experimented with gunpowder, fertilizers, fuses, and pipes and almost blew off his hands. After losing interest in blowing up the neighbor's dog, he focused on flirting with the girls who were obsessed with him. But after a while, his interest in any girl, similar to that in making a bomb, would also fade, as if commitment would gnaw away his flesh. I had seen him

33

with Daphne more than once, spending the money he had stolen from his parents in steak and seafood restaurants. More than once, *Napoleon* would demand his underlings' total attention while he flaunted his sensuality upon us as if we were Bowery beggars. He would evaluate a local steak house's filet mignon or rib-eye, a Napa Valley merlot or Chardonnay, a four-star restaurant's Black Forest cake or Belgian chocolate moose, or the color of Daphne's eyes or the shape of Ginger's nose or the suppleness of Sylvia's lips.

Unlike Jim, I preferred to walk along the Potomac and read *Fathers and Sons*, *Letters and Papers from Prison* and *The Meaning of Relativity*. When Jim, for no apparent reason, bought me *Crime and Punishment* for my sixteenth birthday, I hibernated in my room and devoured it in a week while the other boys went to Virginia Beach to watch girls in bikinis. When I related the plot, Charlotte was so interested in the book she borrowed it and read it in two weeks. We discussed whether innate human conscience or external social values, through religious and moral beliefs, had imposed upon us psychological torment. With Auschwitz glistening in our minds, we both rejected any Napoleons or supermen, above the law and qualified to levy justice.

***

Just as I began to relate the bulldog incidence and Agent Peter was scribbling down notes, the doorbell interrupted us, as if the visitor wanted to prevent the agent from knowing Jim's nature.

"You know, this isn't your local soup kitchen." Agent Peter threw pen and notepad onto the pool table while the maid opened the front door at the end of the hallway.

Father Jones in sunglasses stepped into the foyer and upon seeing me said, "Wow, Father Lawrence, fancy seeing you again. Didn't have a chance to say goodbye the other night. Did you get a glimpse of that sneaky penitent? I'd be interested in seeing his face. Though, of course, I don't know many people here in town. And of course, ha, ha, would be interested in knowing about the confession." He adjusted Jim's statue to direct its gaze at the living room's center. He walked down the hallway rubbing his hands and studied the portraits, the sofa and the pool table. "You know, that portrait's slightly tilted. Of course, it's not obvious, but to a connoisseur, well, it's grossly distorted. Makes the Reverend look crooked, you know what I mean?"

"For someone in such a dull and unproductive profession, you're damn nosy." Agent Peter grunted from the corner and took out a cigarette.

"And with those shifty eyes and crooked lips, you look more like a hit-man than an agent. Are you sure you're not an undercover gangster trying to penetrate the FBI?" Father Jones rubbed his shoes on the carpet.

"Well, if you want to know, that's easy, let's walk down a dark alley in South Bronx. I'm sure you're looking forward to heaven and doing nothing, not that you're doing anything useful now." Agent Peter took out a lighter.

"Hey, as far as I know, this is a nonsmoking room." Father Jones glanced at the sole of his shoe.

"Must be the new priest at that old church. Bones, ain't it? Oh, Jones. Well, just to let you know, don't care for no visitations from no priests. My husband's a preacher, you know. So you're like rivals. And what's with them sunglasses?" Sylvia tramped akimbo through the hallway and growled across the room.

"What're you going to do, fine me?" Agent Peter sneered at Father Jones, but after glancing at Sylvia, just stuffed the lighter into the shirt pocket and the cigarette into his mouth.

"Oh, as usual, doing dirty jobs, running errands." The priest turned to me. "We get no respect, I tell you, no respect. What'd they think we are, office boys or deliverymen or sanitation workers? Hey, we're men of God, holy men, the bridge between ordinary men and God."

"Do you have a cold?" I said. "Or just one whiskey too many? Should be careful with that stuff. You could lose more than your voice." Previously, I didn't notice Father Jones's voice irritates me, but now the rasping seemed to grate against my eardrums.

"Cut the holy crap and tell us what you've delivered, errand boy." Peter sucked at the sides of his cheeks and thrust his hands into his pant pockets.

"That's it. I had it. I tell you: I had it. It's the last straw. I'm going to—" Father Jones said, leaping up and stamping on the carpet. I thought he would cry for his mom.

"Going to quit?" Agent Peter said. "That's fine, but what else can you do? Forget it, at least now you don't have to worry about three meals and a warm bed. I don't want another homeless bum turned psychotic killer giving me more work. I've enough scoundrels to nab."

"Oh my God, watch it, watch it, Father Jones." Sylvia rushed at the priest as her eyes bulged and her face paled. "Know how much that carpet costs? Oh, oh…" She tripped over a cue and fell into Peter's arms, saying, "Oh, you heartless priest."

"Sylvia, you alright?" Peter carried her to the sofa, laid her down, and rubbed her temples.

"Well, ain't that touching, just like man and wife. Ain't that so, Father Lawrence?" Father Jones, while watching the drama, sat on the armchair, adjusted the seat and scratched his face. "Hmm, forgot to bring a camera. Oh, well, better luck next time."

"I'm sure you didn't come here to watch this." I disapproved of their exhibition, but disdained even more Father Jones's pleasure at Jim's misfortune.

"But I'm sure glad I came, just at the right place and the right time, to witness this, shall we say, drama or, if you prefer, romance. Wouldn't miss it for anything, well, besides whiskey and confessions, those are our lifeblood." He rubbed his hands, probably anticipating the scene's climax.

"But you have an errand, I presume." I said.

"Oh, yes, of course," he said, "but wait, it can wait. This is more interesting, more delectable, more…just more than that damn errand, that damn note. After all, it's only a note, nothing compare to this. You know, I'm still waiting for a confession. Can't believe no one came to confess. Must be those shrinks competing with us. But this is better, no need to confess, right? Two priests as witnesses, ha, ha, ha."

"What're you looking at, priest?" Peter said, letting go of Sylvia and rushing at Father Jones, but she moaned, right hand against her temple, and called him for a glass of brandy.

"Oh, dear, never mind that there ass priest. Feels giddy. Oh, how long I got to suffer, poor dear Sylvia."

"Yes, dear Sylvia. I'll go… a glass of whiskey… no, brandy… right away… where are the wines…" Peter kicked the cue and wandered from sofa to pool table to Jim's statue while the maid stepped out of a nook just behind the door and trotted down the hallway.

"The note could be important." I went over to Sylvia, checked her pulse and prescribed some rest.

"Ah, yes, of course, the note. It's important, I think. Must be, why else would the guy need a courier. It's for Mrs. Whitfield." Father Jones thrust his hand into the side of the leather cushion, pulled out a key and slipped it into his pocket. He got up, walked over and handed Sylvia a folded piece of paper.

"I warn you Father, you don't upset me. You given me a headache already."

"Can't upset you with your beau around, right?" Father Jones elbowed me, walked over to the portrait, swung it open to reveal a wine cabinet and took out a glass and a bottle of Chardonnay.

"How dare you, how dare you. Oh, oh my poor head... Peter... Peter... where's that brandy?" She rubbed her forehead and opened the note to read it. "What's this? Best not be one of them sick jokes. Ha, what? Ha, ha, you kidding me? But, but, it's his handwriting. No, can't be."

I tried to look at the note but she folded it and shoved it into her alligator skin handbag.

"Care to share?" Father Jones opened the Chardonnay and poured a glass while the maid walked in with a glass of brandy.

"Sylvia, you look pale." Peter grabbed the glass and walked over to the sofa. "Here, take this." He helped her sit up and she gulped down three drafts. Face flushed, she whined for another minute before turning her diamond bracelet and tapping her fingers on the glass.

"No need to hide secrets from us, you know, since we're priests and all that." Father Jones swirled the Chardonnay, sniffed it for five seconds and sipped it. "Ha, Father Lawrence's a reliable guy, can guarantee with my reputation."

"No question about Father Lawrence's reliability but ain't much reputation there to guarantee nothing." Sylvia gulped her brandy.

"Ouch, that hurts." Father Jones simpered and finished the Chardonnay. "If I wasn't a priest—"

"You don't look or act like one anyway, so don't worry." Peter walked over and snatched the glass from him. "By the way, errand boy, your job's done. So get lost. Oh, I forgot. You're waiting for your tip. Well, here's five bucks. Go get yourself a bottle of whiskey and get drunk in the alley." He slipped a bill into the priest's pocket and beckoned the maid to escort him out the door.

"But...but...the note...the note...If there's anything I could help...I've spare time, plenty of spare time, and I'm very eager to help. Just let me—"

"That ain't none of your business, Father Bones." Sylvia growled at him and pulled my sleeve. "But Father, might could need your help. This here note..." She glance at Father Jones and waited until he was out the front door before speaking again. "It's a ransom note."

"Poor sucker." Agent Peter hummed "Dixie" and started another pool game.

"Kidnapped, the poor dear." With a handkerchief, she rubbed her eyes but didn't smear the mascara. "When he disappeared, I knew, just knew it, something gone wrong, terribly wrong. But hoping for a miracle, yes, a miracle from the Lord. Oh, my poor Jim... he... he..." She sobbed and took out a mirror to check her face. "Donald Larsen, that there fiend, must be him. He kidnapped Jim. Father, you got to help."

"Don't worry, the FBI will track down that greedy banker and find the poor sucker. Don't worry. We'll get him back alive. Yes sir, alive. I promise. You've nothing to worry about. Everything will be alright, will be taken care of." Peter patted her and requested two more glasses of brandy from the maid.

"I'll do whatever I can to help find Jim," I said. "First, his diary—"

"Forget about that there diary. We but need four million dollars. Damn it, four million dollars, what a greedy son-of-a-bitch, like his profit from the Ponzi schemes weren't enough to buy several islands in Dubai." Face even more flushed, she leaped onto the carpet and barked orders to prepare lunch.

"He's not getting anything. I'll make sure. The only thing coming to that greedy banker's a lifetime in prison." Peter grabbed her glass and finished the brandy.

"Father, that there scoundrel want you to deliver the ransom," Sylvia said.

"Him? No, I'll do it. I'll nab that two-time loser." Peter punched the statue in the chest and bruised his knuckles.

"How did he know I'm here?" I rubbed my chin and recalled all the faces in the party. For a new BMW, a diamond necklace or watch, or even a bottle of 2005 Screaming Eagle Cabernet, almost anyone would've helped Donald Larsen.

"Ouch, ah, you've got a point, Father. Something's fishy here. The greedy banker may be watching us, or at least paying someone to spy on us. That loser Chandler—" He turned the stature to face the wall and put a towel over its head.

"Oh, dear Peter, he's just a harmless drunkard," she said.

"And drunkards need money to buy booze. Besides, the Ming vase, that'll cost him plenty. Believe me, I know these petty criminals."

"But he's not a reliable spy," I said. "Donald Larsen should be smart enough not to employee a drunkard." If I were the banker, I would employ Mrs. Walker, whose simple and sincere words might disarm even Attila the Hun.

"You don't worry about the four million. I'll just talk to Jim's flock and we sure to come up with the money, not a penny less. Why, to give is to be blessed. They all want to be blessed special now most facing foreclosures. And besides, they're so eager to have Jim back to bless them and to lead them. Without him, they're like lost sheep. Nobody going to stop them from giving their money. I sure ain't. I sure want them to be blessed. Wouldn't you, Father?" Sylvia grinned and revealed her facial wrinkles. "Mrs. Walker will give everything away even though she don't got nothing."

"Sylvia, what're you talking about?" Peter took down Jim's portrait and slid it under the pool table.

"Oh, Peter, you're such a dear stranger here."

"Why give the money to that crook?"

"You wouldn't want him to kill Jim, would you?" Sylvia giggled and patted Peter on the cheek.

"But Donald Larsen should go to jail for life, for destroying all these people through the Ponzi scheme, and for running down that innocent precious girl." Agent Peter threw the glass onto the floor, wiped his hands on Jim's statue, and marched out of the room.

I wanted to take my leave and go up to my room to read Jim's diary, but Sylvia said, "Almost three years ago, this here son-of-a-bitch Larsen was drunk driving, killed that there pretty girl and got off scot-free. Sonya, poor girl, she—"

"Christmas? Near Harrisburg?" I blurted out without asking how she knew Sonya.

"Well, well, very impressive, Father. I reckon you monks isolated from the world. You know, running away from simple folks. But seem like you might could know more gossips than me. Wow, care to share some of your knowledge?"

Of all the possible futures confronting me when Sylvia opened her mouth, this one, where a tsunami followed an earthquake, selected me, yanked me—along with Camellia and Ichiro—into its bosom. But perhaps Sylvia mistook Donald for another banker, another Ponzi schemer.

Whether it was true or not, at that moment I believed friendship and love would triumph over randomness. But after I read Jim's diary…If only I hadn't known…

39

CHAPTER 9

J IM WHITFIELD CHRONICLES
Part 1: A New Hope

September 1, 1987
  Today, I was ordained the assistant pastor at the church near my home. I used to throw stones at those windows when I was young. In fact, some of them are still broken. But now, I'm the second in command here. What fate, what destiny, what twists and turns this life. All his life, Lawrence wanted to be a priest, but the letter from Charlotte shattered his dreams. On the other hand, I'd never thought about being a preacher until two months ago. And now, goodbye to no-respect used-car salesman, and hello to venerated preacher. Fancy that. Moving up the ladder, from promoting used cars to promoting God.
  I called my girlfriend Patricia to check if her husband was in town. When she said he wasn't, I asked her out for dinner to celebrate the birth of a new dawn, the coming of a new season. Hallelujah.

July, 4 1994
  Sylvia and I moved from Fairfax, Virginia to Gilead, Tennessee. I'd waited for the senior pastor to retire for years but the crone refused to leave his post even when he was walking with a cane. I couldn't wait anymore. When I decided to leave the church, I felt a burden lifting from my shoulders and knew God wanted me to venture into the new land. I loved Tennessee the minute I drove over the border. On the

way here, Sylvia and I discussed how we'd build a new church and gather a new flock and preach a new gospel. Not like those who hide out in the monastery and waste their lives.

The first day I moved into the service apartment, I called the mayor and arranged to have dinner with him and his wife. Sylvia and I went through the phone book and scrawled down the addresses of several local churches. We'd attend their Sunday services and invite folks to a revival meeting that I'd hold in the local park to awaken this sleepy town. And to deliver my message and show them my wisdom and charisma.

I love Independence Day.

October 30, 1994

I woke up this morning singing Hallelujah. After several months of preparation, today marked the official opening of The Church of Jim Whitfield. I wore the new oxford and pinstripe suit I bought yesterday just for the occasion. Sylvia bought a new dress and had a perm. We walked up to the church steps under the cheers of the members and only grieved over having to rent the place. The wreaths from the mayor and the local businesses stuffed the atrium and the scent of lilies and jasmines and even chrysanthemums filled the air. Sylvia almost fell over a bouquet. She blamed her new high heels but I saw her ogling a handsome young man who shook her hand.

I entered the sanctuary and walked on stage to welcome the audience. When I saw four hundred people filling almost two-thirds of the auditorium, I knew the posters in City Hall and the flyers in the mailboxes had done their work. Of course, the core members had been going to other churches during their services and inviting those churchgoers to come and celebrate with us. Definitely chose the right core members from the revival meeting to help out. Must develop an inner circle, the leadership of the church, the guardians, and the most loyal members. Every strong church has a dedicated core team that'd follow the leader to the ends of the earth, to sacrifice everything for him, to devote their hearts, minds and souls to a single purpose, advancing the church and uplifting the leader. That Walker character seems like a good candidate, must invite him for dinner. And cute little girl, his daughter.

Before preaching the sermon, had everyone write their names, street addresses, phone numbers and email addresses. Then, I preached. I preached for two hours and when I saw members of the audience rubbing their eyes and blowing their nose, I wanted to continue. But Sylvia signaled to me to stop and collect the donation. I closed with a moving story and when I saw tears in Sylvia's eyes, I signaled to the ushers to pass the collection plates. After worship, we served the free lunch buffet: clam chowder, smoked salmon, crab cake, sirloin steak.

When we counted the donation, we found about hundred thousand dollars. Just a tiny success, but a nice start. First, consolidate the church, initiate new members, and assure steady attendance and income. I must build up cash, the fuel that runs any enterprise.

At night, Sylvia and I went to the Gilead Steakhouse to celebrate with filet mignon, a bottle of merlot, and Black Forest cake. Unlike Lawrence, drinking whey and eating crud, probably forgotten what steak tastes like.

July 4, 1997

After a year's effort, the cathedral in the center of Gilead opened for business to reflect my new image. Yesterday, I stood in front of the building surveying the five-acre plot of land and admiring the stone-front façade for an hour. Stepped into the atrium to the smell of new wood and caressed the walls. In the sanctuary, surveyed the two-storied theater. Felt the seat's cushion and wool. Looked up at the arched ceiling. Surveyed the three multimedia screens behind the stage and strolled down the aisle, triumph pulsating in my blood. Walked on stage and tested the pulpit. I heard my voice and asked the technicians to adjust the sound effects. I turned around and saw myself on the screen and asked them to adjust the lighting. Everything must be perfect.

In the church gymnasium, I shot hoops for an hour before going to the cafeteria and ordering a salmon salad. Went up to the observation tower and enjoyed the view of Gilead. After lunch, I went to the sauna in the church basement and prepare the sermon.

Jackson had objected to building the cathedral and worried about paying the mortgage. Fortunately, the others, unlike he who only trusted his calculator and spreadsheet, have faith and they drowned out his objection. I hate that faithless pragmatist, bringing that secular virus into the church. He should know great men never count pennies. I know the congregation will rise to the occasion. And it'd be my job to maintain their faith.

January 2, 2000

After working with my lawyer for three months on all the red tapes (just schemes for bureaucrat to stuff their pockets), the Great Commission Missions is registered as a nonprofit organization. Of course, the work is necessary to avoid stepping on the tail of the law. With the organization in place, I could plan my missionary trips, to the ends of the earth, and to solicit the required funding. Three days ago, I made some slides and compile a pitch: a hook, something to seize their emotions, and provide a way for them to participate so they feel like they're making a difference. And of course, a good closing, that's what separates a winner from a loser.

Yesterday, I presented the pitch at the board meeting and the members unanimously approved to give ten-thousand dollars to the fund over the next six months. Today, after worship, I held a general meeting and presented the pitch to the congregation. I received five-thousand dollars of pledge for this year and intended to collect at least four-thousand dollars by the end of the year. With the money in place, I could begin to prepare this year's missionary journey. I opened a bottle of Yquiem to celebrate.

April 30, 2000

After preparing the sermon and having sex with the maid, went to the Gilead Steakhouse to have dinner with that calculating banker Jackson. He wanted to treat me to dinner so I ordered a T-bone steak with baked potato, two glasses of 1982 Mouton, and a double chocolate cheesecake. During the dinner, we discussed about my sermons and I agreed to ease up on bankers. In return, he'd donate a thousand more each month. We smiled, shook hands and toasted to our futures like gentlemen. Yeah right, gentlemen, my ass. Never trusted a banker and never will. They're all crooks, not that I have anything against crooks, as long as they don't steal from me. But got to keep an eye on him, in case he tries to make a profit at my expense. These days, can't trust nobody.

May 14, 2000

During worship, was preaching to the congregation about them losing their jobs their spouses, their children, their life savings to capture their attention and set the mood for the main message. All of a sudden, a tattooed biker stepped into the sanctuary and I was scared shitless. He sat down next to Mrs. Chandler, and she screamed and fainted on the spot. I thought she had a heart attack. So couldn't con-

tinue with my sermon on fear; couldn't warn my flock against scientists, historians, writers and the like. And lawyers of course because
they're the usual suspects. But of course I have nothing against them.
They're just like you and me, trying to make a quick buck before retir-
ing to Maui or Malibu with a young mistress, maybe two if you hit the
jackpot.

Did that biker think this is a bike shop or a roadside café? Couldn't
he read the neon sign out there? Maybe he couldn't read. This is The
Church of Jim Whitfield, not Jim's Motorbike Repair or Jim's Diner.
Just because you smell food, doesn't mean we peddle food here. Next
time, go down the road and you'll find Joe's Big Mouth.

Good thing Chandler was such a fool. Started confronting the biker
as soon as I gave the order to sweep the guy out of the sanctuary where
he doesn't belong. I called an ambulance and sent Mrs. Chandler to the
hospital. Hope she'd be alright soon.

So I had to delay my sermon on fear. Fear was actually gushing out
of the listeners' eyes and they were begging me to continue, to develop,
to amplify, to drive the hammer into the nail. But I had to start all over
next Sunday.

And don't forget the donation. I didn't collect the donation. That's
ten to twenty thousand dollars down the drain, enough for another
missionary trip to the Mediterranean. Damn it.

November 25, 2000

We were having the Thanksgiving service in the sanctuary and the
attendees were sharing their gratitude when a homeless man came in
and sat in the pew next to Mrs. Walker. The trash hoarder probably
smelled lobster and followed his nose. Can't blame him, that's basic
instinct. Mrs. Walker screamed and ran to the back of the sanctuary
where she hid under a pew. Never expected she could run so fast, with
all that weight. And she scared poor Daisy more than that stinker had.

I couldn't allow the bum to ruin our service. Got to make an exam-
ple of him and demonstrate my dedication to defending my flock.
When I asked Chandler and his drinking buddies to sweep the foul
smell from the pew, the drunkard was like a defender of the faith,
chasing the guy out the back door with the broken broom.

After Chandler returned with the broomstick, we continued the
sharing and rebuilt the mood. As soon as the attendees saw the food—
lobster tails, shrimp, foie gras, Black Forest ham, champagne, and fruit-
cake—they began laughing and singing again.

During the feast, Sylvia told me we had two hundred thousand in donation, which, after accounting for the meal's expenses, was still decent for a day's work. And that Jackson thought the monthly mortgage was too heavy a burden. Typical of a banker. Before leaving, I made an appointment with a pretty young lady to counsel her next Wednesday.

With vagrants and tattooed bikers loitering through the premise, I decided to install security cameras, build an alarm system, set up a surveillance room, and hire two or three security guards. I'd also ask the police commissioner for some help. Probably could send a cruiser to patrol the premise on Sunday mornings.

Part 2: Portrait of a New Jim

February 14, 2001

On our anniversary, Sylvia and I stepped into our two-million-dollar mansion and opened a bottle of champagne to celebrate our success. She marbled at the chandeliers, marble floor, and outdoor pool. But I went down to the basement to review the empty cellar and planned the wine collection. I'd need several dozen cases of wine to decorate the cellar, and several sports cars to fill the garage. I walked around the orchard, thinking of the pear I'd eat later in the year. When I passed the fountain and the staff quarters and reached the back entrance, I tried the combination to make sure I could sneak in and out of the house when necessary. I made sure no one else has the combination so only I could use it.

When I returned to the house, I called the secretary to buy three cases each of the 1982 Mouton and 2005 Screaming Eagle Cabernet, one case of the 1921 Yquem, and two bottles of the 1964 DRC Romanee-Conti. That should be a start to build up my wine collection. I called my contractor to turn the cellar into a vault so it could stand a bulldozer. And surveillance cameras throughout the mansion. Have to monitor those greedy servants, keep them from getting into the cellar and other classified locations.

August 1, 2001

Last month, the Church of Jim Whitfield donated a hundred thousand dollars to the Great Commission Missions and we began our second missionary trip in the middle of the month. Since Sylvia and I went to Europe last summer, we decided to go to Tokyo, Seoul, Hong Kong, Beijing, Singapore, and Manila.

Last summer, I wasted my time touring those old churches in Rome and going shopping with Sylvia in London's Soho and Paris's Faubourg Saint-Honoré. When we arrived in Venice, she went to San Marco by herself and I enjoyed the gondolas on the canals and met a pretty woman. For a week, I would go to her place in the afternoon and have dinner with Sylvia in the evening.

So this year, we skipped the Great Wall in Beijing. And when Sylvia was having a ball in Hong Kong, shopping twenty-four hours a day, finding every brand name and many knockoffs, I just went to Lan Kwai Fong to have Thai curry chicken. I met a girl from Greece and went to her place after dinner.

Lawrence might say I waste my time with food, wine and women. But what does he know about any of these things? Zilch. So let me enjoy them and he can enjoy his blank wall in his prison cell.

March 19, 2002

Last September, attended the local congressman's fundraiser dinner. While dancing with the mayor's daughter, I met this New York banker. Real slick. He pitched his financial success and tried to convince me to invest in his portfolio. Of course, I ain't gullible Jim, so I just told him I'd consider it. People always want something from me, but I don't mind giving a burger as long as I can get back a pork chop, a rack of ribs or a T-bone steak. I ain't no cheapskate. So if you're willing to give me something, I'll consider giving you something. After all, life is give and take, even though it's more blessed to take than to give.

A week later, I got my gumshoe to check out the financier. Background check and all that. He was kosher. But the banker turned out to be the husband of an old flame. Had the affair with Patricia about thirteen years ago, while an assistant pastor at my first church, in Fairfax. Bored with her husband to the bones. We'd see each other when Sylvia went shopping in Potomac Mill Mall or New York's Fifth Avenue. We'd go to Ocean City or Williamsburg on weekends when Sylvia went to Los Angeles with her shopping buddies. Patricia's totally devoted to me and even left the church after I ended the affair and asked her not to give me trouble. What a coincidence, what a small world. If I'd known her husband was this banker, would've asked her to get connected to some of his investments. And would've persuaded her to stay in the church after the affair.

If I'd invested with him thirteen years ago, with eight to ten percent return for more than ten years, I'd be rich by now. Just my luck. Last month, invested forty thousand bucks from the church, to test the water. If he continues his streak, I'd invest some of my own money.

During last week's board meeting, when Walker asked to review the bank account, I wanted to throw him out of the building. He should know no one, including any board member, has the right to review the account. They have to trust the annual financial report Sylvia prepared. If he makes trouble, I'd have to get rid of him. With him, it's easy, illegal gambling will do. If not, then stealing from the liquor store, using drug, or beating his wife and daughter. Oh, that adorable daughter. Fortunately, the other board members rejected his request and we went to a seafood restaurant for dinner.

Tonight, the church hosted the Donald Larsen Financial Night, which members must attend. The advertising in the local newspaper and radio stations also drew in as many nonmembers. When I approached the church and the neon displays above the front door and on the front lawn, I felt like I was attending a musical at the Radio Music Hall.

Donald Larsen in his three-piece suit stepped onto the stage and started cracking jokes just like a used-car salesman or street hawker. Talking on stage like a motivation speaker, trying to rescue his listeners from financial ruin. Good communication skill, good opening, good eye contact, good emotional hook. He showed several charts on the return-on-investment and pictures of client's mansions, yachts, and sports cars. The audience stared at the pictures as if they'd received salvation. No wonder the financier is a fat cat. I wanted to walk up to him and tell him I slept with his wife thirteen years ago. But that wouldn't be good for business and I'm too smart for that. He'd promised three-percent commission on the night's investment. So, after his speech, I was running around urging everyone to invest his or her life savings.

About eighty percent of the attendees rushed to give money to the banker. That's about four million dollars and three percent is a hundred twenty thousand. Naturally, anyone with common sense would want to get ten-percent return on his investments. They're entitled to all the gain because they're providing the capital that greases this country. They deserve every dollar just like I deserve every dollar.

August 1, 2002

Third missionary trip: Jamaica. Quiet and relaxing vacation, and without Sylvia, much freer much more enjoyable. Swam in the beach in the morning, what refreshing water under the summer sun, tinkling my every cell. And that girl from Brazil approached me. So will have a good time tonight.

Need to keep an eye on that Larsen, the more I know him the less I trust him, the greedy banker. Probably scheming to rip me off after seeing how much money I've invested. Need a good gumshoe to spy on him, take some pictures of him for my album. Also a computer wizard to hack into his system and check for any anomalies. And of course, to do some transactions on my own, to protect myself. You know how it is, nowadays everybody needs protection.

February 11, 2009

Last night, had dinner with Agent Peter at the Gilead Steakhouse. Treated him to a grade-A dinner—filet mignon with Shiraz—and gave him a Rolex Masterpiece. With his meager salary working for the FBI, he's lucky to have me as his patron. And I'm doing him a great favor, introducing him to Larsen and his sure-bet investments. (Of course, I'm getting a commission. But he doesn't know that.) In return, asked him a favor. At first, he hesitated, probably thinking about ethical issues and all that crap. Though irritated, I kept a smile and reassured him, time after time, that if I said it was okay, then it's okay. I asked him not to let me down. He's a fool and only half a man. But I still need him for the job. And also, to keep an eye on that greedy banker.

This morning, I met Jack, a gumshoe with bushy eyebrows, steady eyes, and a stiff face, who didn't talk much. Had to replace the previous guy who was killed by some thug in Memphis. I liked Jack and knew he'd be a good gumshoe, so hired him to work for me fulltime: two hundred dollars a day plus expenses, money for new and more powerful lenses. And he could go to five-star restaurants for dinner (I'm not your wash-your-underwear-till-it-evaporates cheapskate). But I told him he better get results soon, those bedroom photos that I need, or he could kiss his career goodbye. We shook hands like gentlemen.

February, 15, 2009

When I woke up this morning and was about to complain to a nurse who didn't speak English, I got a call from my gumshoe Jack. He told me last night, Sylvia met Peter for dinner at the Gilead Steakhouse and had the Valentine special and went back to our place afterward. Today, they've gone to Atlantic City.

By noon, when I checked my email, I received good quality pictures of Sylvia and Peter together at the Gilead Steakhouse, in our bedroom, at the casino, and in the hotel suite. This Jack's really professional, must retain him for some more jobs.

In the evening, called my lawyer and asked to start the paperwork for divorce since Sylvia had committed adultery with Peter. I wanted the lawyer to confirm I wouldn't have to pay alimony because it's adultery. I now know getting married without a prenuptial is like walking into the ER without insurance. But everyone makes an honest mistake once in a lifetime.

Now, I must recuperate in this freezer of a hospital room in Moscow. Where's the heat? And the stab wound still hurts like hell. Just couldn't believe my vacation here turned into such a nightmare. And I don't think the guy who stabbed me wanted to rob me.

CHAPTER 10

IN MY YOUTH, I had played with Jim in his Fairfax home and we had fought the bullies together on the school playground. Though he only considered me a lackey and a pawn, I pretended he was my buddy. A child's daydream. At one time, Jim forced us—his lackeys—to kidnap his neighbor's bulldog and sent me to lure the dog out of the backyard and into the trap. Amid the barks, I trembled from head to toe, but obeyed his command and unlocked the gate. The dog shoved aside the gate, almost pushing me to the ground, and chased me across the yard. As my adrenaline surged, I ran down the alley for my life, not daring to pause and check my direction. The barks hounded me through the alley and before reaching the street, I tripped and flew into a bush, scratching my elbows and knees. As the bulldog charged at me, its crumpled face enlarged, and I could only fling a handful of dirt into its eyes. But before it could bite my arm, a stone crashed into its head and a stick gashed its face. Charlotte brandished the branch, struck its neck, and ran down the road shouting. The bloodstained beast roared down the alley and chased after her to seek revenge, while I got up and tried to run after them. But in less than a block, I lost them. Later, Charlotte told me Daphne's brother had punched the beast twice on the head and knocked it out. Jim's lackeys, too afraid to approach the dog, had fled under Simon's scorn.

After Daphne had committed suicide, Jim on his knees had begged me not to reveal that he had fathered her unborn child, especially to her brother Simon and he promised never to seduce another underage girl again. I accepted his performance and kept my promise all these years. I had never met the brother but heard he had broken the football team captain's nose for touching his sister on the cheek and so understood Jim's fear. But even while trembling, his eyes twinkled and revealed apathy toward his deceased lover. From that twinkle, I could've anticipated his escapades but had evaded them and hidden myself in the cabin while carcasses paved Jim's path.

But if I had been present when Jim expelled the tattooed biker from his church, I would've walked up to his face, readjusted it and spat on his cheeks. Of course, his worshippers would curse me and throw me out with the tattooed man. But I would bring back several dozen prostitutes, homeless bums, and juvenile delinquents and sit them among the pious members in the pew to remind the latter of their alter-egos and treat them to a taste of heaven. Jim, the shepherd, had secured their peace and comfort by sweeping away the fornicators and drug addicts, earned their donation, submission, and worship and, by entrusting the trouble makers to social services, saved time for his mistresses and *mission trips*.

What did he see every morning when he awoke from his fantasies and, from his castle, surveyed the thatched roofs paving the town below and listened to the lark singing its melody? New prey and conquest for the day? Another chance to win a zero-sum game? Could he relish life's fragrance fleeing yet majestic when faced with the rosy clouds above the dawning horizon? Would he ever collapse under the sobs of Iraqi widows and orphans? I would admit that like others, I gathered dust to construct my Eden. And within the fences, I guarded my paradise against intruders. Even while we tried to bridge our worlds through a rainbow, Ichiro and I would see a different shade of purple in the same lilac or hear a different trace of purity in the same symphony. And yet, we traversed the rainbow and shared the distinct shades and the unique traces.

Though different in backgrounds, education, professions, and personalities, Jim Whitfield and Donald Larsen shared a common vision of paradise. They feasted on their followers, admirers and worshippers and offered them the *Fountain of Youth*. Though Donald probably had kidnapped Jim, they would soon realize the comrade in the other and would join forces to cheat, steal, and trample on their new worshippers. There would be other Walkers and Chandlers willing to bow before their thrones and offer their first harvests. And though there would also be other Arthurs, the two comrades would also ground these saboteurs into sawdust.

And yet, despite my disgust, within my bosom, the same seed awaits the word or the idea to blossom into greed and narcissism, fear and insecurity, hatred and intolerance. I fear becoming one of them and, even more, one of their worshippers, but only an imaginary line separates them from me.

After reading the diary entries, I also realized Sylvia and Jim, like Bonnie and Clyde, belonged together. Even in junior high school, I had thought they would be together, though Jim had tried to avoid Sylvia while she sought any chance to grab him by the arm and unload her mind. He told me she had once tried to seduce him by undressing in front of him but he just grinned, scrutinized her until she was fully naked and left. I didn't believe him and still couldn't, but Sylvia wouldn't hesitate to use her body to realize her dreams.

But now, perhaps after discovering his affairs with young ladies, married women, strippers and prostitutes, she learned to love the greenback, which turned out to be as dubious and heart breaking as Jim had been. I would've felt sad for her if she had for herself, but she seemed to have discovered a new life, and perhaps a new beau.

After reviewing the first batch of files, all Jim's boasting and flaunting as if directed at me, I still didn't know his and, much less, Camellia's whereabouts. I hoped she was just walking away from the daily drudgery to sort out life's fragments. I walked up to Jim's statue and squeezed its neck and pretended to listen to his squealing. I called Camellia's mom but no one answered. The drizzle outside the window was softening the edges of the fences, the benches and the trees and obscuring the browns, the yellows and the greens, but in my mind glistened Camellia's eyes and lips. I had promised myself to find her and so I would. The more I discovered about Jim and his church, the more I appreciated her and Ichiro's friendship, and the more I treasured those moments with Charlotte in the Arlington Central Library pretending to analyze the Constitution and at the Georgetown University campus pretending to attend classes. Jim Whitfields and Donald Larsens abound in Gilead as well as in New York City and Los Angeles and London and Paris, in hospitals and banks and churches and city halls, but I had found a Charlotte, a Camellia, and an Ichiro. For the occasional oasis in the heat, I would sing through heaps of dung and dance across the sea of sand.

I went downstairs for another cup of tea and stepped into the sun-room. I was about to step into the drizzle and stroll through the garden to clear my mind when the maid emerged from a crevice behind a gun cabinet and handed me a note. Every five seconds she would shift her eyes toward the living room. I recognized the crumbled ransom note, which Sylvia had stuffed into her handbag after divulging its contents. The maid whispered, "The ransom's two million, not four." I mulled over the words for wisdom and opened the note to confirm Sylvia's ruse. The maid's delight shone through her eyes. This shouldn't be the maid in Jim's diary, but to be fair, he probably had affairs with all the female servants. The maid grinned and grabbed the note. She glanced into the living room and tiptoed out of the sunroom and up the stairs, probably to return the note to Sylvia's bedroom. In front of the Stein-way, I sipped my tea, and looked out into the grayish-green, preferring to soak in the rain than to suffocate in this twenty-eight-bedroom man-sion where every plate, every cushion, and every portrait, if given a mouth, would shame the paparazzi into retirement and drive the tab-loids out of circulation.

My right thumb's joint began to ache under the humid air and I re-alized the seconds had been pouring down time's tunnel until one day the last one would reach its goal and my last breath would disperse. After all the springs and autumns in prayer and meditation, I still strug-gled with moments of doubt, which would crowd over and threaten to overtake the meadow of belief. And with all the smiles and handshakes in Mission Hill and Logan Airport, I still struggled between solitude and engagement, like electron and positron, which would attract only to destroy each other. At moments, I even questioned the decision to give up Charlotte and enter the monastery. Only a glimpse of the dis-tant light in the darkness propelled me forward into unknown grounds. And along the way, the scent of wisteria, magnolia, and chrysanthe-mum... Camellia, Ichiro... Walden Pond, Mount Lafayette... Bach, Beethoven... The Law of Large Numbers, The Pauli Exclusion Princi-ple... a stranger passing through a foreign land...

Sylvia walked up beside me and pouted her lips. "What're you looking at out there? Gold coins dropping from the sky? Well, I prefer diamonds." She poked her nose at the window. "Hey, there's better ways to get them than staring at the rain. Yes, Father, much easier—"

"I know. Such as super-sizing a two-million-dollar ransom into four. That's not too hard." I twisted around and, to avoid the red lips, pre-tended to admire a dead fly on the table.

She opened her mouth into a red circle surrounding a dark abyss while the glass shook in her hand and showered brandy onto the piano keys. I searched for fear and shock in her dilated pupils but she, delighted in meeting a connoisseur, finished her drink.

"Well, well, I be darn. Father, ain't you the smart one. I misjudged you... ha... what you know... Can you share your secret?"

"Professional secret."

"Oh, I understand, believe me, I understand perfectly." She tapped the piano key and hammered out the D note several times. "People keeps asking Jim how he became so successful and he never tell them nothing. And of course, professional secrets. Got to have some tricks up your sleeve, in your pocket and in your bag, and so forth. How else you going to make a living, right? But you sure a bag of surprises. Ought to talk to Jim when he come back. Maybe you two can partner. I mean, a venture... something profitable..."

"The extra two million dollars—"

"Oh, ha, ha, ha. Ahem, Father, want a share? Well, finders keepers, right?" The muscles beneath her right eye twitched for two seconds while she beamed. "How about twenty-percent? Two hundred grand. Nice finder's fee."

"No."

"No? So you want more? Oh, come now, you be reasonable. You but lucky, in the right place at the right time. Don't you be greedy now. There's more where they come from." Sylvia hammered out the G note thrice.

"I don't want anything."

"Oh, I ain't no cheapskate. No, no, I said two hundred grand and you gonna get two hundred grand. But just one thing..." She leaned forward, her lips almost touching my nose, and whispered, "Don't tell nobody nothing, you understand, not a single person—"

"You shouldn't cheat those people." I put down the teacup and walked out of the sunroom before she could reply. I began to wonder whether she wanted her husband back. If the police couldn't locate Jim, she could be with Agent Peter without having to divorce her husband and lose half of the fortune. If I were Jim, I would worry about my life.

CHAPTER 11

Part 3: The Art of War, Episode I: Jim Strikes Back

April 5, 1987

During lunch today, I made a proposition to Sylvia, a proposition she couldn't refuse. A simple task, just as a joke to kiss Lawrence. Naturally, I set a deadline. Offer good until we finish lunch, long enough for her to make a bad decision. As expected, she snatched the offer like a hungry dog, before I took another bite of the soggy sandwich that tasted like mud. Anyway, she must've thought it was an offer of a lifetime. And, in many ways, it was. She wouldn't have another chance with me, if she'd dared to reject the offer. I'd find any number of girls who'd do it. Now, show time. I mean, of course, lights, camera, action, Act I tomorrow evening during our annual school dance party. There'll be sparks and fire, and someone will be sizzling in hell during our annual dance.

April 6, 1987

At three in the afternoon, shaved and took a shower. Powdered myself and put on the cologne. Wore the white silk shirt, black bow tie, and matching tuxedo and oxford. I didn't want to spend three hours in that outfit. But it was show time and though I wasn't the star of the show, I was the director and had to sweep those ladies off their feet.

Checked myself in the mirror for half an hour before driving to the hotel.

Met Charlotte at the hotel lobby, my lovely Charlotte, strummer of my heartstrings, wringer of my tear glands. Wished she'd allowed me to pick her up. But no, you heartless gentle beauty, oh, you woman.

Before going into the ballroom, sent a message to Sylvia, the cue to lift the curtain and begin the show. My fingers trembled expecting a Broadway performance, under my direction. If Sylvia had messed it up, I'd never talk to her again. But happily, she followed her direction to the last word and to the last movements of her fingers, a natural actress.

Oh, what a beautiful night. The chandeliers were shining brilliantly; the lovers were dancing beautifully. And I entered the ballroom blissfully. Ecstasy, better than from that foul-smelling grass I smoked three nights ago. The delight, the tingling, the lightness. But, for a moment, I was peeved because Charlotte widened the distance between us, as she entered the room. A slap on my face. I wouldn't have taken it from anyone else, not Sylvia or Gina or Betsy or Lily, but Charlotte. But why, my love? So Lawrence wouldn't misunderstand? Misunderstand what? I'll show her who truly cares about her.

But then, that moment came. We stepped into the ballroom and surveyed the dance floor where a dozen couples were already dancing under the sparkling lights. Oh, the music, the scene, the actors, the climax. Action.

Charlotte stared at the scene. Those gentle eyes, so menacing and that face, so dark under the glittering light. How frightening, that horrendous look, that injured expression, like that of a wounded lioness.

Sylvia should become an actress. Of course, she acts like one already so no need for training. Her red and menacing lips attacking Lawrence's, a vulture devouring its prey. And he looked like he wanted to pee but couldn't find a toilet. Would be nice if he wetted his pants, but no such luck. That defeated expression, that deflated face, I'd pay a million bucks for it but just have to sleep with Sylvia.

Charlotte's eyes, red with sadness; her lips, weak with pain; her face, flushed with anger; her steps, hasty with desperation. She charged out of the ballroom. But what about her heart? Her heart turned to stone. Or is it ice? Waiting for me to caress it, warm it and melt it. The savior, the Lancelot, who is I. Who else would save you, oh my love? I ran after her but when I stepped out of the hotel and onto dung, she'd disappeared. I drove to her place but couldn't find her. I went to a bar in Alexandria and had three glasses of Long Island Iced-Tea. Oh, happy night tonight, happy soul this soul, the end of Act I to this masterpiece, my creation, to rival the greatest dramas.

Now for Act II, escalation of conflict, further development and complication of plot, toward the unavoidable happy ending.

I felt like a new man with a new heart waiting to do something great like Alexander or Caesar or Napoleon. Even now, I still felt the rush, the high, and the sweet aftertaste, just like flying through the air. When I returned home and couldn't sleep, I called Sylvia to come over to celebrate.

April 7, 1987

This afternoon, I visited Charlotte and comforted her. I persuaded her to write a letter to Sylvia: to stop that easy girl from contaminating our virgin boy by telling her he's not chaste. Naturally, my dear Charlotte hesitated in the beginning, not wanting to slander her virgin boy as well as herself. But I told her, with loose girls like Sylvia (how I have experience with them), got to take drastic actions. Devastated, defeated, abandoned by that son-of-a-bitch, naturally she depended on her savior. And for the first time she listened to me, her true lover.

After helping her with the letter, I wanted to spend more time with her, comforting her and consoling her and being there for her because that was the best time to exert my love. But she threw me out as if I was still plotting against her. Alas, I could only lament. But anyway, end of Act II, toward the climax with more complications and conflicts.

April 10, 1987

This morning, I went over to Sylvia's place and we read Charlotte's letter. She was shock and I was shock. I wasn't sure Charlotte would mail it out to Sylvia. Gutsy girl.

Anyway, we got a good laugh though Sylvia felt sorry for them. She tried to make a pass at me, but I was too clever for her. Told her I'd destroy the letter to prevent anyone else from seeing it. She got angry, and said I was trying to protect Charlotte. Good, I like that. She'll tell everyone, including Charlotte, I wanted to protect my true lover. That'd confirm I'm the guardian angel and savior. Eventually, Charlotte will be convinced I love her like the jewel of my heart.

But got to find out which seminary Lawrence is applying to and send this letter there to *help him out.* End of Act III. Can't wait till the finale.

CHAPTER 12

THE SUMMER BEFORE HIGH SCHOOL, having just stolen six-hundred dollars from his parents, Jim wanted to celebrate Independence Day out of town and though I believed New York suited him, he preferred to sample Boston's firework. We took the bus from Union Station and by noon arrived at South Station. We lunched at Faneuil Hall and strolled through Government Center toward Back Bay, éclairs in hands and sweat washing our foreheads. The crowd began to converge at Beacon Street and by the time we reached the Esplanade, black, blonde, and brunette hairs like toilet brushes were rubbing against our faces and arms. Like a child in a toy store, Jim sang and danced and flirted with some college girls. In the middle of thundering but distant laughter, I sweated, the shirt wet against my back, and felt lost among the faces and sounds. I didn't belong there, not in that crowd and not under those stars and not with Jim, but I couldn't figure out where I should be. From another world, Jim addressed me but his eyes frolicked across a redhead's pristine face and his mind probably distracted by a less pristine fantasy. All around, eyelashes flapping, lips moving; all around, laughter, dancing, hugging and kissing. I stood alone at the center of the universe and glared into a night deep and dark. I searched for a wormhole to tunnel through space-time and return home but found only ripples after ripples of nothingness. Now, Jim's words jeering at me, the same feeling, the same predicament: no bridge, no tunnel, no wormhole. Nothingness extended a hand but I dared not shake it.

Under the kaleidoscopic firework, amid sweat and bodies and laughter pulsating along the Esplanade, I recalled Jim's refusing to pick me for his basketball team. The 1812 Overture's notes resonated into my ear and wedged a tune into my mind. Across the water, M.I.T.'s Building 10 stood under the firework. When I discovered Jim had stolen the money from his parents, I bought a ticket and returned to D.C. On the way, I meditated on the shadows around Interstate 95, George Washington Bridge's triangular lights and Delaware River's bobbing water.

Now, after reading Jim's scheme to separate Charlotte and me, the same ache gnawed at my abdomen. I dropped onto the leather sofa next to the bed and drank the tea, but it tasted bitter. I smashed the mug against the tile floor, dispersing the liquid across the tiles toward Jim's statue. The image of Charlotte surfaced onto my mind—an image of a friendship unfulfilled.

I went downstairs for some cold water but it couldn't dispel the fever. I stepped out of the mansion for fresh air and under the clouds strolled across the garden past marble statues of J. P. Morgan, Andrew Carnegie, and J. D. Rockefeller, whom even as a boy, Jim had worshipped as other boys had Superman. Beneath my feet the crushed stones crackled a dirge and the daisies drooped on either side. At the end of the path, a bronze Cupid urinated into the golden fountain and a marble Aphrodite gazed into the northern sky. Beyond the fountain, against the clouds, an apple tree dangled half-ripe fruits.

The torrent from the Cupid celebrated Jim's victory and incited an eddy in my guts. Along my path, stones and twigs, feces and carcasses, and once in a few thousand miles, a ruby or an emerald, but trampled and crushed.

Jim trampled and crushed the gem Charlotte and I had shared. He sneered at our wrinkled cheeks and twisted lips and throbbing veins. He probably savored these images on many stormy nights.

One day, one day, if only one of these days... But, the sound of "but" echoed through the firmaments.

To destroy Jim, first obliterate Lawrence.

I wandered beyond the apple tree through the sculptured bushes unsure of the path. The stench led me to a dead skunk rotting on the ground. A vulture yelped and hovered overhead probably impatient for its afternoon snack. The marigold's aroma attacked my nostrils. As I confronted the lone path ahead, gray between green shrubs, a mist descended into my heart and I lamented the fragments of crushed gems.

I had refused to see Charlotte when she tried to amend, and dealt her a blow stronger than any punch Jim could offer. The apple I had offered her sank into my stomach, the aftertaste lingering among my taste buds.

I walked around the mansion to the front yard, and saw Edgar stepping out of his BMW and slamming the car door.

"Hello, Father, fancy seeing you here again." He handed the keys to Sylvia's chauffeur and marched through the drizzle. His eyes shifted; his brows danced; and his lips stretched from cheekbone to cheekbone. "What a coincidence, must be my lucky day. What're you sulking over? A pretty girl? Your old flame? Well, they come and go. What can you do about it? I say money is the most loyal companion, won't let you down in times of trouble. Not like women, or for that matter, men also." He patted me on my shoulder. "Remember the proposition I made during that funeral party? It still stands and I'm waiting for a reply. But don't take too long because another entrepreneurial priest, when he realizes the opportunity, the reward and payoff, would immediately seize the day. After all, in today's world, especially in this economy, those with the sharper eyes, the quicker legs and the stronger hands will win, usually just by a nose. I don't know why but I like you, so I want you to have the first chance to seize this opportunity. You know the shooting in the post office? Well, three people dead, and they're now my customers. When people mourn, when they cry, and when they stamp their feet, I smell opportunity. I'm like a poet who can see new things in the mundane, but of course in the world of money, capital, and the good old greenback. And I'm telling you again, the funeral business will thrive in this recession, just like bankruptcy lawyers. So get on the bandwagon while there's still a chance." He gave me a bundle of business cards and whispered, "Just like now, I smell opportunity. Just in case… oh, ha, I don't mean to be coldhearted, no, as you can see, I'm a warm and friendly guy. But heck, life is life, as they say, and things happen. If, I'm just saying if, if the preacher were to meet with some, eh, shall we say, misfortune, or if you prefer, calamity, it's all the same to me, you know what I mean. Well then, Mrs. Whitfield would have to make some arrangements. Right? A less proactive salesman would've waited until the milk's been spilled, but not me. I'm here to preempt any other salesman from taking my business. That's right, before the sales pitch and the closing, there's the presales calls, laying the groundwork, creating the mood, smoothing the path, building relationships. You'd be amazed at how many salespeople miss it and end up losing not just initial business but recurring ones. That's where the big profits are, with returning customers and no more acquisition costs. And every man and every woman I see is a potential customer, a potential business, and a potential profit. Oh, I'm saying all these just to let you know you can trust me to make money. And you'll benefit through the partnership with me. And with a potential customer like the preacher, his mansion, his sports cars, his wine cellar, that's right, I know about it, and though I can't confirm, all his mistresses' houses and cars. Why, I could make tons of money, providing the supreme-luxury version of our service to him, a funeral fit for a king. Oh, here's Mrs. Whitfield. Got to go. Wish me luck, not that success has anything to do with luck."

The mortician's timbre irritated my ear and tormented my head, so, after he followed Sylvia into the house, I stood in the drizzle and listened to the white-noise, which usually would spawn alpha-waves to order my thoughts, emotions and decisions. But now, even as the raindrops cooled my forehead, Jim's words, ever clearer in this mist, had lodged into the crevices of my mind and, through various renditions, their nuances haunted me.

Would I be willing to damn myself just to destroy Jim? After reading the next section of his diary, I realized his minions—those I called my friends—had been tiptoeing behind my back, ready to plunge a dagger into my heart.

CHAPTER 13

Part 3: The Art of War, Episode II: The Return of Sun Tzu

September 1, 2007

Camellia left for Boston this morning for her mission. I saw her boarding her flight at 8:00 a.m. A dreary dawn but soon a happy afternoon will come. She'll accomplish the mission, my faithful agent. I have confidence in her. Nothing can stop her. She's not the throwing-up-hands-at-the-cliff type. So much like me, the determined winner. And, we'll soon celebrate, with champagne, with caviar, and with a diamond-encrusted Black Forest cake. Maybe even a trip around the world.

October 10, 2007

Camellia called and said she'd befriended Lawrence and he trusts her. I complimented her and told her I'd wire three thousand dollars for her new apartment and furnishings. Everything is coming along, just as I've foreseen.

She wanted to seduce him. But I didn't want to sacrifice her, not her. Get him drunk and have a prostitute finish the job. If not that, then work on his Achilles' heel, Charlotte. That'd get his blood boiling and he'd lose his head and his heart. If anything, the sound of her name can stir up his dreary emotions. But I needed Lawrence to commit a sin and expose his hypocrisy.

I told Camellia to think up something. With that witty brain of hers, I'm sure something innovative will come out of it. Drunkenness? That's easy, but a bit too common. Sloth and avarice? Not his style. Abandon his nonexistent God? That'll do it. He'd leave the monastery, and he'll become a nothing, a nobody, a bum.

Hope Lawrence enjoys my gift, with all my planning and Camellia going to that freezer of a city. Even if he doesn't enjoy it, he should thank me. After he loses his virginity or faith or both, I'll visit him in the Bowery and hand him a flask of whiskey.

April 20, 2008

This afternoon met this computer wizard in my office and he hacked into my computer in one minute. And didn't talk much. Just the man I'm looking for. I told him I needed someone to monitor what Donald Larsen's doing with my account and make sure he's not embezzling my money. I also needed a guy to log into the church members' email accounts and help me prophesy their needs. So I can be more effective ministering to them, and cut the weeds and prune the branches to make the church a safer place for worship.

But before anything, this guy will have to earn my trust. I told him to go to Boston and steal the letter Daphne wrote to Lawrence. Then hack into his email account and send me some damning revelation, so I could forward the information to Camellia.

Lawrence, one day while you're walking down the street like any nitwit, you'll tumble down a hole so deep you'd think your hell is real. But your hell doesn't exist. You'll disappear into nothingness, vacuum, empty space and not have to burn forever. While I sip my colada in Maui and race along the Road to Kana. Can't blame anyone, we choose our paths.

June 2, 2008

Received Daphne's letter from Ichiro. I thanked him and paid him a thousand dollars for his trouble and expenses. Told him I'll soon have him break into Larsen's system and transfer a few million to my bank account. But now, he could take a vacation and enjoy life with the money.

Lawrence could've destroyed the letter but he kept it and probably wanted to blackmail me with it. Well, I have the letter now and you aren't getting none of my money. Good thing I have Mr. Soseki, and the monk thinks he's his friend. Still, that monk will pay for my humiliation. I should've never begged him.

Ichiro also sent me some of Lawrence's emails for my leisure reading. This man is good. But when I poured a glass of whiskey and read the first email, I found out Lawrence was trying to get hold of the original scroll of *On the Road*. What nonsense, searching for toilet paper. That's just like Lawrence. I drank the whiskey to wash the staleness from my mouth and hoped to find some juicy gossip. But in the second email Lawrence was telling a friend he went to Harvard Square to have salad for dinner. What'd I care what he has for dinner? I couldn't find anything about Camellia, or about Charlotte. And no emails about his reactions to losing Daphne's letter. Does he ever let anyone know his feelings? Well, at least Mr. Soseki can hack into his account. But I have to tell him to filter the junks before forwarding the gems.

July 1, 2008

When I woke up in the morning, I had a headache and kicked the bedpost and I knew it'd be a lousy day. Wanted to expel my bad luck by burning Daphne's letter. But when I opened the safety box, it was gone. Thought I'd misplaced it, but I recalled putting it in there. Should've burned it right away, instead of waiting for a chance to waive it in front of that virgin boy. That really makes my day. I thought maybe Sylvia found it and stole it. But it meant nothing to her. Hopefully, she didn't give it to Mad-Dog Simon to spite me. But any way, nobody knows where that creep went. And she, like I, probably had never seen his ugly face either. But who the hell stole the letter?

CHAPTER 14

Two years ago, on Father Theodore's advice, I entered the Irish bar in Boylston, expecting to meet some drunkard, lonely heart or fraternity boy, but found Camellia, through her whiskey breath, babbling about the search for happiness and intimacy as well as some incoherent philosophy of life. When an athletic young man, after ogling her for half an hour, bought her whiskey and tried to make a pass at her, I interfered and would've earned a black eye and a broken nose had the bartender and security guard not intervened. After the guard expelled the young man, she wanted to buy me a drink for fending off the *loser* but, unwilling to lower my guard in that lion's den, I refused the offer. She kept inquiring about me and, at one time, asked me to dance, but I again declined.

When we left the bar and strolled along Commonwealth Avenue amid the September breeze, she said, "You monks like to pick fights in bars, too? How about discos?"

"Do you expect us to do it in the monastery, after Laud or Mass?"

"But why with guys who think with their muscles?"

"In my experience, alcohol doesn't solve many problems, maybe insomnia, but even that—"

"You going to counsel me with that God stuff?" She grasped a lamppost and danced around it. When some college students passed by, she grabbed one of the boys and tried to dance with him but he slipped away and hastened down the street as if avoiding a leper.

"I didn't become a parish priest so I wouldn't have to counsel people. Why spread half-wisdom and pseudo-nonsense?"

"Now, you're talking like a sage." She slapped my back, thrusting me forward into the lamppost but I swirled to avoid it.

"Will you be alright?" I said.

"What if I won't be? Are you going to help me? Of course, your prayer and meditation are probably more important than helping people." In front of the hotel, she gave her phone number and requested that I call the next morning.

I wasn't aware of the trap so I called the next day to check on her condition. She again thanked me, this time her tone sober and hesitant betrayed her sadness. We chatted for an hour about her adjusting to Boston after two weeks there and decided to meet next Saturday to find her an apartment.

During the next three weeks, we checked apartments in Brighton, Allston, Watertown and Back Bay and I stepped deeper into the snare while learning of her childhood.

"When I fell on the sidewalk and scratched my knee she didn't care… when I wanted to go over to Susie's place, he wouldn't let me…when I got a D in algebra, they didn't even notice…when I reached puberty and… and… I was so scared…"

I listened to her childhood episodes and recalled an afternoon at a playground when that steel-like fist crashed into my jaw and the pain traveled through my gum. I had forgotten the bully's name or the event leading to the fist but remembered the tears flowing down my cheeks and Charlotte screaming and kicking the ruffian in the shin. While Camellia wiped away her tears, I wanted to embrace her and share my past.

Camellia disliked her mom and detested her dad. Although Mrs. Larsen tolerated her daughter, she had checked any affection and intimacy toward her flesh and blood as if an embrace or a kiss or a chat would damage her arms or her lips or her liver. And Donald Larsen, reaping a fortune from his cons, had never bought Camellia any presents. Not for Easters, not for Christmases and not for her birthdays. And for as long as she could remember, he would invent expletives to insult her, as if halting such abuses would damn him. Once, he had barged into her bathroom and scrutinized her naked body, not lustily but spitefully. She could no longer bear the shame and humiliation and two days later ran away from home.

At an early age, I had lost my parents to cancer and could empathize with Camellia, who had lived as if without parents. Except for Mrs. Larsen's snubs and Donald Larsen's abuses. No matter how different our views and our lifestyles were, we bonded together as fellow orphans, who early on must learn to defend against the indifferent and sometimes cruel world and throughout our short childhood had to face similar storms and billows. She was attracted to me perhaps because for the first time in the journey through mud and thistles, she encountered a fellow cripple, marred by similar scars, sporting a familiar limp, showcasing a related hunchback. Though neither strong nor capable, I promised to protect her from Donald Larsen and similar monsters.

Along Storrow Drive, Camellia and I would discuss and disagree on the purpose of our lives—hers for the friends to share joy and grief and the lover to share everything, and mine for the mountain or wilderness to reach beyond myself toward enlightenment—but we shared a common passion to trot through the desert, despite the sun and sand and more sand, for the oasis.

"Just wanted a stable job with decent money, friends to hang around and gossip, a man and a home, but of course not necessarily a husband and a family and lose my freedom. But of course, if the right man comes along... That's not too much, is it? It's not even the American dream. I'm not greedy," she said. "You're so eager to help me, but I can help you more, by showing you how a mother can steal her son's savings, how a father can violate his daughter, how a teacher can seduce her student to murder her husband and get the life insurance, how a tenth grader can shoot his teachers and classmates point-blank as if playing a video game."

Her sincerity had shielded her treachery, planted through Jim's benediction. Probably, as a loyal lieutenant, she would report my every syllable and my every twitch to Jim and he would snigger, hand to mouth and shoulders bouncing, at the ignorant monk's silliness, his compassion. All our moments, beside the Charles River next to the water, along Route 3 between two walls of birches, maples, and oaks, and among the crowds in Faneuil Hall, mutated and the cancer threatened to infect all other experiences. But had I known the intrigue, I would've helped her, then confronted her and fought Jim until my last red blood cell.

This Valentine's Day, she had invited me to candlelight dinner at her Back Bay apartment. While I stood in front of her apartment and regretted having come, the door opened to a lady in a black dress. After dinner, she kissed me and began to undress, but I held her hand and said, "They said something about destroying friendship."

"You could've come up with a better excuse," she said. "All I want is to be happy, to find someone who'll make me happy and to make him happy. Be with me and save me from a life of misery."

Under the candlelight, I examined before me two paths: matrimony or celibacy. To marry without love or to contemplate life and the universe without lifting a pinky to flick away suffering? To be a fool or a hypocrite?

"You must be thinking what your Jesus would do. Just know I love you more than anyone else and I'll make you happy. Don't you love me?" She snuggled against me and shivered and I embraced her and shielded her from the darkness. While the wind whistled outside the window.

"Not in the way you want it." At that moment, Charlotte's specter emerged upon my mind and though afraid to startle Camellia, I bared my soul. The candle's flame cast on her twitching lips an unsteady light.

We sat on the sofa for about half an hour before reviewing the laughter at Sturbridge, Newport and Cape Cod and the tears along Storrow Drive, on Boston Common and at that Newbury Street café. She told me she wanted to hurl away the past, to amputate the pain and suffering and to journey into the land of sunshine and beaches. Before reading Jim's diary, I had believed her words and wanted to help her find the long incinerated Eden, not meant for mortals along this segment of time. Now, I could only bask in a sea of snake venom and with bile quench my thirst.

***

And Ichiro? Since the lecture at Harvard University, after which Ichiro and I had chatted for two hours in a coffee shop, he had delved into Zen to liberate the body, the mind and the psyche from the bondage of knowledge, memory, emotions and matter. But, he couldn't abandon Sonya's ghost, which continued to haunt his mornings and afternoons and evenings and nights. He had fasted; he had abstained from alcohol; he even had lived alone in the mountains for several months; but Sonya's spirit continued to circulate through his arteries and nourish him. His reasoning sharper, his memory clearer, his feelings more refined, his music more like Beethoven's Symphony No 6, the brook followed by the storm followed by the paean.

Love and pain coexist and interact and annihilate each other, only to create a refreshed day, a refined feeling, a rejuvenated energy. Sun and rain... laughter and tear... electron and positron...

On a June evening, amid the music from Simon and Garfunkel, Ichiro recounted his meeting Sonya in a walkathon against human trafficking. He was enjoying the view across the Charles River near Watertown, a flock of geese in formation over Harvard Business School's red brick buildings, when a middle-aged woman, face flushed, wobbled on the walkway and fainted from exhaustion. He eased the woman onto her back and sprinkled water onto her face while, from behind, Sonya glided over and performed CPR, the movements graceful yet sensitive, like a painter's strokes across the canvass. After the woman woke up and thanked them, he and Sonya walked along Storrow Drive, beside the widening Charles and Cambridge's converging skyline across the river, and chatted about nanotechnology, the human genome project, and the cure for cancer. After finding out he had grown up in Seattle, she recounted her adventures on Mount Rainier's trails, which would receive snow even in September. And after finding out she had also graduated from the University of Chicago, he recounted his fruitful but lonely times on campus, while studying mathematics and philosophy. By the end of the day, he made a friend.

When Ichiro finished his story, the music outside the café had ceased, the crowd had dissipated, and the waiter was rushing us out the door. But we stood outside Harvard Yard near the bus stop and, holding our cups and sipping the brownish liquids, continued our conversation, drifting from his romance to my monastic journey to the futility of war to the economics of greed and materialism to the topology of the space-time continuum. In the end, I recommended he travel to Europe, where time had etched wisdom into the landscape of its cities and towns, and leave behind for several months the dark cloud that would disperse through a shift in the wind. When I sneaked back into the abbey, I had only enough time to clean up and prepare for laud. I tried hard not to doze off to the tune of Veni Creator Spiritus, but afterward had a headache and the next night dancing images in entangling dreams. Yet, I had enjoyed the time with Ichiro and cared not about a few sleepless nights or the Kafkaesque dreams.

When Ichiro went to Paris to study music, I awaited a new dawn of morning clouds and chirping orioles, a new Ionian piano quartet with contrapuntal melodies and plagal cadence, and a new algebra of linear operators and rotational transforms. I wanted to share in the purple striations, the iambic beat, the structural beauty of a new pseudo-symmetry.

But my reverie had dispersed. Ichiro was only performing a drama to deceive the monk, a fool.

***

Above, the chandelier twirled. Beneath, the bed tossed. The sunlight poured through the drapes. My head ached and my breath reeked of alcohol while the bottle of whiskey sat on the desk.

I tried to get up but the mattress tossed me onto the floor. The floor spun and bobbed like an amusement park ride. When the ride ended, I sat on the floor and held my head, while the memory continued to pain my mind.

Jim's statue, perhaps an illusion like the diary's fiction, stood across the room smirking, enjoying the misery that the fiend had planted with his diary's words and phrases and intended to reap when it ripens. Construction of reality from words, from a mouth or a pen or a keyboard, from a friend or a stranger, so long as we grant these syllables authority and credibility. Should I grant Jim that power? But those paragraphs, those entries and those pages would create a new reality independent of their accuracy. Just as in the Prisoner's Dilemma, without knowing truth from bluff, I must choose and create reality.

Though unable to fulfill at once truth's and love's demands, I must choose the next step and the next word and accept the grief, the frustration and perhaps the regret that would linger in my mind until Alzheimer should relieve me of the suffering. Eighty-percent truth and twenty-percent love, or perhaps fifty-fifty? Embrace Jim's gospel and send Camellia and Ichiro to hell? Ignore the madman's delusions and return to our Garden of Eden?

I couldn't pray or meditate or chant Veni Creator Spiritus. Treachery had clouded my pupils, stuffed my eardrums, and embittered my taste buds. Serving food in a soup kitchen in Mission Hill with Ichiro and Camellia, dining with them in Back Bay ... I couldn't focus on a single contour among the images swirling in my mind. Nor could I isolate a single word among the voices clamoring within my ears. I hadn't eaten for two days but wasn't hungry; the fumes had filled my stomach and would satiate me for days and days.

Ichiro and Camellia had worked with me as a team on the lawsuit against Pi Epsilon Naught Chemical for dumping chemicals in the water. And with the help of our lawyer Jan Moscowitz, we won on behalf of the town's residents and celebrated justice and camaraderie. But while we were fighting our opponent, they were waiting for the chance to thrust the dagger into my back. With my back wide open to them. And now, the nectar of laughter and embraces after that victory sickened my stomach and irritated my throat.

Jim's claws had severed my bond with Camellia and Ichiro and his breath had poisoned my memories of the Easter rainbow, the Independence Day fireworks and the Christmas snow.

Before coming to Gilead, I had gone to meditate at Walden Pond. That morning, under the rising sun, the water sang and danced to the rhythm of the morning breeze, and the ripples crisscrossed to weave a lattice of light. The clouds drifted in the stream of air. No one else to taint the birches or to corrupt the morning or to smear the lark's melody. I chanted Veni Creator Spiritus. Peace. Yet, a squall-laden peace.

I wanted to search for peace, for kindness, for love in hypocrisy's rubbles but the desert had opened its arms. I would enter, not hesitating, and choke on the dry air and collapse under the sandstorm. And yet, among the sand dunes rippling into the horizon would sprout an oasis if I could endure and embrace the desert as it had me. These hands and feet of flesh and bone, this heart of fear and hunger, under the sun and in the sand, to seize the fleeting peace at Walden Pond.

***

In less than two weeks, Sylvia had raised four million dollars through the church. On the day I was to deliver the ransom, I met her in front of the mansion. She told me most members had defaulted on their mortgages and sold their refrigerators, ovens, washers, chandeliers, and air conditioners before moving out. And Mrs. Walker sold her dowry— an emerald ring and a diamond necklace. They raised one million dollars from the proceeds. Sylvia also sold the church to Edgar Cunningham for three million dollars, but complained the mortician had shortchanged her.

"The chandeliers, the Steinway, the cherry wood pews, the computerized kitchen, the multimedia system, the workstations... Damn it, should get at least a million more. But, at least I sold the wine on the side, made some side profit." She cursed Edgar and marched into the house.

Before delivering the ransom, I strolled around the mansion. I trampled on the crushed stones past the fountain and under the apple tree plugged a fruit hanging low and ripe and dug my teeth into it. The flesh crunched in my mouth and the juice filled my tongue. Above, the nimbus drifted and below, the crickets tapped their iambic rhythms, but here Lawrence stood at the cliff ready to leap across the chasm, ready to cross the thin red line.

I longed to stand before Camellia and Ichiro and pour out my grievances. I longed to yank out the nagging ache and endure the gaping wound.

Oh God, don't let me hate Camellia or Ichiro, let my anger dissipate before the sun rests for the day. But let me scorn Jim ever more, until my veins throb beyond redemption, until I leap into the desert or plunge into the infernal. Oh, let it be, let it be.

A bean goose coasted across the sky as if savoring the September rain and fog that had softened the contours of the trees, the poles and the distant houses. Then a roar, as if from a jet engine, echoed through the air and the bird plunged into the fountain and spawned plumes that leaped into the sky and beads that fell onto the earth. Agent Peter, rifle in hand and cigarette in mouth, strolled along the path to the fountain, grabbed the goose by the neck and yanked the bird out of the water.

Five days ago, I had also delighted in the sky, the clouds, the sunlight, and the meadow. But now, my eyes had opened and I saw the darkness beyond the sky, the mists among the clouds, the agitation in the sunlight, the maggots in the meadow and the gun-barrel among the rosebushes that would continue to bloom after the gunshot.

That bean goose had enjoyed its last few seconds as if the bullet hadn't existed, before plunging into darkness. But I would continue to look into the barrel, waiting for the roar to echo through the air and the bullet to pierce my flesh, knowing the sky, the clouds, the sunlight, and the meadow would abandon me and the rosebushes would betray me. I searched for the happy fool but knowledge had transformed rainbows into mists, music into vibrations, friends into frauds, and tomorrows into illusions.

Oh happy, happy fool. If I hadn't known the truth behind Charlotte's letter, or Camellia's affair, or Ichiro's mission... if... if... if... the door into lost worlds once possible but now extinguished after *if* mutated into *is*.

And yet, I had chosen to read the diary and, for all the dung and bullets and daggers, would choose again if necessary, to plunge into the desert and savor the dust. Just as I had chosen the monastery rather than Fermi Lab. I must seek to be Lawrence and more so each day, and not the *ifs* of another soul. I must walk through the desert to find the oasis and I must walk through the night to find the dawn. In the sea of sand, the ocean of stars, Lawrence would search for Lawrence.

After I had finished the apple, I returned to the house and grabbed the bag to deliver the ransom—yesterday's newspaper—to Jim's kidnapper. When I left the mansion, Agent Peter was barbecuing the goose on the porch and said he would come along soon. Had Sylvia given me the cash instead of saving it for her retirement in Fiji, I might've hidden it and delivered an empty bag anyway. But now, without my intervention, Jim might still never leave his dungeon. How delicious the thought, the feeling, the endorphin surging through my brain. Never thought damming my soul would be so satisfying. But no amount of endorphin could fill the void left by Camellia and Ichiro, their lies, their deceit, their hypocrisy.

I headed for the brothel.

CHAPTER 15

WHEN I WENT INTO THE MEN'S ROOM of the local brothel to deliver the ransom, I found taped to the toilet bowl's backside a note directing me to St. Barnabas Church. As I walked out of the building, a young man in pinstripe suit inquired about the brothel's service. I apologized for not being able to enlighten him and left for the church. I passed a spa where two ladies were arguing whether to have sirloin steak or barbecue ribs for this afternoon's *Eat and Buy* party. At the church's footsteps, I bypassed Father Jones's whiskey breath and went to the altar. I found the second note soaking in the silver basin's holy water. When the priest offered me whiskey, I declined and left the sanctuary. I went into the graveyard and, before a cracked headstone, dug up a GPS-enabled mobile phone. Beside the bowing fence, I waited for the phone call while the crow scattered the flies and pecked at some carrion. Had I known the banker would be playing hide and seek, I would've borrowed Jim's bicycle to save some calories. But Agent Peter and his comrades, smart enough to follow in his sports car, should be enjoying their lunch—barbecue goose and beer. At one o'clock, when my sweat had cleansed my face, the kidnapper phoned and, in a muffled voice, directed me to the Million Dollar Café. I accepted a sandwich from Father Jones and rushed to the rendezvous.

At the café, a young lady and two middle-aged gentlemen were cursing New York bankers, Washington politicians and Texas oil executives. And a couple near the window discussed the strategy and tactics to sell all appliances and furniture and leave town before the bank could realize they had defaulted on mortgage payments.

After the real-estate bubble had burst and the financial markets collapsed, I anticipated the authorities unmasking more risky mortgages, imaginary oil fields, sanitized financial statements and other con games for the twenty-first century consumers, who had disentangled from the trickery of the travelling preachers, the professional beggars and the local magicians. And after learning from Sylvia of the families, marriages, and careers collapsing under Donald Larsen's Ponzi scheme, I realized the carrion had dispersed its scent across Gilead to perhaps other towns, penetrating banks, diners, and churches and settling into the carpets of every apartment, townhouse and single family home. I had toured Jim's twenty-eight-bedroom mansion, marble hallway and arched ceilings and chandeliers and Victorian furniture and wine cellar and ten-acre garden. I had seen his Lamborghini and Armani and Rolex Masterpiece. I had walked through Main Street, where foreclosure signs for million-dollar mansions lined the sidewalks. I never had more than three thousand dollars in my bank account and so strolled through town like a New Yorker walking through the Roman Forum trying to ferret out the history behind every reclining column and every headless statue. What the atomic bomb had done to Hiroshima, the greenback had done to Gilead.

Before I could order a cup of coffee, the waitress handed me an envelope, which two hours ago someone had left for me—*a sad-looking man with a neon phone*. I thanked the waitress and took out a car key and a note directing me to City Hall. I walked along Happy Valley Road past foreclosure signs and broken fences and reached the red-bricked building where a gilded statue of the mayor extended both hands to welcome visitors. I went to the back as instructed and located the BMW and I got into the sedan and started the engine with the car key. After driving along Main Street for five minutes, I returned to Jim's mansion and though surprised the car had his garage door opener, I entered and waited in the garage for further instructions.

The kidnapper called and instructed me to get into the Porsche. It took me more than ten minutes to open the door and scratch the side. Fortunately, the next call didn't come until half an hour later, in which time I had adjusted the driver's seat, turned off the stereo, threw out the condom packs and finished the sandwich tasting of whiskey tuna. While staring at the plasma TV on the garage wall and recounting the millions of dollars Jim had filched from the church or laundered through the Great Commission Missions, I wanted to relay my location to Agent Peter, but received an SMS: *Don't you dare contact the agent*. Camellia said her father had engineered complex derivatives to sell to clients but his planning revealed a man as cautious and calculating as Napoleon and a mind as twisted as my delivery route.

By the time the call came, Agent Peter, who would shoot a fly for disturbing his sleep, probably had lost me and was boxing his car door. I drove as instructed to Whitfield Park, where birches flaunted their yellow oval leaves and the crickets' iambic tune hypnotized the squirrels. I located the trashcan and put the bag into it. I retrieved a package—my *reward* according to the kidnapper. After returning to the car, I opened the package: a picture of Sylvia kissing me at the annual dance.

Frustrated at the kidnapper's game, I threw away the picture and drove the car out of the park and I returned on foot toward the trashcan and, mobile phone in hand, waited behind the bushes for the fiend. I despised Jim's venom, tainting not only my friendship with Charlotte, Camellia and Ichiro but also the air and the water. Yet, I wouldn't allow myself to relish his demise. Not like Sylvia. She probably would've given up her alligator-skin handbag for that treat. If Agent Peter could arrive in time to nab Donald Larsen, perhaps Jim could reunite with his Lamborghini and wine collection. But if the fiend had only sent an accomplice, Romeo might not be able to thank his wife, much less visit his mistresses and girlfriends. I was about to call Agent Peter when footsteps interrupted the crickets' rhythm and a face emerged behind a birch.

A phantom. In a dream. I couldn't match the eyes with the birch leaves or the lips with the cricket's tune or the body with the breeze. The hands that had caressed my hair and the lips that had kissed my cheeks. I still wondered when I had entered this nightmare.

I was so focused on delivering the ransom as to forget my purpose in Gilead that Camellia's apparition flashing out of my unconscious mind and appearing beside the trashcan, though dispersing my worries, dislodged me from my dream into another space-time continuum. A world not of Sylvia, Father Jones and Agent Peter, but of Camellia, Ichiro and Father Theodore. But the shifting wind stirred the fallen leaves and reminded me the two worlds converged at a locus: here and now, where Camellia collided with the ransom. She came to pick up the money.

I stepped out of the bushes and called after her, but upon seeing me, she dashed away and exclaimed, "The trashcan. It's in the trashcan."

"Camellia? Don't tell me you're helping your father, with kidnapping and extortion. I want to know the truth, for once." Though afraid of the reality around the corner, I chased after the truth within her. But she leaped and sprinted and, while I scrambled through the path, she reached the park entrance and slipped into a Lamborghini Gallardo, which screeched down the road leaving the smell of burnt rubber. Along with her, the truth fled into the horizon.

I couldn't believe she would help Donald Larsen and, after huddling down and panting for several minutes, returned to the trashcan, in which I found a package—a memory stick and a note from Camellia indicating the storage device contains Jim's other diary, all the secrets hidden from Sylvia. I clasped my hand and shuddered at the scent of his cesspool and I prayed that only drunkenness, fornication and orgies filled his diary, but my mind's eyes foresaw an abyss.

CHAPTER 16

J IM WHITFIELD CHRONICLES
Part 4: Inferno

March 3, 1986
Came home and found seventeen messages on my answer machine. All
from Daphne. Spent almost half an hour deleting them. Afterward, my
index finger hurt like hell. And after listening to her voice for thirty
minutes, I had a headache and had to take an aspirin. Wanted to turn
off the answering machine, but Ginger might be calling any time.
Damn it, Daphne, stop messing with my life.

March 19, 1986
One of those days when you wake up and your joints tell you the
storm is around the corner. Was eating bacon and scrambled eggs
when I heard the news on TV. Daphne had committed suicide. Almost
choked on the eggs. Thought it might be another Daphne. But no, her
picture appeared on the TV screen. The naïve smile, the blonde hair
over her shoulder. Jeez.

Must be because I wouldn't marry her. The silly girl. Why'd she
have to make such a big deal of some innocent fun? Now, the mess is
threading to spill into my backyard.

Mad-Dog Simon. If he finds out I got his sister pregnant, but no, he
couldn't. I was scared shitless and didn't finish my breakfast. Thought
about not going to school but didn't want to draw suspicion onto me.

When I walked into the schoolyard, I scanned around searching for the Frankenstein monster. But only saw Sylvia coming after me. I charged into the school and escaped her but bumped into Lawrence who was reading some book with a foreign title. Grabbed his shirtfront and told him we got to talk after school. Didn't want to stay in the corridor so for the first time, arrived in class on time. How humiliating.

Didn't know what came over me. Must be fear. Fear must've made me stupid. Rushed home before the last class ended and waited for the Lawrence to arrive. He took his time, the creep. When he came in, some virus must've attacked me. I knelt in front of him. I wept. I begged. I begged for him not to tell Simon about my involvement with Daphne. I was in a daze for the rest of the day.

Only after dinner when the sky darkened did I realized what I'd done. I'd humiliated myself in front of the virgin boy. I felt the shame and smashed my computer monitor. I swore I'd get even with Lawrence. I swore he'd pay for seeing me like that.

I went over to Ginger's place and felt better. Later, while she was sleeping and I was having a cigarette, I paced around the bedroom worrying that Lawrence might still snitch on me. But no, the gutless coward wouldn't dare. I vowed to castrate him and unscrew his head if he squeals.

I looked through the window down at the street and saw a shadow around the corner. I dropped the cigarette thinking it might be that lunatic Simon. But it was only a dog. What a scary creep, the Mad-Dog. Where in hell did this monster come from anyway? And I don't even know what he looks like, damn it. Right now, better keep a low profile and avoid him.

July 5, 1986

This morning, when Lawrence walked into my room like a saint, saying Charlotte didn't want a date with me, I knew he'd betrayed me. Was probably sniggering in his heart, thinking I'm a damn fool. Shouldn't have trusted the double crossing virgin boy. Should've asked Charlotte for the date myself. Just didn't think that shrimp would dare to stab me in the back but he has more guts than I thought.

Followed him to the ice-cream shop and saw Charlotte waiting for him. I knew it. He'd arranged a date with her, the double-crosser. She was scribbling something and laughed that carefree laugh. Wished I could be there holding the cone instead of that conniver. They talked until the ice-cream melted on their hands, damn it.

Went to the local bar and had a Bloody Mary. Felt like a Bloody Mary, too. Wanted to pick a fight with some shrimp but there were only tattooed bikers whose arms were thicker than my legs. After having a drink, I felt nauseous. Was about to leave when a biker walked up and bought me a drink. He started to hit on me, asking me to go to his place. I was scared shitless and ran out of the bar leaving one shoe behind.

February 7, 1987

Bought a new shirt, a new pant and a new pair of loafers. Bought a dozen roses for Charlotte. Will be asking her to go out with me on Valentine's Day. My last chance at happiness, love and life. Mustn't fail. Must defeat Lawrence.

I'd practiced how I'd approach her and how I'd smile at her and how I'd praise her and how I'd ask for the date. Just as in the sales manuals.

But when I looked into the mirror. Hated the flashy shirt. Hated the hillbilly pant, like those in some sixties sitcom. Hated the loafers, like some used-car salesman's footwear. And the damn roses were withering like they were scared shitless.

Oh, God, if you exist, please make Charlotte like me, please make her love me, please make her adore me, please make her worship me.

February 14, 1987

Last week, when I asked Charlotte for a date, she laughed in my face and walked away. She gave Lawrence the roses I bought her. Okay, I was cool. I brushed the locks of hair from my forehead and headed home. On the way, I punched a poodle and bruised my knuckles. But I was still calm like the eye of the storm. I went home. I took the bat. I smashed the TV pretending it was Lawrence's round head.

Sure, Lawrence can spit in my face and kick me in the butt whenever he wants to. Sure, the son-of-a-bitch can shove my head into the toilet and I'll thank him, maybe beg for more. Sure, I'll smile, and offer him a glass of cyanided wine. I'm a cool guy, not like Mad-Dog Simon.

Last night, woke up in an alley in Georgetown next to a homeless man reeking of urine. Puked on his trouser legs and urinated into a trashcan. Then wandered through the streets in the half-light waiting for Valentine's Day. I passed a florist where bundles of roses had been stacked against the display window. Wished I could buy my beloved Charlotte a dozen. My image in the window scared me. The damn sports jacket: it's not silk, it's not cashmere, it's not Armani. But I was cool like Alaska in the winter.

Bought a bottle of whiskey and finished a half by noon but the stuff tasted like vinegar. Vowed to reveal Lawrence's wicked soul to Charlotte. She'll find out that I'm her most loyal, most devoted, most submissive, guardian angel.

September 3, 1987

Lawrence had left Charlotte for the seminary, as I'd expected long ago. She should've trusted me instead of that virgin boy. Yesterday, I went to Charlotte's place to comfort her and found out she'd left town. And her grandmother didn't know where she'd gone. Damn it. Oh my poor Charlotte, what kind of God-forsaken place have you gone to? I love you so much I'd take all the money from my parents' accounts and flee with you to the Bahamas, or whatever islands you want. And we'd live happily ever after. I swear I'll find you.

September 15, 1987

A week ago, I hired a gumshoe to locate Charlotte and yesterday the man gave me her address for three hundred dollars.

496 Perfecto Lane,

Edison, NJ 08820

To celebrate, went to the bar and had three glasses of Long Island Iced-Tea. Danced with several women before passing out. Woke up in the morning in bed with a middle-aged woman I didn't recognize. Took a shower, got dressed and left her apartment. Bought a bagel and went home. Before breakfast, I turned on my computer and wrote a letter. I imagined how Lawrence hated Charlotte and assembled the words he didn't dare to write.

In the afternoon, I left the church secretary in bed and sent Lawrence's letter to Charlotte. In the letter, he said he hasn't forgiven her for writing that hideous letter. He blames her for all the pains and troubles he's gone through. Of course he would, that unforgiving son-of-a-bitch. He hates her. He'd never forgive her as long as he lives. He never wants to see her again. Not even when he's dying of cancer. He forbids her from visiting him.

Hope she finally sees his true color and despises him so she could forget him and move on with her life. And realizes how caring I've been, comforting and supporting her when she was in hell. I'm here, always here, ready to take her into my arms, my dearest Charlotte. Can she ever find someone more loving, more caring, more and generous than Jim?

CHAPTER 17

I DROVE DOWN PERFECTO LANE past a row of pre-W.W.II ranches, and came to several colonials, number 496 the second to the last unit before Route 28. The two-story house rested against a row of oaks and behind a pear tree bearing greenish-yellow fruits. Withered leaves jitterbugged on the driveway and the lawns on either side, while a squirrel, chasing an invisible mate, bounced from branch to branch on the tree. As I drove my car onto the driveway, a delivery boy threw the newspaper over my car and knocked once on the storm door, helping me overcome my dread of approaching the concrete steps, the storm door and the dark-green front door.

After reading Ichiro's SMS that he had found Camellia, I stepped off my car. A woman in her late thirties opened the front door. She peered at me. She staggered against the door but gripped the handle and regained balance. Charlotte had aged, as had the spruce in her previous home, the lines on her forehead and between the brows distinct against her hair's faded color. Traces of the summers and winters, along with those of the morning fog, draped her face and even sank into her body, which swayed behind the storm door. Against the swishing leaves, a silent sadness and a still grief expanded from my guts toward my chest and spread to my head. Time had gnawed at her just as it had the faded colonial, the cracked driveway, the warped street signs, and the man at the driveway. We couldn't escape entropy anymore than U.S. residents could avoid federal income taxes.

From those eyes flowed streaks of tears to remind me of time lost, happiness dissipated and relations severed. Youth's folly, that wise clown, lifted its head and taunted me, implicated me and showed me the sand dunes stretching to the horizon.

Eternity in an instant: what Ichiro sought in an everlasting union with Sonya. But I sought a different satori, a different obscure knowledge, a different dark night, not through seppuku, neither smothering breaths nor arresting heartbeats.

Charlotte flung open the storm door, rushed out of the house onto the driveway, and embraced me, her tears against my cheek. "Forgive me. Forgive me."

"Actually, I came to ask your forgiveness, for refusing to listen to your explanation and your apology, for severing our bond, which should've been stronger than any Jim, than any letter, than any seminary."

"Oh, I was so scare that I'd pass away from this life without seeing you again, without your forgiveness, without consolation… just like the oak that collapsed during last year's snowstorm, or the backyard fence that toppled this summer, or the stop sign that dropped onto the road."

I smelled her familiar scent and tasted the tear as it seeped through my lips. I embraced her emaciated body, recalling the brave girl who had chased away the bulldog. I caressed her face and studied the wrinkles that revealed all my pigheadedness, insensitivity and selfishness.

"Once in a while, I would inquire about you at the monastery, and though desperate to see your eyes again, respected your wish. I knew you would forgive me but time's not on my side." She touched my cheek but didn't move her fingers, as if she were afraid to damage it.

I related Jim's scheme to destroy our friendship, from Sylvia's kiss to the fake letter, and swore to avenge our suffering. My voice trembled and my face flushed. She listened and rubbed her forehead, but again embraced me.

"Oh, I'm so happy," she said. "All the dark clouds are gone, dispersed. Instinctively, I knew you didn't write that letter. Oh, you never said you never want to see me again. You never said you wouldn't forgive me. You never said any of those things in the letter. Oh, all the pain, all the suffering, what does it matter? And that evil Jim Whitfield, what does he matter? He's nothing, an ant, a flea, an ameba." She kissed me, and the girl who had chased away the bulldog and saved me from the canine teeth returned to my side. A withered leaf bounced off my nose onto her cheek and in an instant she closed her eyes and dropped her head. She let go of me, as if she had also severed from a branch, and, in the mid-September wind, fell along with the leaf. I held her to prevent her from dropping onto the pavement and tried without success to wake her up. I carried her into the house, which reeked of sandalwood, and put her on the sofa. I rubbed her temples and after a minute she woke up.

"You scared me. What's the matter?" I helped her sit up.

"I'm sorry. I was so excited..." she said, rubbing her head, "my blood must've..."

I went to the kitchen counter and picked up the thermal flask beside several bottles of prescription drugs. The chair against the table, the pot on the stove and the fork and spoon and bowl in the drying rack seemed to recount her daily solitude. I ignored their silent reproach and the back door's grumbling and poured warm water into a glass. When I returned to the living room, Charlotte's sad smile greeted me.

"What are those drugs for?" I handed her the mug and sat down beside her.

She took the mug and drank a draft. "I left Fairfax two months after you went to Boston. There was nothing there for me. Moved here and had been living here since. A quiet place, but with supermarkets and malls close by. A decent place to live and many pharmaceutical firms around the area so I can easily find a job. I had switched jobs twice and it wasn't a problem finding work. Even now, in this recession—"

"That Thanksgiving, I looked for you and found out you'd moved, but no one seemed to know where you went. I guessed you didn't tell anyone so I wouldn't look for you."

"No, I wanted you to know, but didn't want anyone else to. I didn't know how that evil man could've found me." She reached out and grabbed my hand, her hand cold and trembling.

"Because he has money and money can incite people to walk through walls, plunge into fires, and jump off cliffs, and turn water into fuel, lead into gold, and saints into demons." I rubbed her hand to warm it.

"Might have been a good thing we didn't see each other. If you had let me talk to you, in my desperation, I might have tried to change you." She leaned against me.

"Then, perhaps we'd have a boy and a girl by now." I held her, her fragile body.

"Now, I'm glad it didn't happen. After a while, I would've regret it, taking away your dream, your aspiration, making you less of what you could be, just for my selfish desire."

"I would've been happy with you." I took her mug and put it on the side table, next to a picture of us at Great Falls, the roaring rapids to the left beyond the lookout.

"But incomplete, and so always searching for the missing piece. Anyway, you don't seek happiness."

"I've always wondered how you knew me so well."

"Because I love you, though, a tainted love. And these many years I suffered, knowing how limited my love for you is. Can there be pure love? I wish I could—"

"If you believe in God's love."

"But I don't. I tried to believe in your God, so I would understand you more, but felt so hypocritical, not that I don't believe in a metaphysical or spiritual realm, just not the miraculous tales in the Bible. Another word, not your God."

"And I respect that."

"This is what kept me going all these years." She leaned toward the side table and grasped the framed picture. "We were so happy. We were such good friends. And I destroyed that with my jealousy."

"And I with my grudge..." The evening discussions in Arlington Central Library, the autumn hikes at Great Falls, the morning picnics at Bull Run and the laughter at the National Mall burst through memory's floodgate. Had it not been for Jim's interest in her, I wouldn't have discovered her feelings and we wouldn't have become best friends. During a picnic at Bull Run, she had told me how her father had died trying to save a fellow coworker, when an ex-employee with a semiautomatic handgun shot his way through the hallway to the corner office, killing half the workers before shooting the general manager in the heart and jumping off the seventh floor. Later, I discovered Daphne's father had been the shooter.

"We've lost so much time. When I was young, I never thought of time as being scarce as it was with money, but after I moved here and as I grew older... I've squandered so much time, wasted, contaminated, dumped into the ocean. And now—"

"We can make up for lost time. The experiences we had, even though they bring us pain, they'd also help us value the precious time, the precious friendship, the precious aspirations." I handed her the picture retrieved from Jim's Bible.

"Oh, I thought I had lost this picture or someone had stolen it. But you have it. I'm so glad all this time you had this by your side. Even if you had been angry with me, even if you had wanted... it doesn't matter, as long as you had this picture with you. Even if it hadn't comfort you, it comforts me to know you had it and my picture was with you all this time. I'm so happy." Her face flushed but her eyes couldn't focus on my face.

I wanted to reveal the truth, but her thrill and my nausea prevented me from dealing her the blow. My fingers twitched and I wanted to squeeze Jim's neck. "There's something you must tell me." Though the room was warm, my voice trembled.

She put the picture on the side table, looked through the living room window at the swirling leaves and suggested going to Hoboken for lunch.

"Do you need your medicine?" I helped her stand on her feet and walked her to the kitchen.

After drinking some more water, she entered the bedroom and took out a letter from the desk drawer. "The letter Jim wrote on your behalf. From now on, we stand shoulder to shoulder, as comrades against the evil Jim. Together, we'll fight and defeat him."

"Are we still friends?" I grasped the letter.

"I caused you so much pain."

"That picture I gave you—"

"I want you to have it, to keep it."

"Tell me about the medicine."

"We will defeat Jim."

"Do you still love me?"

She lifted her tired eyes and wanted to turn away, but I held her and kissed her on the forehead. Tears ran down her cheeks and hung at her jaw. I caressed her face and wiped away her tears while the leaves clamored outside the window.

"I have liver cancer, terminal." She kissed me. "Let's go to lunch."

CHAPTER 18

CHARLOTTE,

What have you done? Why have you written that untruthful, destructive, and self-serving letter? Why have you destroyed my dream of becoming a priest and helping all those helpless and lost sheep, those folks who just want a few words of comfort?

Now I got nothing, zilch, nada. What else could I be except a priest? You tell me. What else could I do except listen to people's confessions? You tell me. Oh, you've taken that from me; you've taken everything and more from me. And all for what? Your pitiful lame jealousy. How I hate you; how I despise you; how I loathe you. How I wish I'd never known you. I swore to God that I'd never ever forgive you as long as the sun continues to shine, as long as the earth continues to rotate, as long as there are bankers. Yes, I won't forgive you, not even if you beg me, not even if you get the Pope to beg me. I've written everything down so I'd remember all the details as long as I live. Hear me again: I'd never forgive you, no way, not in a hundred years, not if Mad-Dog Simon becomes a lousy wimp.

I don't want to see you ever again, not when the government abolishes income tax, not when monks can marry, not when the sun burns out, not when the universe explodes, not ever. Never, do you understand? Your sight sickens me, churns my stomach and makes me puke, even though I'm used to puking. I'd never come visit you, not when you've gotten sick, not when you've gone loony, not even on your deathbed. And don't come see me, never, ever. I'm sure you'd be able to find me—there aren't many places I could go—but don't come visit me, not ever, you hear. Even if I'm dying of cancer, I wouldn't want to see you. Now, you understand how much I hate you, how much I loathe you, how much I despise you?

Lawrence

CHAPTER 19

UNDER THE SEPTEMBER STARLIGHT, which shivered against the oak foliage, Charlotte and I burned the letter in the back yard, where chrysanthemums yellow, white and jade lined the fence's interior perimeter. We toasted with green tea Charlotte had purchased during her Kyoto trip. She had wanted to drink red wine, but I, though high on endorphin, couldn't allow alcohol to destroy the remains of her liver. I took out two chairs so we could sit around the trashcan and watch Jim's venom go up in flames. Though he had tricked his friends out of their lollipops even as a five-year old, I trusted him all these years, believing, or fantasizing, he would value friendship. But his diary revealed a viper more venomous than Donald Larsen could ever aspire to be. Since a scorpion stings on instinct, I must blame myself for letting Jim poison and paralyze me. I couldn't fold my hands and blame God, fate, causality or entropy.

I added dry leaves to kindle the fire. The flame crackled while I held Charlotte's hand and relishing her warmth. Her eyes, sparkling against the flickering light, sliced through my grief and brightened my heart more than did the starlight and the flame leaping beyond the trashcan's edge and dancing in the air. An occasional car passed to anchor me upon reality, but her hand would remind me of a distant world where snow danced on the lake. A spark leaped out of the trashcan but faded before hitting the ground.

"I'll come here and stay with you, until... until..." I said.

"We must help the FBI nab Jim," she said, tightening her grip, "for embezzlement, for money laundering, for conspiracy, for every evil deed."

"I'll ask Father Theodore for an extended leave, probably would kick me out of the monastery for asking. Extended leave for a monk, like long-term disability. Then again, Father Theodore's a bit different from the usual abbot. Still, it'd mean I haven't detached myself from worldly concerns. They still bind me."

"You haven't changed. Still struggling, searching, journeying." She removed a string of hair from my sleeve and caressed my hand. "But I'm glad. Because once you stop, your faith would become a fossil, your aspiration would evaporate, your vocation would become routine, your God would become an excuse to vegetate, and you would wither, as I had."

"You must let me take care of you."

"But I want to take care of you."

She went into the house to cook dinner while I extinguished the fire with ashes and put the trashcan near the fence, next to the chrysanthemums. Through the kitchen window, under the lamplight her graceful smile, simmered through time and grief, touched my heart and it ached for the lost time, the lost memories and the lost discussions by the riverbank. A squirrel, bobbing along the oak branch and shaking off a shower of leaves, distracted my daydream, but the uneven eave, the open backdoor, the flagstone path and the bobbing shadow of the branch reminded me of that dream, long ago in Fairfax, where Charlotte divulged her feelings. Not even a skunk could distract me from that dream.

A young couple from next door, Mr. and Mrs. Singh, strolled across their backyard to the fence and introduced themselves. They worked at pharmaceutical companies, he on cancer research and she on software algorithms. Since relocating here five years ago, they had dinner with Charlotte almost every weekend. Charlotte would invite their daughter Shakti and three other children to her place for parties. She would listen to their aspirations and help them toward their dreams of becoming playwright, neurosurgeon, nuclear physicist and social philosopher. Recently, she was preparing the children for the SSAT, and all four wanted to enroll in a specialized high school. When she was diagnosed with cancer a year ago, Mr. Singh had recommended two specialists, fellow classmates from Johns Hopkins University, but since the cancer was terminal, they could only delay the inevitable with dendrimers.

"We were devastated. She was so kind to Shakti and the other children." Mrs. Singh shook her head and sighed. "We tried everything we can, but most of all she needs someone to take care of her. And she deserves it. You must be one of her friends. I'm so glad you're here."

Charlotte was preparing dinner and humming an allegro when I led the young couple into the kitchen. I prepared the table and went to the living room to admire the etchings of the Washington Monument, the Lincoln Memorial, Great Falls and Healy Hall, and beside them on the coffee table, pictures of Charlotte and several children, around a BBQ pit roasting marshmallows, in the backyard scattering dry leaves and on the sidewalk throwing snowballs. She would've doted on her children.

She prepared grilled rib-eye steak with sauté onion and mushroom, just as she had two nights before Jim, with Sylvia's help, staged his Shakespearean drama. That evening, Charlotte's parents were playing bridge with the next door neighbors while the smell of onion and mushroom tickled my salivary glands. The last snow had melted the previous day and the daffodils began to bud in the backyard. We discussed Maslow's Hierarchy of Needs, which the teacher broached in psychology class, and she inquired whether a hungry artist could paint *Madonna* or a sexually frustrated philosopher could write *The Republic*. I thought for a while but couldn't answer her, never having been either. I promised to solve some partial differential equations while fasting and report the results. I fulfilled my promise and would've reported my findings the next night during the annual dance, had Jim not severed the bond between us.

On that distant night, after the steak dinner, while discussing *War and Peace*, she said I would always prefer Andrei to Pierre, forsaking the girl for eternal life. I divulged my struggle between my Pierre and my Andrei, one very different from that between the id and the superego. I wouldn't want to be Pierre at the novel's conclusion—abandoning his search for meaning to become just another noble and husband and grinding through the days and years—and had wondered whether there could be an alternative to Andrei's forsaking the world to its own misery and destruction.

Now, after these many years, again I wanted to enjoy her cooking, her gift. So, I prevented my ascetic mind from suppressing this indulgence, and sampled the steak as a connoisseur pate de foie gras. I said, "You have a good memory."

"I know that since you're in the monastery—" She cut a piece of steak and examined it.

"Why do people think we starve in the monastery?"

Camellia had also erred when she cooked me steamed lobster and scallops in white wine sauce. Though I never fussed about my meal and would enjoy any food nutritious enough to nurture my body and energize my cells, I would look forward to steamed lobster with a dash of lemon juice and steak with red wine.

"Monks are supposed to be ascetics. You certainly didn't go to the monastery for lobster feasts or sushi buffets." Charlotte showed me a smile that melted my heart.

"I wish I'd been here sooner." I put down my knife and fork to feel the warmth in the room.

"You are here now."

"You must've been lonely here."

"I never got married. Had an affair with a married man, but didn't last. Didn't love him. Didn't enjoy being with him. Didn't know why I carried on that affair." She put down her knife and fork and took my hand.

As her thumb moved across the back of my hand, I tried to experience her loneliness, her pain, her yearning for love, to love and be loved. If I had been her friend, if I had been by her side, if I had dined with her once a week, if I had listened to her, if I had comforted her, but I didn't, only abandoned her to the dust of time.

"It doesn't matter now," she said. "The past, the memories, the scenes, the laughter, the picnics, the conversations have been redeemed, yes redeemed, by your arrival. I'm sure you understand it. Oh, I want to have some wine, to celebrate the renewal of our friendship, to celebrate Jim's defeat."

I went to the cabinet, took out the cabernet and pour two quarter glasses. I drank to her smile, the joy of redemption seeping into this moment and intoxicating my mind. The wind continued to moan and the leaves continued to hiss, but I only wanted to hear her joy, a tune lingering in silence, trumpeting over a tide of tears and echoing between cliffs.

She recounted the time a coworker with a shotgun came into the office and started shooting anyone in sight. He had shot about fifteen coworkers including three managers, when he reached her cubicle by the window. Without life in his eyes or cheeks, he pointed the gun at her head. Outside the window, snow was falling to remind her of a Christmas in Georgetown and another winter's laughter. She wanted to take out my picture. But before she could reach her handbag and before the coworker could pull the trigger, the security guard, dressed as Santa Claus, shot him in the back, the bullet piercing his heart. She spent Christmas next to the fireplace reflecting on her apathy under the gun barrel and, my picture in hand, the desire to see me.

"I thought about my father and about how strange it'd be for me to die the same way. But I knew I couldn't die at that time. Not yet. I hadn't seen you. I hadn't apologized to you. I hadn't cooked you the rib-eye steak. And I hadn't asked you whether Anna Karenina was to blame for seeking happiness." She took out my picture and put it on the table.

I could see myself pointing a gun at Jim Whitfield, demanding he beg for mercy, and shooting him between two streams of tears. Then I would pour out a glass of cabernet to celebrate his death and my demise, which like the Roman Forum's decay would linger through the coming and going of the seasons, the rise and fall of regimes and the birth and death of technologies. But tonight, I would defer the hellbound path and enjoy this glass of wine with Charlotte and celebrate victory, over mistrust, over deception, over alienation, over Jim Whitfield.

"You must meet Camellia and Ichiro one of these days. Camellia's studying nanotechnology so you two would have much to talk about. And Ichiro, his cooking is almost as good as yours." I finished the wine and tried to feel drunk. But no luck.

"I'm jealous." She sipped the wine and cocked her head and an eyebrow. "They let you out to meet people, to interact with the world?"

"Father Theodore requires it of me, to leave the monastery once a week, like a weekly chore, and report back to him my day's adventure. But it's only me." I told her how Brother Anthony, like Father Jones, thirsted for chitchat but couldn't even meet visitors and suffered each day in solitary prayer and last year lost ten pounds.

"That's not fair. Even though I'm happy you're not stuck in the woods day after day after day, I feel sorry for this Brother Anthony, unless he's overweight. You must do something about it. Make it more egalitarian, more democratic, with more of a balance of power, Montesquieu and all that." She finished the wine and her face flushed.

"Like you said, we don't go to the monastery to enjoy the gourmet."

"But we must fight for equality and fairness. And you see what a Jim Whitfield had done."

"Father Theodore isn't Jim Whitfield."

"But power corrupts and you, all of you who kowtow to him, are like devils tempting him to step over the line and abuse his power."

I had missed her simplicity, her no nonsense pragmatism and her hatred for injustice, all of which had inspired me and tampered my tendency to reflect rather than to act. I revered Father Theodore but agreed that the humblest, noblest and holiest person could stumble over power, as a man distracted by an apple would catch his foot on the tree's exposed roots. He had listened to and even sought counsel, not just on the monastery's affairs but on his spiritual growth, but I was too focused on my edification and sanctification to worry about my friend the abbot and, along with other monks, had been luring him toward the ledge.

Before I could comment, Charlotte fell off the chair onto the floor.

CHAPTER 20

J IM WHITFIELD CHRONICLES
Part 5: Jim in Love

February 12, 2006

   Today, after worship service, while everyone was enjoying the buffet lunch at the visitor's hall, Johnny Chandler took Walker's daughter, Daisy, to a Sunday school classroom and tried to kiss her. She would've allowed him if I hadn't intervened and lectured him on a pure heart and a pure mind and so on and so forth. When he left with his head hanging below his shoulders, I gave her the Valentine's card I bought yesterday. She blushed and thanked me and I dreamed of kissing her. But I just told her to get lunch. When she left, I looked out the window at the snow in the front yard and swore to defend her against predictors like Johnny. He looks like a high-school dropout, a troublemaker, a gangster, a drug addict, even a sex offender, and has no right to come into my church. One of these days, I'll expel him from the church.

   When I went into the visitor's hall, Johnny had left. Daisy was sitting in the corner next to her mom, who was wolfing down a chicken breast. I filled a plate with barbecue ribs, corn, and baked beans and handed it to Daisy. Then, I went to talk to the newcomers and persuaded them to return next Sunday.

March 15, 2006

Johnny's homeroom teacher found marijuana in his knapsack and the school may be expelling him. When the school janitor came to inform me, I gave him five hundred dollars and went to the bar to have a Screwdriver. And I bought a round of drinks for everyone there, including the bartender, the waitress and the security guard.

I contacted the church board members for an emergency meeting this Saturday and would propose expelling Johnny from the church. I'd announce it during worship just before the sermon, which would focus on this issue. I'd emphasize the enormity of the situation. I couldn't allow a wolf to roam among my sheep, especially with Daisy Walker around. It's my duty to protect her. If Chandler causes any trouble, I'll expel him, too. Don't much like his drunken face anyway. I left the bar and went to the gym for a swim before having dinner at the mayor's mansion.

March 19, 2006

When I called Johnny onto the stage and announced that the board had decided to expel him for drug possession, I thought he'd charge at me. But good thing old Walker was standing between us. And Chandler was too drunk to understand anything, that useless bum. I would've taken any excuse to expel him, too. And poor Daisy, how pale her rosy cheek turned. From now on, I must spend more time to console and take care of her.

I talked to Walker after the service and requested meeting with Daisy to counsel her. He agreed. With her boyfriend expelled for drug possession and them breaking up because of it, she needed a hand to guide her and a shoulder to cry on. So I talked to Daisy, and set an appointment for this Thursday.

Went out with Sylvia to the Gilead Steakhouse to celebrate the eventful day, but she had to rush to the airport and fly to Los Angeles with her girlfriends to shop for some limited edition perfume and attend an auction of a movie star's wardrobe. I went to the bar thinking about Daisy and ended up drunk.

March 23, 2006

As expected, Johnny begged Daisy not to break up with him, and claimed he'd been framed for possessing marijuana. When we met on Thursday in my church office, I told Daisy that all drug addicts lie about their habits, not just to others but to themselves. Advised her to drop him like a hot potato, before he scorches her. She wept and I wanted to kiss her, the pretty face. But what's most attractive about her is her innocence, gullibility and obedience. Told her Johnny's bad news and she believed me. Told her to never see him again and though she hesitated, she promised me to do so. Told her we should meet every Thursday for counseling until she gets better and she agreed. I could've kissed her and she would've let me, but I wanted her to like me. Not since Charlotte did I want a girl to like me. Her eyes aren't as alluring as Ginger's, her lips aren't as seductive as Candy's, but there's something marvelous. I've been thinking what I should get her but know she doesn't give a damn about diamond earrings or pearl necklaces or crocodile skin handbags. Won't be able to sleep tonight, so might as well think of something. Wish I could see her. Even just a picture of her. Should've taken a picture of her in some event. Maybe last week's picnic, but no, she wasn't there. Maybe during New Year's celebration, but didn't recall seeing her there. I'll take a picture of her this Thursday. But tonight, a cursed night, I couldn't see that innocent face.

March, 30 2006

Today, during our counseling session, congratulated Daisy for breaking up with Johnny, but could see she was very depressed. Wept through half the session. But I comforted her; joked about myself; told her about this wimpy kid who followed me like an obedient dog and how I used him as bait to catch a dog and how a ruffian smashed the dog's face. When she didn't laugh, I returned to how I fell into this puddle and had to drag my muddy clothes home. She was so concern she forgot to weep. So I pulled a flower from the back of her ear, one of the magic tricks I'd learned in high school while performing on stage. She finally smiled. Oh, the delight, the happiness, never thought a smile from a girl could make me so happy. If Charlotte had smiled at me, but that wasn't to be. Daisy's smile couldn't make up for that, but it's close. So close, like a dream almost coming true.

Daisy told me how sad she felt at seven when her puppy disappeared one day and never came back. She didn't looked at me, just stared at her shoes. I listened to her and enjoyed it. Never enjoyed listening to Sylvia babbling about the dolls, the dresses, the handbags, and the perfume that her parents gave her for her birthday, for Easter and for Christmas. Daisy and I had tea and some cookies and all of a sudden I felt so angry that my ears were burning and I crushed the cookie in my hand. Not at Daisy, but at that Lawrence. Just realized happiness was what was missing all those years. Not being able to be with Charlotte. Missing out those ecstatic moments. The happiness that I was entitled to, my inalienable right, just like my mansion, my Lamborghini Gallardo, my Rolex Masterpiece, and my Mediterranean and Caribbean cruises. Deprived from me, yanked out of my hands. Oh, the wretched monk. Daisy spilled her tea. Her face became pale and her hands trembled. She was scare stiff. I apologized to her and got her a towel to wipe the tea from her dress. Her blue dress, so simple, so pure, just like her. Wanted to tell her how I felt, but of course I couldn't. Just thanked her for allowing me to help her. Didn't want her to leave. So asked her about her favorite food, book, and place, her high school experience, and anything I could think of. After she told me all these things, she even asked things about me. And I knew she didn't want to leave either. But Chandler walked in and wanted to talk about Johnny. So she had to leave. Didn't have a chance to confirm the next appointment. But she'd be here next Thursday at the same time, I was sure.

That Chandler started chattering before she left. But I was thinking about Daisy's smile and her voice. Now, I couldn't remember what the hell the drunkard and I discussed.

April 13, 2006

Bought Daisy a puppy. Think it's a spaniel, but what do I know about dogs. She (Daisy is SHE now) was so happy that I would've bought her a diamond necklace, or a condo, to see that expression. I swore to protect her, as her knight in shiny armor, her guardian angel.

We drove to Memphis for lunch, barbecue ribs and champagne. As we walked into the restaurant, I held her hand. She was trembling, but didn't resist. She wasn't sure if she could drink, so I gave her permission and saved her from her guilt. She relaxed and enjoyed the champagne. I told her that whenever she's not sure if something is okay, she should ask me and I'd tell her. She smiled and agreed. So we toasted to a new beginning. I just wished she'd disagree with me once in a while. I'd never allow anyone else to disagree with me. She drank just one glass but I finished the bottle. I'm entitled to such bliss and ecstasy. Won't let anyone take them away from me.

When the phone woke me up in my office, my head was pounding and I couldn't remember how I'd returned there. Got really drunk in the restaurant. When I picked up the phone, I heard Sylvia complaining that she hadn't received a check to pay for the renovations of our spa and sauna. I said something and hung up. I wanted to call Daisy but before I could, she called me to check how I was doing. Turned out she'd driven me back and taken a taxi home. After I hung up, I watched the sky darkened and yearned to kiss Daisy.

June 23, 2006

Yesterday, Daisy and I went to the local park for a picnic. As I held her and watched the clouds drift in the sky, I realized three months had passed. I felt pure bliss, but still remembered Charlotte and my archenemy Lawrence. I kissed Daisy's forehead and swore to avenge myself. Lawrence had taken what I deserved and given me that nausea in the stomach, that fever in the head. I'd been unable to enjoy steak, wine or woman. Now that Daisy had taken that pain from me, time to give it to Lawrence.

July 5, 2006

Yesterday, Sylvia went to London and I invited Daisy to celebrate Independence Day in my mansion. Had the servants cleaned the place until the shelves and windows were gleaming. Ordered lobster tails, foie gras and Champagne for dinner. Went to the spa for a message, manicure and mud bath. After the sauna, I drove to her place to pick her up. She was happy to see me and she showed it. And I knew she loves me. Love. Not like Sylvia, who just wanted to own the most popular lady's man, to show off to the entire world her precious possession, like her diamond earrings, ruby necklace, and tailor-made nightgowns and shoe collection. Should've dumped her like a hot potato.

But Daisy's different. Beautiful? Yes. But there're prettier women. She's so innocent, so attractive, so Daisy. She cares about me and wouldn't give a damn what other people think. Would I love her? Could I, after Charlotte? But Daisy, unlike Charlotte who was so independent, would never disagree with me. Would I like her if she starts disagreeing with me?

My heart felt younger when I saw Daisy's radiant face. We arrived at the mansion and I danced with her to celebrate Independence Day. I hadn't danced for ten years and my vigor returned to me.

We ate dinner under candlelight and she told me about the orchids she was planting. I made her promise to give me a pot. And I'd give her whatever she wants. We drank Champagne and toasted to us. We celebrated independence and freedom and no more crap.

I took her up to the observation tower, and we could see as far as Memphis. I held her and kissed her and we watched the firework. The red, yellow, orange, and green sparkles spreading like showers. Crackling noise from far away. I never cared much for firework. But tonight, how beautiful, how magnificent. Celebrating us.

We danced and she was such a good dancer. She was delighted, her eyes shone and her smile gleamed. I kissed her, her soft supple lips, and felt the firework in my heart. Afterward, I took her into my bedroom.

August 1, 2006

The liner had stopped off Montego Bay, Jamaica where the blue sky meets the sapphire sea. Some empty soda cans lay on the crystal-white sands of the beach. A young couple was playing in the water. In the afternoon we'd go down to the beach and play around like silly kids, too. I feel like a kid, at least a young man.

Daisy had never been on a cruise and would watch the sky and the water on deck like she was in a dream. She even forgot to eat and I had to drag her to the restaurants. We tried Italian, Greek, and Japanese. At first, she was afraid to eat the sashimi, but when she tasted it, she loved it. Last evening, we watched the sunset on deck and I almost felt life was complete. But I remembered Charlotte and wished I could've gone on cruises with her.

When the captain announced that soon we'd have to get off, Daisy was still sleeping so peacefully, like a baby, no, like an angel and the sunlight through the window was caressing her face. I wanted to wake up sleeping beauty. But how could I be so cruel? You angelic face, I gave you a condo and you thanked me. I gave you a limousine with a chauffeur and you thanked me. I brought you on this cruise in the Caribbean and you thanked me. But I wanted to see that delight on your face when you got the puppy. Where's that genuine delight that'd made me so happy? I'll buy you a bigger condo, with a chef and a maid. I'll bring you to Paris, Rome, Vienna, Moscow, Tokyo, anywhere you want. What do you want, my love?

March 15, 2007

I bit into the steak and it tasted stale. I sipped the wine and it tasted sour. I inhaled the air and it smelled foul. I'd been so happy when I celebrated Valentine's Day with Daisy. Then, a week ago, after I spent an afternoon with Daisy and walked into my office, Sylvia introduced me to a girl. Now, I can't sleep. I can't concentrate on my sermons. I don't even enjoy being with Daisy. This ache in my belly is back. And that girl's face wouldn't leave me. The pretty face, the perfect nose, the delicious lips. She's so much prettier than Ginger at her best. But there's something else, not her lips, not the way she smiles, not the way she drinks her coffee, but something. Just don't know what. It isn't the innocence and pureness as with Daisy.

After meeting the girl, I spent that night in the bar thinking where Sylvia had dug up this girl to taunt me, to make me miserable. I didn't and still don't believe she'd met the girl at Donald Larsen's trial, though she went to his trial for killing someone while drunk driving. She's hiding something from me. Why'd she introduce such a pretty girl to me? Ain't she jealous? Must be to taunt me because she thinks I couldn't have this girl. But, I'll show her. Anything is possible if I believe it and act on it.

This morning, I scanned the catalog for a painting to buy Daisy, to make up for being so mean to her. But, all the while I was looking at the paintings, this damn ache continued to gnaw at me. After I held my head for two hours, staring at the catalog, I swore to win over that girl and relieve the ache.

March 17, 2007

Camellia, my sweet Camellia, your look, your smile, your twist of the legs taunt me through the day. So sweet, yet so aloof, so magnificent, yet so mysterious. Curse my soul for meeting you. I'd been damned by your lovely smile, wretched person that I am.

Last night, donned glasses and mustache and wig. Drove to Greenwich Village in New York. Waited for Camellia at Bleecker Street across from Washington Square Village hoping she'd eat at her favorite sushi bar, at least she told me it was her favorite. Cold outside but burning with a fever inside. Almost a delicious fever. Wanted so much to just glimpse at her face, to see those pretty eyes, to hear the sweet voice. Just to be next to her without her knowing it. Was scared shitless when a damn ruffian approached me, but lucky a policeman was nearby. Damn this New York. Why'd she want to live in this place? I mean, Gilead's such a nice and cozy town. My heart thumped and my chest heaved, at every woman who walked down the street. And the disappointment took as much toil on my body as the anticipation. Dreamed that the next girl would be her and her smile would suddenly greet me. And what'd you know, she recognized me. No, just a prostitute. Then a beggar approached me. And those sinister eyes peeping out from the side streets and near the stairways. After a while, the wind chilled my heart and all the faces took on frightful appearances. She never showed up at the restaurant. Damn it, felt as bad as when Charlotte rejected me.

As I walked toward the West Side where I parked my car, the wind slapped my face. Yeah, laughing at me, I was sure. But I cursed it like I cursed everything I hated, which included Lawrence. May the wind be damned for all eternity. As I approached Sixth Avenue, all of a sudden, from nowhere, as if in a dream, I heard her sweet voice. Coming around the corner like a phantom suddenly materializing. My heart made a painful thump against my ribs and almost leaped out of my chest. I threw myself into the depression at a lizard shop's entrance and came face to face with a crocodile. But didn't dare to make a damn noise.

Camellia appeared and turned the corner. A sickly middle-aged executive with a vulpine face held her hand. And laughed at something she said, prostituting himself, clinging to her like bees to honey. I didn't dare to move. Afraid they'd notice me. The crocodile opened its jaw and exhibited its knifelike teeth. And I held my breath, hoping the glass could withstand the beast's attack. But it shut its mouth, that two-time loser.

Camellia was laughing as they walked down the sidewalk. I followed. My stomach churned. Wanted to drink whiskey to numb the pain. Passed a prostitute soliciting two men in suits and an art gallery with some strange paintings. The man held her and kissed her. I wanted to stab him in the heart, to shoot him between the eyes, to castrate him, the son-of-a-bitch. But I ran into a pole and bumped my forehead. They went into a motel. I collapsed onto the ground, panting, aching, and burning with anger. A dog came to sniff me and I growled. A middle-aged man in Armani suit holding a young pretty lady in his arm threw a five-dollar bill at me. I became delirious with a fever, mouth dry, forehead burning, and sweat drenching my back. Didn't know how I got back home.

Camellia in the arms of that philanderer, they were kissing and walking into the motel. The same image kept rerunning in my mind. In my dream, too. Couldn't dispel it. I'll fix him like I fixed Johnny. Hell has no fury like Jim's.

This morning, during worship, I walked onto the stage thinking about Camellia while my mouth moved and spewed out words that I didn't recognize. Afterward, Mrs. Walker praised me for my preaching.

She was deeply moved. Whatever. I'd forgotten what crap I blabbered. Just wanted to see Camellia. Called her but no one answered. In the afternoon, I had a fever. Drank several glasses of whiskey but the fever worsened.

March 23, 2007

This morning, I bought a dress and a pair of shoes for Camellia and she liked them. Wanted to ask about that man she was with last Saturday, but every time I thought about it, pain would pinch my heart. Even when I was with Daisy. The same pain, reminding me of how I'd lost Charlotte and why I hated Lawrence's every cell. But now, Camellia's smile, like opium, relieved me of the pain.

During dinner at a sushi bar in midtown Manhattan, when I asked if she had a boyfriend, she sipped her green tea and grinned. She asked why I wanted to know but she understood perfectly well. How unlike Daisy she is and how she tortures me. While having green tea ice-cream, she mentioned she was renting a place in the Lower East Side. I told her I had a condo in Memphis and she could stay there. Just help me take care of the place. She hesitated as she licked the spoon. But, I knew she was interested. Could see it in her eyes. I told her I could get a limousine and a chauffeur so she could go to New York if she needed to. She said she had to think about it. Just to torture me.

After dinner, I drove her back to her place. Then drove around the corner and parked the car. I crossed Hudson Street to the corner opposite her building and looked up at the matrix of windows. Searching for her unit. When one of the windows lighted up, I stared at it to find Camellia's profile against the light. After a while, when nothing happened, I became sad, like that time when Charlotte chased away the bulldog and saved Lawrence.

I stood in the cold, with two shady characters down the street whispering to one another and occasionally eyeing me. The lighted window went dark and I became depressed. If that was her unit, she'd probably gone to sleep. I was about to go when I saw her coming out of the building. I walked into the phone booth to hide my upper body and tracked her to the corner, where a BMW approached and picked her up. Inside the car, a middle-aged blonde man kissed her. I raced to my car, started the engine, and sped down Hudson Street. After three blocks, I saw the BMW and followed it along Lexington Avenue toward midtown. The car stopped in front of a pub and they went inside. I didn't have my glasses and mustache and wig so just waited outside the pub, staring at the neon signs and groups of youngsters going in and out of the place. I felt feverish and wanted to smash someone in the face. I checked the watch every minute, and became more impatient as midnight approached. I wanted to rush in and right-hook the son-of-a-bitch. Sylvia called me and asked where I was and I told her I was playing detective and tailing someone. She guffawed and hung up. I banged on the steering wheel and pressed the horn. Two passersby glanced at me and walked down the street. But a bulldog barked at me for fifteen minutes. Later, a prostitute approached and solicited business but I shooed her away. Slightly past midnight, they left the pub. The guy drove the BMW past the Museum of Modern Art and up Broadway and Columbus Avenue to the Upper West Side. I tailed the sedan but almost crashed into a taxi that cut in front of me and was rushing to hell. Lost them at a traffic light near the Museum of Natural History, behind some dying clunker. I horned at those New York snails and sped through two red lights, but couldn't find that damn BMW. Circled around to Amsterdam Avenue, 72nd Street, Central Park West, but no BMW. This hostile city, these potholed streets and clanging cars. I went around three more times before an obese cop pulled me over and gave me a ticket for running a red light. By the time he left, I was so exhausted that I didn't have the energy to drive back to Gilead. What a nightmare.

I rented a hotel room near Central Park. Looking out of the hotel window, I could see the lights beyond the park. As I drank whiskey, the thought that Camellia could be with the lecher tormented and depressed me. I wanted to strangle that satyr, who was trying to steal Camellia from me. I would give anything to be with her. My kingdom for Camellia.

March 26, 2007

Called the real estate agent and bought the penthouse condo at the outskirts of Memphis. Asked him to furnish it with leather sofa, plasma TV, cherry-wooded dinning set, king-size bed, a dozen dresses and shoes, two mink coats, and, three cases of wines. I went there and stood on the balcony, thinking of the moonlit dinners that Camellia and I would enjoy there.

Last night, while we were having dinner in Greenwich Village and I was pouring a glass of cabernet for her, she agreed to take care of the condo that I didn't own. I kissed her hand and we drank to our future. I told her that she wouldn't regret the decision and that she'd love the place. Promised to hire a chauffeur to drive her between Memphis and New York so she could eat and shop in Manhattan and return home for the late night news. After dinner, we went to a discotheque and danced until three in the morning.

As I was driving back to Gilead, I rebuked myself for not believing what I'd taught. Only fools doubt, and greater fools believe but not act. Should never have doubted. Should always believe that I'm entitled to happiness. Almost forgot what I'd learned. Almost let my emotions get the better of me. And I realized with Camellia, like with Charlotte and Daisy, when happiness and even life depended on her decision, I still lacked faith. But from now on, nothing's impossible with Jim, not even the impossible.

After the agent came in with the papers and I signed them to seal the deal, I went to the florist and bought a dozen pots of orchid for Daisy. She'd suffered my moods and I wanted to make up to her. I ordered steak dinner for two delivered to her condo and took a bottle of 1921 Yquem to her place. When she opened the door, I held her and kissed her and we forgot about dinner.

July 5, 2007

Camellia and I celebrated Independence Day in her condo, which had become my second home. My first home is still Daisy's condo. When Camellia moved in three months ago, she had almost nothing. Her clothes and shoes were old, her jewelry imitations, and her personal items nonexistent. When I showed her the dresses, the shoes, and the mink coats, her eyes gleamed and I was delighted. She thanked me, kissed me on the cheek. And I kept recalling her kiss as I drove back to Gilead. The air so fresh, the day so bright, the music so sweet. When I returned to the church, Mrs. Chandler was waiting for me. She complained about her husband's drunkenness. I nodded. I smiled. I drank my coffee. I gave her my blessings. I returned to my daydream: Camellia kissing me.

Tonight, we celebrated with champagne and foie gras. I also bought a diamond-encrusted cheesecake from that gourmet restaurant in midtown Manhattan. Those crazy New Yorkers, love them and hate them. Maybe should buy a condo there and enjoy the night life. But still have nightmares about that creepy night and those two-time losers.

After we finished the foie gras and had a slice of cheesecake, we danced and watched the fireworks from the balcony. We made love on the balcony during the firework and had another slice of cheesecake.

Even after the firework had disappeared, the lights still shone and the music still sounded, as if the city was having a rock concert through the night. I love Memphis. I love Independence Day.

Long live freedom and liberty. Free to love Camellia and Daisy and any other mistresses. Free to drink Yquem or Romanee-Conti like water. Free to fly to Orlando or Los Angeles or Prince Edward Island in my private jet. Free to take a dip in Jamaican beaches on weekends, have lamb stew in a Roman piazza on Easter, and sample sushi in Tokyo on Memorial Day.

Camellia slept in the bedroom while I finished the champagne. I always enjoyed watching her sleep. Something angelic and even divine about that expression. Her silky hair covering her smooth skin, her peaceful lips kissing the pillow, her eyelids moving once in a while, maybe searching for something in her dream. All stored in my mind, like in a computer's memory, to be replayed time and again. Like a timeless movie classic, always refreshing, always moving, always renewed with each showing. This is the life I deserve, the life I was born to live. Life according to Jim.

Still, happiness reminded me of what I'd missed with Charlotte, what Lawrence had taken from me. I sat in front of my laptop looking at a picture of Charlotte and I vowed again to seek justice for the wrong done to me. Only his suffering could lessen my pain and my grief.

With Camellia by my side, the future's mine, the possibilities are unlimited. I've relished youth again, tasted love again, that love that belongs to the young. Everything's possible, with Jim: a New Man.

CHAPTER 21

AFTER CHARLOTTE HAD FAINTED during dinner, I wanted to stay for a few days to take care of her. But when she woke up, she insisted that I return to the monastery and prepare to fight Jim Whitfield. She wanted me to prepare my body, mind and soul for the clash because she couldn't. I couldn't resist her plea. I had never been able to.

A few days after I had returned to the monastery and sampled more of Jim's confessions, Camellia appeared at my cabin's front door, the same sad eyes and the same trembling lips, this time against the autumn foliage and the piles of firewood. A phantom, a hallucination. Unsure whether I was still dreaming, I grabbed her by the shoulders, my hands cold and trembling.

"Things would've been simpler if you'd agreed to marry me." After embracing me, she raised her hand to caress my cheek.

"I thought that was just a charade, brilliant playacting to set a trap for an ignorant monk." I said as grief and anger churned in my stomach into a bitter cocktail.

Throughout last year, Camellia and Ichiro had been supporting each other in their searches—his for perfection through loss and death and hers for happiness through love and intimacy. Amid the July winds of Cape Cod, in the September sounds of Harvard Square, and under the January snow of Mount Lafayette. This January, after several noon-to-midnight discussions with Jan Moscowitz on the Pi Epsilon Naught lawsuit, she suggested hiking through Mount Lafayette's knee-deep snow, but I excused myself from the cliffs and gorges so they could challenge the elements without worrying about the monk. When they went to Washington for the cherry blossom festival, I rejoiced over their sharing each other's suffering and hoped a sparkle might burn incense in their hearts and spread the aroma through the deserts of their memories. Ever since Sonya's death, Ichiro had always gone alone to the cherry blossom festival and his sharing the memory of Sonya would mean opening to Camellia his sanctuary. But she returned under rain clouds, the cherry blossom festival having forecasted a storm. She had been avoiding him through the summer before disappearing among the September winds. When I tried to probe through those clouds, while we were lunching at Faneuil Hall, she grabbed my hand and expressed her love for me. I detected carcasses raising their heads. During those months, I spent most weekdays chopping woods near the cabin and, with every stroke, felt the heartache. But after I had read Jim's diary, the clouds dispersed to reveal a skeletal mountain. Enlightenment.

Now, after hearing my words, Camellia jerked away her hand as if flinching from a flame, and she twisted her lips while her cheeks twitched.

"Ah, but you weren't helping Donald. You were trying to save *him*." In that instant, I was enlightened. I began to assemble the pieces into a picture. Donald Larsen wouldn't dare to risk his financial-engineering brain while Agent Peter and his associates continued to scour mud and dung for any stench of his greed.

"No, no, no."

"If I had to guess—"

"Don't... don't..."

"Since you prefer telling me everything, I'll listen."

"Forgive me." She collapsed onto the ground, the spot where the snowman had melted last winter.

Amid her uneven breath, I lifted her while. I tried to hate her but could only embrace her and she wept against my ear, her tears washing my neck.

"Would've been better if there's nothing to forgive."

"You and Ichiro are the two people I least wanted to hurt." She swayed in the wind as if about to collapse again.

"Guess you failed." Bile surged into my mouth as I recalled Sylvia's words and I wanted to scream away the knot and fire in my bosom.

"I failed you and I failed him. When the chasm opened up between Ichiro and me, I thought things couldn't get any worse, but now...

now…" She buried her face in her hands while the wind played with her dress. "I meant every single word I said on Valentine's Day and I wouldn't take back anything I did. That was not playacting, not a charade," she said, her calm and steady voice seizing my attention as a lasso would a calf's neck. "I was determined to help him when I first came to Boston but then… then… you…you were kind, you were patient, you were sensitive, you didn't judge me."

"But you returned to help him when he was in trouble." I wiped away the dry leaves and sat on a pile of firewood, trying hard to believe her words.

"I loved him once, but you're all that matters to me now." Camellia picked up a fallen leaf and gave it to me. "I wish I didn't —"

"But you're not my mistress and I don't want you to be mine or anybody's." I had hoped she was only helping him defeat me, but as I recalled Jim's diary entries, my cheeks burned though a gust swept across the clearing and slapped my face. "You should've chosen Ichiro over that scum."

"You'll never forgive me, will you?"

"I've no right not to forgive you. But apparently, you still care for him."

"I'd planned to leave him and I did. But I had to get something from him."

"Of course, you couldn't abandon him when he's been kidnapped."

"No, he wasn't, not by Donald, not by anybody. It was a sham to get the money."

"And you still helped him."

"And I still love you."

"I trusted you. You were my friend."

"He was gentle and loving." She sat on the firewood next to me. "He cared for me when I was alone and desperate for love, when no one cared for me. I'd lived under bridges, sometimes next to drunkards and prostitutes for several months and then I met him. Can you understand how that's like, after all those years of being unwanted? I wanted a roof over my head, food to fill my stomach, someone to care for me and, why not, a decent living. When I first left home, I was so happy to be free like a bird. I'd never return to that hell called home even if I had to live like a homeless bum. And yes, I cared about him and still do, but after I met you, everything changed."

"What does this scum have that Ichiro doesn't?"

"He was running away from someone name Simon, the brother of a girl he'd known from a long time ago. For some reason that I don't know, this guy was trying to get him. He was very afraid of this Simon."

"I hope so." Every time I recalled Simon's breaking that football team captain's nose, I would imagine that Jim like a worm would cringe under his bulldog eyes and gasp for breath in his eagle claws. Now, I relished that image more than ever as the leaves slapped my face.

"And that day, while preparing me to get the ransom, he joked about having confessed to a priest. I thought this guy Simon was getting into his head and I was scared. But his sly smile showed that he still had his marbles. No, I don't want him to go loony." She tried to grab a leaf but it slid past her fingers.

The rasping voice, the musty smell, the rat-like steps. Another slap in my face. Jim the Penitent was kicking me into the ditch before escaping from Simon's claws.

"I wanted to tell you everything but I was so afraid of losing you, and now... now..." She leaned against me and grasped my hand.

"Guess you found out there was nothing in that bag. Sylvia kept everything." I wanted to pull my hand away but didn't. I still cared about her. I still considered her my friend.

"Guess she wanted the two-million on top of his life insurance." After Camellia explained that Jim had a ten-million-dollar life-insurance policy, I realized the wife had another motivation for keeping the ransom, but wondered how love could turn into hatred in eleven years. I still could remember Sylvia dressing in her lingerie to impress Jim and, with her polished nails, threatening other girls, including Daphne and Charlotte, to stay away from him. The same passion, from infatuation to malice, in the course of a decade.

"You still don't believe I love you. But whether you believe it or not, I was going to take the ransom and leave him even though he will divorce his wife. A smart woman should go for the man who loves her, not the man she loves. But I'm just an ordinary woman. I wanted the money so I wouldn't be dependent on him anymore and we could start a new life. And I gave you Jim's secret diary to show I love you more than him."

"Do you know Ichiro has cancer?"

She twirled the leaf as if trying to understand the foreign tongue, before dropping it and grasping the firewood beneath her. "Where's he? Where's Ichiro? I have to find him. Tell me, tell me..."

"He said the same thing when I last saw him." From the corners of her eyes, glimmers attempted to break through the sadness.

"There's something I must tell him." She marched through the leaves and ran down the path toward the main building as a gust tossed her hair and flapped her dress.

CHAPTER 22

O N A S EPTEMBER E VENING TWO YEARS AGO , at the Java Coffeehouse in Harvard Square, with The Sound of Silence seeping through the front door, Ichiro raised his cup and announced, "Good news. The polarity of the nitrogen atoms in the air are aligned, so the Dow Jones will reach another peak."

"Sure, and El Niño is back, so divorces are on the rise." I raised my cup and toasted to our truths.

"You would've believe me if I were an economist, or a physicist, or an econo-physicist. But because I'm only an ignorant mathematician—"

"When I was young, I used to depend on so called authorities for knowledge—"

"Of course, scholars and politicians like to monopolize the truth. Well, it used to be priests and kings."

"But, when I discovered that a law, a theory or a whole discipline had to anoint fudge-factors for salvation, I ended up banging my head against the wall."

"If you'd lived in the seventeenth century—" He wrote "enlighten-ment" on the napkin and pushed it toward me.

"I might've accepted Newtonian mechanics as gospel and dismissed particle-wave duality as cult, voodoo or quackery." I crossed out the word and wrote "alchemy." "But, perhaps one day we might resolve this duality at the center of black holes and render quantum physics as heresy or plain old superstition."

In the middle of chatters on genocide, global warming, monetary policies, corporate morality, competitive advantages of nations and social construction of reality, I declared a new doctrine, "Let's dismiss Albert Einstein, Sigmund Freud, Milton Friedman, Edmund Husserl, and Karl Barth. No general relativity, no psychoanalysis, no monetarism, no phenomenology, and no neo-orthodoxy." Freeing the mind from clutter, junk and pollution, for creativity, for analysis and for inquiry.

"But even if we have enough time and energy, could we rely on reason, logic and the scientific principle to test these theories? Could we trust our eyes, ears, nose, tongue, and fingers to gather impartial evidences? In the end we could only doubt. And live in our own world with our own doubts. Then what? Negotiate, compromise, and vote? Yes, facts and truths by majority, by popularity, by the spirit of the times." Ichiro toasted to this last truth.

At one moment, a sparrow flew past the windowpane, glided down Mount Auburn Avenue, and disappeared behind the church tower. I tried to track its path, to validate the laws of aerodynamics. But even with telescopic eyes, I couldn't pinpoint its location and speed simultaneously. Duality, uncertainty, the fundamental nature of reality. Nature toying with us. As mere mortals, we could sip coffee and eat cheesecake, but not transcend space-time toward enlightenment. That elusive enlightenment.

I wanted to negotiate with Ichiro on a new physical law. Hoping our friendship would allow me to tune a constant, to my benefit.

Around us, young men and women were debating the politics of peace, the rights of androids, and the nature of dialogue between text and audience. With their own opinions, their own biases and their own prejudices. Ichiro and I glanced at them, listened to their conversations. We sipped our coffee and tried to figure out the game of life, where each player must roll a loaded dice and, without dirtying her hands, break the rules and deceive the other players. Ever since the Charlotte disaster had thrust me into multi-plot nightmares, I had questioned while still yearning for friendship, which like El Dorado had lured many adventurers to their demise. I wanted to reach out to Ichiro across the sea of sand, but confronted around me a wall that had protected me against sandstorms.

Now, the same coffeehouse, the same seat, a similar autumn day, but a different waiter, a different menu. A different Lawrence waiting for a different Ichiro.

The young man at the next table, hands and hair waving, was portraying his plans to join a top management consulting firm's Hong Kong office after receiving his MBA and outlining the milestones to become a partner, while the young lady opposite him sipped coffee and glanced out the window. The waitress handed me the cup of hot chocolate and walked to the next table to serve them, smiling at the young man, as if congratulating him for the achievement. At the piano, a man who resembled Ichiro played Beethoven's Moonlight Sonata, the tune reminding me of my friend's piano concerto.

After reading Jim's diary, I had wanted to divulge his *Autobiography in Eight Parts* to Agent Peter, but the thought of back-stabbing him ached my stomach enough to lasso my tongue. I couldn't expel my integrity and betray my soul, even to crush this devil. The more so after suffering from Ichiro a left hook. Perhaps, I was too selfish to sacrifice myself and rid the world of this scorpion, which would scour the land and sting every exposed ankle.

I intended to seek out Arthur, a rare gem like Camellia and Ichiro in the waves of sand, who dared to challenge Jim Whitfield. I wanted to share in his courage, his intellect and his struggle for a personal faith. I hoped the tumble, a test of strength and courage, hadn't discouraged him and he would stand and join me shoulder-to-shoulder in the fight against the evil that is Jim.

I was enjoying the music and the Java beans' aroma when Ichiro appeared at the entrance, the sad eyes hovering over the gaunt face. Reluctant to confront his treachery, I had avoided him since returning from Gilead, but couldn't fling from my mind the sculptured face that continued to haunt me within my cell's four walls. When I prayed, when I meditated... The images of Storrow Drive, Harvard Square, and White Mountains, the discussions on Fermi-Dirac Statistics and the Topology of Black Holes and the smell of cappuccino and oolong. Dream fragments that surfaced upon my memory, though once nurtured my soul, now pained my heart and liver. A scene thrust forth: Ichiro tiptoed across my cell from the door toward the desk, sifted through my documents, and simpering yanked out Daphne's letter. He offered Jim this gift and received a hundred-thousand-dollar check and a pat on the back. To slash my flesh, to pinch my nerves, to crack my bones, Jim would've delighted in burning a million dollar-bills.

I should slap Ichiro in the face. I should lift him by the collar. I should shake him like a dusty jacket. But all I could do was ask about his health. I worried about his health and his fight with colon cancer.

No matter what he had done, no matter how much he had betrayed me, I still considered him my friend because he wasn't Jim and his betrayal didn't define his character, his disposition or his personality. On the other hand, with the algorithm seared onto his ASIC chip, Jim's character compelled him to cheat, steal, and manipulate.

Ichiro sat opposite me and said, "We live as if we would never die. Sure, we know we would die, one day. But our day to day living, our conversations, our decisions don't take into consideration this ultimate reality, a reality we know but want to avoid until it's unavoidable." He picked up the menu and examined it. "The end of the road, the end of the journey."

I knew he had thought about death ever since Sonya had died and, long after her burial, her death continued to massage his muscles and tinkle his nerves. Despite being drunk for a while, he had awakened into a new day, not of blue skies and white clouds, but of a cumulus merging into mist. With a dash of northeaster purifying the heart. But his quest to dissect *the finale* had not only tossed him into a storm but also had dragged Camellia and me along.

Even when I was searching for my direction, the news of Daphne's death had revealed my segment on that timeline, which passed through the birth and death of kings and beggars and the rise and fall of monuments and empires. From the segment's endpoint, I could review the snow, moonlight and blossoms, the faces, melodies and fragrances, which would dash past me and disperse among the seconds. And every once in a while, I would imagine standing at the finish line and reflecting on the books and papers, the sandwiches and cheesecakes, the slope behind the monastery and the café in Harvard Square, Charlotte and Jim, Camellia and Ichiro… One day I would arrive one second before the end and ponder the memories, search for missing gems, and perhaps rate the journey and assess the man. To squander the minutes and seconds—steel-blue lake or ashen-white graveyard, moonlight serenade or battlefield thunder—would be to mangle pieces of myself.

Even as the thought of losing Ichiro pained me, I refused to toss my rifle or raise the white flag, but began to search the Internet and ask Harvard Medical School professors for treatments and surgeons.

"Let's have dinner tonight. I have something important to discuss with you." I didn't know how to mention Daphne's letter and his betrayal, but in his current health, couldn't and wouldn't allow Jim's venom to poison our friendship and our remaining days.

"Sorry, not tonight."

"I thought we're friends." I dropped my cup onto the plate and splashed hot chocolate onto the table.

"Maybe my face and my voice will disgust you."

"You better have a good excuse, turning me down. Of course, having a date would be acceptable."

"I invited Camellia over for dinner tonight. Just the two of us." He wiped away the hot chocolate, leaned onto the table and studied my features.

I would think nothing of it were it not for his eyes divulging a joy as sad as a tear. He put down the cup and spun it on the plate. He lifted it to his lips but only examined the liquid and returned the cup to the plate. I sipped my hot chocolate and watched a mosquito circled his head. The chatter and laughter and the jingles of spoons against cups and plates rose and fell, but Ichiro's silence drowned out the noise. In the next table, the young man continued to exercise his mouth and hands, probably spewing out fragments of the same reverie, while the young lady bit her lips and glanced at Ichiro.

"We decided to give it a try. She told me about Jim." Ichiro caught the mosquito, squeezed a fist and with a napkin wiped his hand. "That letter—"

"Jim can go to... Hmm, I think it's a good idea. I've been waiting..." In my heart, joy and ache surged from an answered prayer. I recalled Camellia under the candlelight kissing me: her soft lips, her uneven breathing. I imagined having accepted her and renouncing the priesthood...

"Aren't you jealous?"

"Of course, nothing less would do." I wouldn't mind living the monastic life and having a happy family and a successful career and a ten-acre mansion facing the Mystic harbor. But I wouldn't want to fall into a black hole, whose gravity would bind me, or at least my liberated atoms. I had always wondered why only the monastic life would quench the thirst in my soul and lead me to the real Lawrence. Perhaps, one day I would be enlightened.

"Aren't you angry?"

"Did she know?"

"She didn't care much about her father. And then, she was optimistic. And she said even if..." Ichiro glanced at the red and black spot on the napkin, folded his hands and again leaned on the table. "I didn't want pity. Listen—"

"She wouldn't. I'm sure." I wanted to walk over to the next table and tell the young man to look at the lady and evaluate the cost and benefit, if he can, before deciding on their future. But I knew the Siren's song would lure the young man into the management consulting firm's bosom, and reward his servitude with fame and wealth and success. If I were young, if I had graduated from Harvard Business School, if I had wanted to make a name for myself, if I had wanted to rub shoulders with the business world's head honchos…

"I wasn't sure. I feared substituting Camellia for her. I feared any happiness would betray Sonya. I feared any love would betray myself. I feared—"

"Fine, go ahead and fear. Enjoy the fear, only don't become addicted to it. And don't let it stifle your life, or prevent you from becoming more of Ichiro."

In June, during one of our walks along Storrow Drive, Camellia had glanced at the frolicking sails and asked, "Can there be healing when pain touches pain?" I knew she and Ichiro had been sharing their sufferings, and rejoiced in her raising the topic. Though pain would sharpen pain, I had hoped love would blossom among pain's ashes. I felt sad at being excluded from my two closest friends' intimacy but rejoiced at a possible new dawn. That day, the sun, mimicking my mood, shone periodically above the zigzagging clouds. But throughout the walk, the wind whistled an aria through the foliage.

Perhaps Camellia would forsake happiness and be with Ichiro and thus find joy, but he wouldn't allow her to abandon her pursuit. Sonya would remain in his mind and heart, a distant cherry tree, blossoms flowing across the stream of time, undisturbed by a black hole's gravitational pull.

I sought to discern the note between C and D, to distinguish the shades of violet in lavenders, to slice the nucleus into protons and neutrons and them in turn into quarks and gluons. But now I must forget Sylvia's words and pretend…

Pretend. Perhaps that would be my revenge on Ichiro for betraying me. Sweet revenge to quench the evil in my soul.

I opened my mouth but couldn't say a word. I didn't have the right to be a prophet, an oracle or a torturer. Only Camellia, her privilege and responsibility to sprinkle droplets of pain and usher grief into Ichiro's and her heart.

"But…" he said.

"Yes."

"So…"

"You betrayed me." Amid my voice's timbre and the mocha's fragrance, I regretted having said those words—words that would slash his heart just as his action had mine. And taking them back wouldn't reduce the tears or shorten the scars.

"I would make her happy." Ichiro finished his coffee and went to the counter to buy a carnation. He gave it to the young lady at the next table and went to the piano to play Bizet's Intermezzo from *Carmen*. While the young man stared at the flower, I walked over, patted him on the shoulder and said, "Best of luck." I strolled over to the piano, sat next to Ichiro and listened to the melody while Jim simpered in my mind. The melody, like arthritis winding its way through my bones during the first taste of winter, pained my heart and mind.

Ichiro stopped in the middle of a tune, fingers hovering above the keys.

"I have no doubt." I inhaled the minty air while my facial muscles twitched.

"I had to do it," he said. "And I was desperate, desperate to do something for Sonya, anything. Only by doing, by acting, by moving forward could I harvest the mixture of pain and love into strength. Without a purpose, I would've collapsed. To bring down Jim, to destroy evil … the only thing to make sense of her death. It was love, unceasing love, love after death." Grief clouded his eyes while the staccato escaped his mouth and quivered in the air.

"Do you know how precious that letter was to me? But even more, do you know how much your betrayal hurts me? Why Jim Whitfield? Why?" My voice burst forth. I heard but couldn't understand his words. The letter linked me to the breath and warmth that was Daphne and reminded me of my conceit and naivete, which couldn't prevent her death. I had failed her, but wanted to treasure her as a friend while my memory hadn't faded with the seasons and my compassion hadn't frosted over losses.

"I had betrayed you for nothing." He banged his fist on the keys. A note grouched through the chatters and laughter and everyone shut their mouths, turned their heads and waited for Ichiro to hammer out the next tune. "No, I'll get him. I'll get him wherever he is."

"I thought we're friends."

"I have promised her father. The self-assured man, drunk, broken down, without hope. I understand how it feels like knowing the sun might not rise tomorrow, how it hurts when snow might drift year after year…but it was for her…Did I tell you she was killed on Christmas Day on the way back from her father's place? We were to marry that afternoon. That afternoon…" He jumped up and left the coffeehouse while the customers' silence followed his path.

I paid the bill and ran after him, toward Massachusetts Avenue. I grabbed his shoulder and said, "We're friends."

He stopped and glanced across the street at Harvard Yard probably reminiscing his college days at the University of Chicago. He grabbed my shoulder and said, "She regretted having to deceive you. Please forgive her."

"Only if you promise to take care of her."

When a bearded man in a raincoat charged out of the café and through the crowd, and the café owner, blowing the whistle, chased after him, Ichiro thrust a letter into my hand and said, "She's pregnant. Jim's."

CHAPTER 23

October 2, 2008

Last night, at the bar, while drinking a Long Island Iced-Tea, a baby face tough guy with broad shoulders approached me. Thought he was trying to hit on me. But turned out he was an FBI agent, Peter's his name, investigating financial scams in the area. Couldn't stand his in-your-face attitude. And usually wouldn't give a damn about any agents, but this guy looked stupid and could be useful. Won't hurt to have an agent on my side, just in case I got into trouble with the law. So, bought him a few drinks, to soften him up and milk some "FBI most wanted" kind of gossip. Bloody Mary, Screwdriver, Manhattan. By the fifth drink, the alcoholic breath told me about several investigations into financial scams. I wonder whether the FBI was checking on Larsen. Didn't want my cash cow to be a dog in disguise. Never trusted the greedy banker anyway, but couldn't find anything wrong. Still, needed to know if I should exit. Bought Peter three more drinks and asked him about Donald Larsen. At first, he didn't seem to know the name, but when he checked his notepad, he told me crooked Larsen was kosher. Lucky break. But I couldn't trust this incompetent fool. By the time we left the club at night, he was drunker than the Bowery bums. But I got his number for future uses.

December 25, 2008

After the Christmas service this evening, I was enjoying the Champagne with my flock when I heard Arthur the rabble-rouser sprouting nonsense about doubt. Corrupting my flock, messing with their minds. Twisting and contorting my truths. I wanted to spit in his face to stop his gibberish.

Probably thinks because he got a Master of Theology from the University of Chicago, he could pretend to be a savior and spew craps. Just because he took some courses in a big-shot university, thinks he knows all about philosophy, theology, faith and all that crap. But his philosophical mumble-jumble means nothing here. Just blasphemy, sacrilege, profanity.

"Must have doubt to have faith." "Without doubt, superstition." Even when I walked over with a knife in my hand, he continued to spew the nonsense, the lies, and the blasphemies. We all know that doubt is the tool of the devil against us. These folks don't want doubt, they just want to believe, believe in me and in my truths. Can your doubt make them feel good? Can your questioning give them peace of mind? Can your analysis of predestination and freewill mobilize them into committees against the enemies? Can your false teachings motivate them to donate? A disrupter, a usurper, an agitator. As I put the lobster tail into my mouth, I was determined to stop him before the cancer spreads. I must prevent these dangerous thoughts from poisoning my followers' minds. A bad, bad man, an anarchist, an anti-Christ.

I cut out a slice of the apple and bit into it, showing my teeth. But the self-made theologian continued to rave as if I didn't exist, just to cross me—the founder and leader of this church and the creator of these truths. I saw through his hidden agenda—hitting on the pretty girls here, trying to build a name for himself, taking my share of the pie, trespassing into my territory. Well, it's personal. It's war. And all's fair and all that crap. Watch me hit below the belt where it hurts.

I smiled as my deacons circled Arthur. After the reception, I called an emergency meeting to discuss strategies to defeat the antichrist. Chandler the fool wanted to break into the guy's apartment to scare him off. But I suggested keeping a watch on him for illegal activities and gather the necessary evidences. Arthur looks like a drug addict. So we should check his bags and belongings for dope.

January 2, 2009

I was whistling at a pretty girl and trying to stop my car at the intersection near City Hall when I found out the brake didn't work. My car charged through the red light and the van from the side street screeched along the pavement and spun around to avoid me. I was scared shitless. My car continued to glide down the street and ran over a skunk. I kept stepping on the brakes and shouting for help from the pedestrians. But they only lined up along the curb to watch my car pass by. Some waved their hands. My car stopped only when it hit a sedan that had stopped at the next red light. When I tried to get out of the car, I found out my legs were shaking and I couldn't stand. I sat in the car for half an hour until the sheriff came along and greeted me.

Later on, after the mechanic had checked my car, he said the brakes were defective. I cursed the Mercedes-Benz dealer. I swore to sue the bastard's pants off. If I'd gone onto the highway, I would've kicked the bucket. Close call.

February, 21, 2009

Last week, Daisy and I arrived in Moscow and had our Valentine's Day dinner at a five-star restaurant. We had lamb stew and borscht but I preferred the vodka.

The next day, we visited Lenin's mausoleum. We waited on line for three hours and saw the dead man for ten seconds. And for the first time in many years, I learned something. I'd like to be embalmed like Lenin, so all future generations around the world could wonder at my majestic face and glorious stature and praise my magnanimity and magnificence. I'd build a marble memorial hall in Gilead, no, in New York, to showcase my achievements and the man himself.

Daisy was such a naïve child, marveling at everything, like a hillbilly walking through midtown Manhattan. These Muscovites must think we're indeed hillbillies. But, what'd I care what they think. I like her just like that, wouldn't want her to change into, God forbid, Sylvia.

But while we were returning to the hotel, a thug in a trench coat stepped out of an alley and stabbed me, the son-of-a-bitch. I was scared shitless and when blood oozed out of my abdomen, I cried and was sure I'd die in the winter streets of Moscow. Daisy was so brave, jumping at that thug. If he was really a mugger, she'd be dead. Even when her hand got cut, and couldn't say a word of Russian, she still grabbed people by their sleeves trying to get help for me. If it weren't for her, what'd I do? I must get her a new cook, a new condo, a new diamond ring. But she doesn't even care about the ones I'd just given her for her birthday. Well, a trip to the Far East then. She'd like Tokyo and Hong Kong.

Fortunately, the thug left because of the commotion. And someone called the ambulance and I was taken to the hospital. When I began passing out, I thought I'd never wake up. The last thing I remembered was holding Daisy's hand. And I was wondering whether Camellia would've also fought off the thug.

When I woke up, Daisy was sitting by the bed, her eyes red and puffy. I took her hand and kissed it. She kissed me on the cheek and her tears dropped onto my lips. I tasted the salty tears. I believe I love her.

I spent one miserable week in the hospital. Didn't even dare to taste the lame food here. Never know if someone might try to poison me with borscht.

Something's rotten. That was no mugger. Wasn't after my Armani suit or Rolex Masterpiece. I was the target. He was after me, the coward. But I don't know anyone in Moscow and couldn't have pissed off anyone. Someone back home must've put a price on my head. That guy could've stabbed a second time and killed me, but he didn't. Just wanted to scare me. Make me suffer until the next time. I remembered the brakes not working. The same person was toying with me. Couldn't be Arthur or Johnny. They don't even have the money to eat filet mignon, much less to pay a thug here and certainly not the connection either.

I'll need Peter's help. I knew he'd come in handy. Probably can give me some protection and, with the FBI's resources, would be able to find my enemy. Better buy him some vodka and a Rolex Masterpiece.

The damn scar down my abdomen still hurts. Fortunately, I'm getting out of this living hell today. But what if someone outside the hospital is waiting to plunge a knife into my guts again?

Earlier in the day, I glanced out the window at the courtyard. And saw two *horse-faces* smoking under the tree. They could be waiting for me. And a *raisin-face* on the bench was pretending to read a newspaper. He might have a knife hidden in the sports section. I couldn't go out through the front door. They're waiting for me to step into the trap.

When Daisy returns from buying me new clothes, we'll sneak out the back door and grab a cab. No, better walk and disappear into the crowd. But, how do two Americans disappear in a crowd of Russians?

It's been three hours already. I hope Daisy is okay.

March 15, 2009

Two weeks ago, a drug addict slipped Rohypnol into Arthur's tea while he was having dinner at Joe's Big Mouth. He passed out near an alley on the way home and two thugs threw him into a van and took him to a motel where a prostitute was waiting for him. They took off his clothes and threw them into the trashcan outside the motel. While the prostitute did her work, a thug videotaped the scene and another guarded the doorway.

Two days later, I received the videotape at a cost of five hundred dollars. I reviewed the tape and called an emergency board meeting on Saturday. We voted unanimously to expel Arthur from the church and afterward celebrated with New York cheesecake and sparkling wine that members had brought for the occasion.

That night, I took Daisy to New York to celebrate the occasion. We had dinner at an Italian restaurant and after we strolled around Greenwich Village, we went to a hotel near Central Park. That night, I thought about Camellia and hoped she could accomplish her mission soon and return to me.

Today, during morning service, I invited Arthur on stage and announced the church would expel him for soliciting a prostitute. I showed him the tape and invited him to review the evidence with the board members after the service. When the congregation denounced him and several members, including Chandler, threw their hymnbooks at him, I rebuked them and asked them to repent. Those sadistic, blood-thirsty parasites. Their shouts of righteous indignation. They disgusted me. Though I enjoyed expelling Arthur, I did it mainly for my church. I must prepare a sermon to chastise my flock next week. Arthur stood on stage rubbing his chin. I thanked him and asked him to leave and never come back. He bowed, walked off the stage and marched down the aisle.

Tonight, Daisy and I had dinner in Memphis. After I'd gotten rid of the kidney stone, I relished the barbecue ribs and finished a bottle of Champagne. Now, only one enemy: Lawrence.

April 1, 2009

This morning, while having breakfast, I heard that Pi Epsilon Naught Chemical had announced it'd be filing for Chapter 11 after losing the lawsuit and having to compensate local residents. I dropped the cup of coffee on my lap and scorched my leg while Sylvia grabbed the poodle and ran away from the coffee. I'd invested four hundred thousand dollars for five percent of the company and now all gone down the drain. All because of Lawrence. The impotent monk is still messing with me. Putting his nose where it didn't belong. And that fool Johnston, should've kicked his butt out of the Board during the previous meeting. After breakfast, I called my lawyer and discussed my options. We decided to sue the board of directors for negligence, for mismanagement, for being fools. I hate April Fool's Day.

August 24, 2009

This morning, I woke up with a headache and knew it'd be a bad day. Just didn't know how bad it'd get. I turned on the TV and listened to the news as usual. And I found out the FBI was after Donald Larsen for his Ponzi scheme. Called the son-of-a-bitch, but his line had been cut off. I dropped onto my chair panting and was scared shitless. My money, stolen by that greedy bastard. And all the money I borrowed from the church account also. I'd known something was fishy about him. But how come Soseki took so long to hack into his system?

I pulled my hair trying to figure a way out of the mess. When the creditors come knocking on the door, there'd be nothing left, not the church, not my mansion, and not my precious Lamborghini Gallardo, and not my poor wine cellar. Glad I finished the DRC Romancee-Conti with Camellia and Daisy.

Took a bottle of Yquem and went to the sauna next to my study. I drank and sweat. I thought and thought. With his Ponzi scheme exploding in his face, the con man would been running like a deer with a lion after his butt. Then, he probably would kidnap me and ask for ransom. So I finished the wine and left the sauna. Decided to disappear before Sylvia returns. Packed several sets of shirts and pants. Went down to the wine cellar and took a few bottles of Yquem and Screaming Eagle Cabernet and lamented not being able to take more.

Called the plastic surgeon Dr. Moltmann to make an appointment for tomorrow. Hope he lives up to his reputation. Don't want an ugly face like Lawrence's. I called Camellia, told her about the greedy bastard and asked her to return right away. Need her beside me during this storm. As long as she's with me, wouldn't give a damn how much I've lost. With the ransom, Camellia and I could start a new life. But poor Daisy, I have no time to take her along.

I was about to leave when I realized that Lawrence would be looking for Camellia after she disappears. I smelled an opportunity and thought up a gift. If he's smart, he'll come see me. So I left my *diary*, these files in the storage device, all organized into themes. Lawrence should be able to find the password. I have a surprise for him. Bon Appetit.

CHAPTER 24

*D*ARK NIGHT *black-hole days dark as night plunging into space-time singularity among gravitons overpowering electromagnetic forces and sucking in electrons neutrinos and photons particle or wave crossing the threshold into chaos without dimensions in distorted recursive Euclidean space-time like a Mobius strip in a spatial-temporal loop. Darkness overcomes photons and vacuum swallows up probability waves reversing the Big Bang dark matter annihilating matter. Entropy sticking its tongue at the Canonical Ensemble singularity stretching toward infinity and eternity expanding and contracting forward and backward in space and time consciousness enfolding upon thinking upon reflecting upon recursive thoughts creating repetitive themes and patterns spiraling toward the Omega point backward toward a recreated nothingness and a rejuvenated annihilation no here no now no I no no.*

I was meditating on space-time when Jan Moscowitz phoned and informed me Pi Epsilon Naught Chemical had paid the damages. I thanked him. If he hadn't reduced the fee, out of his friendship with Ichiro, we couldn't have afforded him.

Under the dawning sky, beside a copy of *Moral Man and Immoral Society*, I wondered whether I had fought Pi Epsilon Naught out of compassion for the town's residents or of hatred for the corporation's executives. The same lawyer, the same lawsuit and the same indictment, but divergent and even opposing attitudes could've seeped into my flesh and marrow and either salted or pickled my soul. On any day, at any hour, would love or hatred dominate? I wanted to believe my love to be stronger than my hatred. But I hated apartheid, the holocaust, and genocide in the former Yugoslavia—all of which arose from hatred, of another race, creed or religion—just as I hated Jim Whitfield with all my heart and with all my soul and with all my mind and with all my strength. My hatred would kindle the flames of those atrocities and yet I couldn't cease to spit on the inferno across the globe. Of course, the stream of love would flow through the valley of ashes and reduce the flames to sparks but only to delay the strife for another month, another season, or another year. My love for Charlotte and my love for Camellia and Ichiro would remind me of another love. Could I cease to hate Jim on one of these tomorrows, when the rainbow would bridge across the horizon through clearing clouds?

He, like everyone else, should deserve a chance to amend his wrongs. But if he wished to wage war, I would fight him until the mountains crumble under our hatred, until we drown in a sea of red, until the galaxy's stars collapse into black holes.

After my meditation on space-time, I left the cabin to chop firewood. Under the morning sky, while I was dreaming of dinner with Camellia and Ichiro to celebrate their engagement, Father Theodore strolled into the woods and informed me that a salesman-like, whiskey-breathed priest had come to see me. I tried to explain the conspiracy behind my meeting Father Jones, but the abbot just rubbed his bald-head and said, "Nice job. Would've taken me six months to find such a character and what a character. Well, good luck. Just make sure he's a real priest."

I thanked Father Theodore and wanted to raise my doubt about Father Jones's calling, but only mentioned my conversation with Charlotte on equality, fairness and power, and he invited me to meet with him and Father Xavier.

"Father Xavier mentioned something similar to me, so let's chat and brainstorm some ideas. We can discuss the ideas with the other brothers. As an abbot, I don't get much feedback, especially after Father Francis passed away. It saddens me to hear about parish priests molesting altar boys. I'm sure many are tempted and some have fallen. We all need keepers to guard our souls, but trusted brothers, not gossip mongers." He winked and I knew he had in mind Father Jones.

I gathered the firewood, cleaned my hands and under the gray sky ascended the browning slope. An east wind delivered moisture, dispersed leaves down the slope and played with my habit. I expected from Father Jones an avalanche of gossip, followed by inquest into my ransom-delivery adventure and so pondered my counterattacks while savoring the last autumn winds. I signed a greeting to a novice and entered the visitor's building. I noticed on the wall new icons of Paul, Peter and John, icons that I had never used to hinder my reaching the God who transcends matter and energy, space and time, existence and nonexistence.

"Hello, Father, so good to see you again." Father Jones in sunglasses, as if meeting an old friend, shook my hand. "Wow, you have a nice quiet place here, though some of your fellow brothers refused to talk to me, just making strange signs. And of course, could use some renovation, like this wall here," he said, pointing to the cracks on the wall, "and that sofa, that's an antique. But, hey, all in all, a cozy place. Oh, by the way, did you know—"

"Father Jones, I'm sure you didn't travel from Gilead to Harvard to report the town's current events." I beckoned him to sit on the *antique*, the handle torn, the linen cover faded and the cushions sagging.

"Oh, why, of course not, but you know, since I'm here, why not make the best of it? Like killing two birds with one stone. It's not everyday I get to talk to a fellow priest and exchange information, you know, mutual edification and learning. Do you know still no confessions since you left? Not even dull ones like having an affair with a neighbor's wife." He slumped down sideways onto the sofa and almost lost his balance.

"Father, do you have some important news or message?"

"For a monk, you're quite impatient. Oho, but I understand, time is money and in this economic downturn, why, we must all be frugal." He leaned forward, glanced around and hissed. "But you know, there's a few ways to make a quick buck, even for priests, even in this economy, if you're interested—"

"I'll have to get back to my dull work, without any profit." I stood up and folded my hands. I nodded to him and walked toward the doorway.

"But you haven't even shown me around." He leaped past me and blocked the exit.

"I'll get Father Xavier."

"Wait, wait. Here, here's a message." He yanked out an envelope and waved it in front of my face.

I tried to grab it but he pulled back his hand and snickered. "Come on, at least let me tell you some news. I mean, after all, I traveled all the way here to this wilderness, just to deliver the message for YOU. You know, a monk should be gracious, not that other people shouldn't, but monks especially, with your vocation and all. Well, anyway, you know Mrs. Pastor's mansion's been broken into? Oh, I should say Edgar the Mortician's mansion. Can you imagine that with all those locks, dogs, guards and security systems? Nowadays, isn't safe anywhere, not even here, I'm sure. So, Father, you should look after your belongings, not that you have much."

"Did you take the preacher's statue? I imagine the wine collection is more interesting to you. Perhaps next time I visit, you'd share the Yquem." I extended my hand toward his chest and waited for the envelope to drop onto my palm.

"Ah, ha, ha, ha, you're funny, man. Didn't know you had it in you. Wow, should do your own standup comedy. Oho, ho, I wish I could get hold of a bottle of Yquem. Yeah, scrumptious. But no, the cellar's safe and sound, just the safe got broken into. Can't imagine what could be in there, right?" He snickered for a while and handed me the envelope.

So, Jim had retrieved his ransom after all, but I wiped his snicker from my mind and opened the envelope. I took out the postcard of Jim kissing Camellia and, with my shoulder blocking the priest's outstretched head, read the note: Jim's request for another *confession*.

"What'd it say? What'd it say?" Father Jones tried to roll his head around my shoulder, but banged his nose into my back, as I twisted around. His sunglasses fell onto the floor, but before I could bend my knees, he had stooped down and replaced them in front of his eyes.

"Who delivered it to you?" I tightened my fist as if grabbing Jim's neck and wringing the scum out of his flesh. For once, I wanted to be Simon and have the knuckles to break Jim's nose. He probably wanted to provoke me and might be watching me from a distant hill and savoring my anguish.

"Come on, that's not fair, should share and share alike. We're fellow priests—"

I sidestepped the priest, twisted around, and exited the guest lounge. But as I trotted down the hall past the new icons, his breath reached the back of my neck.

"I'd found the note on the altar, under the cross, with a ten-dollar bill, only ten-dollars, the cheapskate—" He rushed forward and walked beside me, trying the glance at the note.

"Tell him I'll be there." I shoved the note into my pocket.

"You know what happened to dear Daisy?" Father Jones's grin blocked my path as I exited the building. I wave my hand to disperse the whiskey breath, but couldn't brush aside the smirk.

"You know, that nice looking girl," he said, ignoring my gestures and continuing to talk to the wind, "you must've noticed her at the funeral party. How could you not? Well, anyway, poor girl... so sad... with her dad committing suicide and now her mom going to the cuckoo house—"

"So, you've decided to minister to patients in a mental institution. I'm sure you'll hear a lot of confessions there. Won't be a shortage of people who'd want to talk to you." I could imagine the priest thriving in that community.

"Aha, thought that'd get your attention." He rubbed his hands and wiggled his brows. "Have a thing for her, eh? Oh, that's alright, after all, we're human, right? I once had a thing for this pretty girl and... Well, maybe another time."

"Father Jones, thank you for bringing the message. I'm sure you'd find Boston much more interesting than this quiet town. So I won't delay you. And I must get back to my *dull* work." I crossed the dirt road and began to descend the slope.

"Oh, but don't you want to know about Daisy. Why, that poor girl, she's devastated that her mom went nuts. Of course, we could all see it coming, with the dad's suicide and the foreclosure and bankruptcy... that son-of-a-bitch Larsen... I curse him in the name of God." Father Jones spat on the ground.

"It's not nice for a priest to curse." I continued down the slope, as a cloud mass approached from the horizon.

"Wait, wait, you know, her granny's remains had been dug up and the plot recycled, for another body. And she didn't know about it until now. Poor Daisy."

I stopped and, recalling a case of grave recycling in Texas, turned around and said, "Edgar the mortician."

"Ha, Father Lawrence, you're a modern day Sherlock Holmes. That's right; it's Edgar's funeral parlor so the authorities had shut down the place. But they hadn't arrested the caretaker because it seemed like Donald Larsen had recycled the plots before selling everything to Edgar. Oh, and some crazy caretaker from Atlanta came in town and accused Edgar of stealing his identity. Let you know when I get more details. Well, tough luck for the caretaker. Have to make a living some other way. But my business arrangements with him, all gone south, damn it. But the funeral business is recession-proof, I must say. Rotten luck."

"The higher the potential return, the higher the risk. But I'm sure you have other business arrangements, perhaps with casinos, strip bars, and of course, liquor stores." I grunted out my disgust at his shifty eyes and stained teeth. Had I considered him a priest, I would've been ashamed of my vocation, but having considered him another cow dung like Jim Whitfield or Donald Larsen, only shunned him.

"You interested?" He rubbed his hands and stepped down the slope but, after losing balance and falling on his hands, crawled back to the original spot. "Between you and me, priest to priest... why not, I considered you my comrade... and ain't greedy, share and share alike, especially with fellow brothers in faith. But you've got to act quickly... the chance of a lifetime."

I turned and trotted down the slope, toward the valley and the approaching rain, which ignored the whiskey breath's gibberish and showered on his blond hair. I felt sorry for Daisy and, on returning to Gilead to confront Jim, intended to visit her. Her dedication to Jim would blossom into tragedy and enslave her. But if Jim could disappear long enough to release her from the trance, she might discover a new sunrise and find a Joe worthy of her love. Or, if Agent Peter, with my help, could get his hands on Jim...

I knew what I must do.

CHAPTER 25

I ARRIVED TEN MINUTES BEFORE SIX O'CLOCK at Ichiro's place to the smell of onion, garlic, tomato and pepper. Camellia, skipping the usual half-an-hour-late entrance, had arrived and was helping prepare garlic bread and linguine in Marinara sauce. In the living room, the coffee table, the tatami mats, the circular cushions, and the Renoir and Monet on the wall excited a simplicity that resonated in my heart. And outside the window, Alewife Station, Route 2 and the Cambridge and Arlington nightlights inspired peace.

"Remember our celebration after the Pi Epsilon Naught case?" Camellia hopped over the tatami mat and embraced me, pushing me out the door. The night after the victory, like other occasions when she had invited Ichiro and me to her place, he ended up cooking dinner: paella with zinfandel and T-bone steak in mushroom sauce. But afterward, she treated us to Beethoven's Symphony No. 6 at Symphony Hall. So, tonight, I was surprised that she had stepped into the kitchen.

"You are my friend." Ichiro, holding a can of tomato sauce, walked out of the kitchen. Since our last meeting in Harvard Square, he had written to apologize for his deception, explaining his need to gain Jim's trust and to access the preacher's financial transactions.

I waved Daphne's letter, which he had returned to me at our last meeting. "You could've confided in me. That's what a friend would do." To help him gain Jim's trust, I would've given him the letter, but he didn't trust me enough to divulge his plan and his intention, perhaps afraid my monkish hands would fumble the ball and forfeit the game.

"I didn't want to implicate you. And sorry, Jim probably ate that corner."

"I don't accept that excuse." Perhaps, on a bad-hair day, I would again bang my fist over this incident. And perhaps upon misplacing my journals, I would suspect him. But two years ago, while we were fishing at Cape Cod, I had promised to be his friend and so I would work hard to overcome the wall between us, for him, for me, for Camellia. "And what about those fake emails, about my looking for the original scroll of *On the Road*? I don't even like that book."

"Deliverables, milestones, achievements," he said, "to build his trust in my ability and my loyalty. It's not your nine-to-five job working for a schemer and scoundrel, and no sick-leave."

"We were so happy," Camellia said, hugging a cushion. "At least you were."

"I'm where I should be. Confronting the truth and trusting that our friendship can sneer at it. What other way can there be? Anyway, forget that now. I came to celebrate your engagement. Yes, I'm happy. And that's enough for now." I went over to Camellia and embraced her; then went over to Ichiro and did likewise.

"I was not worthy to be your friend." Ichiro shook his head.

I shook his hand. He turned toward the window pretending to enjoy Cambridge's winter night. How I wished to swivel him around and expose his tears to Camellia and me. Jim would've done it and sneered at his tears, but I refused the scoundrel's way.

"Oh, Lawrence, you'll forgive us, won't you?" Camellia squeezed my hand. "I didn't want to ruin anyone, even before I met you, but he was fixated on destroying you. And he had done so much for me."

"I want to be the child's godfather," I said.

"What else can you be, the godmother?" She patted me on the cheek.

Ichiro came over and with his palm touched her belly. "We expected no less of you for our child."

"Ichiro will have an operation in two months. The doctor's optimistic because he detected it early. Did I ever tell you I am four-million-dollars richer? That's right, so Ichiro can have the best doctors and facilities." She smiled as tears tumbled down her cheek.

"I'm sure Sylvia was dying to give you the money." I shook my head and slapped Ichiro's shoulder. "Where's the champagne?"

"Ha, more like crying." She clapped her hands, a crispy note ringing in the room.

"I thought monks aren't allowed to drink." Ichiro handed me the can of tomato sauce and strolled into the kitchen.

"And most monks aren't allowed to leave their cloister." I would've been happy chopping wood during the day and reading Merton or Moltmann in the evening, but was grateful for the chance to volunteer at Logan Airport. Sharing my joy and grief with Camellia and Ichiro rekindled my faith in humanity, which had been smothered by Charlotte's letter. Perhaps, Father Theodore had detected a blind spot in my soul's recess untouched even by God's hands.

"So what does that make you, a whiskey priest?" She followed Ichiro into the kitchen and poured water into a pot.

"I thought Father Jones has taken that honor." Ichiro handed me a can opener.

"Ichiro, tell me. What does 'the Tao that can be told is not the eternal Tao' mean?" I opened the can of tomato sauce and handed it to him.

"Is it something like your 'cloud of unknowing'?" Ichiro said.

"His cloud? What cloud? I didn't know you have any clouds." Camellia looked from me to Ichiro and back to me as if scrutinizing two madmen.

"It's not my cloud." I put down the can opener and cleaned my hands.

"Your Church's then. But what do I know about Tao, still less about clouds." Ichiro poured the can of sauce into the pan.

"I was thinking about the difference between the Word or Logos and Tao." I said.

"Do you mean the Greek philosophers' Logos or your Church's Logos?" Ichiro turned for a second and resumed preparing the Marinara sauce.

"Can you guys turn off your brains for one night?" Camellia frowned while putting a tablecloth on the coffee table.

"Does she tell you to do that all the time?" I peeked into the oven at the garlic bread.

"Hey, did I tell you you're becoming more like Edgar the Mortician?" She came into the kitchen, slapped my shoulder and, with a frown, flaunted her happiness. She took forks and napkins into the living room.

"That's better than Jim Whitfield." I took out a copy of Erich Fromm's *Being and Having*, and put it on the counter next to Ichiro. "For you. Nice bedtime reading. Very relevant for our times."

"One of these days, your Church will excommunicate you for reading banned books." Camellia stood akimbo at the doorway, her face reminding me of Charlotte's gentle cheeks.

"You've mistaken me for Father Jones."

"Oh, that's hitting below the belt," she said. "Now I'm sure you're becoming like Edgar. By the way, his voice sounded familiar but I just couldn't figure out where I'd seen him before."

"I could imagine Father Jones taking a Playboy magazine to the confessional." Hands steady and face rigid, Ichiro poured the sauce onto the linguine.

"Who's hitting below the belt?" I brought two plates of linguine into the living room and set them on the coffee table while Camellia, still laughing, played a CD of Vivaldi's *The Four Seasons*. I walked over to her and whispered, "You have a minute?"

She dropped her smile and the CD jacket. "What is it? What's wrong?" As if sensing a storm and bracing for the disaster, she sat on the tatami. "Don't scare me."

"I'm sorry. Didn't mean to scare you. I have something to tell you. Just concerned how you'd take it."

"Ah, so you know." She grabbed the cushion, while in the kitchen Ichiro hummed the melody from his symphony. She said, "You going to tell Ichiro?"

"Where're you two? Dinner's almost ready." Ichiro called from the kitchen.

"He's flirting with me," she said.

"Okay. Never mind." Ichiro resumed his humming.

"You're right. If I'd met Ichiro before Jim… but I didn't want to be a homeless bum, much less a prostitute and he cared about me, I can't deny that—" she whispered.

"Ichiro? Why'd I tell Ichiro? What does it have to do with him?"

"You're his friend. You don't want him to be deceived. I understand. Do you know how much I wanted to tell him about it? But how can I? How can you? How can we hurt him like that especially now? Maybe we should call it off. What right…" She was wringing the cushion as if it were a wet towel and managed to subdue her voice but not her tears.

I realized she was talking about Sonya's accident, so I grabbed her cold and sweaty hand and whispered, "That's for you to tell him. I have no right to interfere. One day you must tell him. I don't and couldn't know how painful it would be but you'll have to. It's better for you to tell him now. The longer the secret drags on, the more it will erode your relationship. But it's not my call."

She wiped her tears with a tissue and glanced toward the kitchen. "I couldn't, maybe you…"

I shuddered at the load she had thrust upon my shoulders and imaged Ichiro's face twisting into a frown, before returning to a pretended nonchalance. I said, avoiding that image, "There's something else I have to tell you."

"Can anything worse happen now? We've been through…" She dropped the wrinkled cushion and surveyed Alewife station through the bay window.

"Actually, it doesn't directly concern you. Just some news I have to tell you."

"Bad news, I presume."

"About your mother."

"What do I care about her?" She waved her hand, then punched the wrinkled cushion. "She didn't care about me. She didn't defend me against him. She just wanted to avoid me like the plague, no, like a bastard."

"Hey, what's going on? If you want to keep a secret from me, you'd have to go into the bedroom to talk about it." Ichiro walked into the living room, a plate of linguine in the right hand and one of garlic bread in the left.

"Lawrence is just trying to make me unhappy." She jumped up from the tatami, helped Ichiro set the plates onto the coffee table and kissed him for a minute.

"It can wait. There are more important things." I leaned over the coffee table to grab a piece of garlic bread.

"No, tell us the news now. We might as well listen to the bad news before dinner. I'm not afraid anymore." She grabbed Ichiro's hand and bit her lips. "In fact, I have something to say also."

"But we might as well deal with the bad news with a full stomach." Ichiro caressed her hand and like a statue gazed through the window into the night.

"Okay, your mom—"

"I told you it doesn't matter to me," she said. "For all I care, she can have cancer if she wants."

"Camellia, sit down." Ichiro touch her lips with his finger and seated her on the tatami.

"She had an affair." I said.

"Well, good for her. You should tell my dad instead. But of course, I'd be interested in knowing who her lover was." She smirked.

I shuddered and after realizing Ichiro hadn't seen her smirked, continued, "Jim, Jim Whitfield."

"The scoundrel," he said. "One of these days, I'll get my hands on his accounts and transactions and put him away for a long, long time."

"Ichiro, let's forget about him. I don't know what to think of him," Camellia said.

"While you're getting your hands on his accounts, I don't mind getting mine on his crunchy neck." I tightened my fist, trying to feel Jim's neck in my hands. But I wasn't sure I could snuff out his breath.

Camellia put the cushion on her lap and twisted the engagement ring on her finger. She opened her mouth but the doorbell prevented her from releasing her burden. I held the garlic bread in my hand, not sure whether to eat it or put it down.

"Ah, that must be Sonya's dad." Ichiro got up from the tatami and wiped his hands on the apron. "He's here to congratulate us, but won't be staying for dinner."

Camellia dropped the engagement ring and it bounced on the hardwood. Ichiro bent over, picked it up, grasped her hand and said, "You're freezing cold. You alright? What's the matter? Don't be nervous, everything will be okay. If you want, we can postpone it."

"Let me take her for a stroll. The fresh air will do her good." Although I believed for love to flourish one must confront the truth, the moment, when inappropriate, could nip its bud.

After Ichiro rushed to the kitchen to clean his hands, I urged Camellia to leave through the backdoor, which exited onto the side stairs, before Sonya's father could come through the front door. But when she tried to stand, her legs gave out. If I hadn't caught her, she would've fallen onto the coffee table. I seated her on the tatami, but before I could inquire about her condition, three buzzes from the doorbell, like a secret society's code, echoed in the room and startled me.

As Ichiro walked to the door to open it, I tried to help Camellia get up. But her legs wouldn't obey her. Her cold trembling fingers squeezed into my arm until I twitched from pain. I wanted to try again, but she shook her head and leaned against the coffee table. I poured her a cup of hot tea. She took the cup and fixed her eyes at the doorway, where the intruder stood.

"Well, well, Father Lawrence, what a coincidence. What an unexpected pleasure. Didn't know you knew Ichiro." Agent Peter extended his hand.

I shook his hand and tried to match his eyes with Sonya's but his aquiline nose betrayed their kinship.

"Stay for dinner. We have more than enough food." Ichiro took out a bottle of cabernet and four glasses.

"Well, good that you two know each other, two good men. Not easy to find these days." Peter glanced at Camellia and continued, "Dinner smells good, I'm tempted to stay but I'll have to take a rain-check." He handed the gift to Ichiro. "Just wanted to say a word before I leave. But you won't be able to get rid of me when you have surgery."

"Could this wait?" I blocked him from Ichiro and thrust my nose at his cheek. I knew Camellia was trembling without looking at her.

"Some things are better said sooner rather than later."

"And some things are better left buried." I was angry at how much he was torturing her.

"What's the matter?" Ichiro walked over, sat down on the tatami and held Camellia's hand. "Are you ill? Your hands are very cold."

"Before you decide to marry her, you must know the truth," Peter said.

"Father Jones came by to see me two days ago." I intercepted him before he could reach them.

"He can go to the bar or the brothel, for all I care. But if you want me to nab him——" Peter said.

"The truth is that I'll marry her," Ichiro said.

"Another request to hear a confession," I said.

"Then go ahead, why tell me about it. You don't need my approval to hear a confession and I certainly wouldn't chaperone you to a confession." Peter waved his hand and turned to Ichiro. "She has a dark secret."

"What made you think he wants to know. He has a right not to know?" I eased myself between Peter and the coffee table.

"We all have dark secrets," Ichiro said. "I've not told her every one of mine. So what if she was a mistress? Did you come to celebrate or to disrupt?"

"It's Jim, Jim Whitfield." Desperate to distract Agent Peter, I said Jim had requested that I hear another confession. Having taken the priestly vow, I had promised to honor the confession's sanctity, but now by disclosing the appointment, I chipped off a piece of my soul and would begin to decay into Jim. After Jim had asked me not to divulge his relationship with Daphne, I kept the secret throughout the years. Though at times I felt that I had wronged her, I still could find my foothold on the boulder facing the storm. Now, the foundation holding up Lawrence began to crumble one stone at a time, until one sunny afternoon under a breeze...

"That bastard?" Agent Peter clenched his fist and his knuckles crackled.

"He's toying with me," I said, "probably wants to confess some more secrets that I cannot reveal. You can set a trap and ambush him. This is your chance to nab him, to eliminate those vulpine fangs from the world."

"After you've heard the secret," Peter said to Ichiro, "if you still want to marry her, that's fine. I love you like my son and want the best for you. When I lost Sonya and the whole world came tumbling down, you were the only one with me, getting drunk with me. So I promised to protect you and couldn't allow you to marry her without you knowing the truth."

"He's right. It's not fair for you to be kept in the dark." Camellia grabbed Ichiro's forearm, which slipped away as he tried to caress her.

"You don't have to tell me." He put down the wine bottle and glasses.

"I must," Peter said, stamping his foot, "because I love you like a son."

"What can stand between our love? What can severe our bond? What can destroy our fellowship in pain?" Ichiro, sensing the storm, raised his voice, almost to a roar, against the winds of random events.

I wanted to interfere, to preserve the illusion, to maintain the façade, but against that desire, lassoed my tongue. Truth must shower on that heart and test its resilience before the seed of love could bud from the sand. Only then would the roots, the stalks and the flowers last through the coming snowstorm.

Oh happy fool, sing and dance of your ignorance. But Ichiro and I couldn't join you, we the greater fools.

"Sonya." Peter almost whispered.

Like a spell, the name of the departed turned Ichiro into a salt pillar. Camellia gazed at the linguine and breathed evenly. The smell of garlic bread and Marinara sauce began to sicken me and the drizzle beyond the window thwarted my flight into the peaceful night.

"No, it won't." Ichiro extended his hand toward Camellia but stopped in midair and she, coordinating with him, raised her hand but stopped at chest-level. I prayed for the two hands to join in love and companionship, but the still air blocked their path.

"Her father is Donald Larsen." The agent's face twitched.

"So what? What does it have to do with her?" Ichiro said, "We're no longer in those barbaric times when children must pay for the sins of the father."

"I knew what Ichiro had done and I'm proud of him." She poured a glass of cabernet and sipped the wine.

"But he's—" Agent Peter raised his fist.

"He's a rich banker scheming after any money he can get his hands on. Nothing more. And nothing unique about him." I pointed at Alewife station. "You can find a few dozens down the street right now."

"Then listen, because this matters. This matters to Sonya, my dear daughter."

"What does the greedy bloodsucker have to do with Sonya?" Ichiro rushed past me and thrust his face into Peter's.

"Before you say anything," I said, pouring a glass of cabernet, "make sure you're able to bear the responsibility for the consequences, especially for the course of Ichiro's life." I downed a draft and walked to the window.

"What else can I do?" Peter smashed his right fist onto his left palm. "Pretend as if nothing had happened? Father, I thought you seek truth and reality, unlike your peers who seek illusions, peace of mind, and an uneventful path to death."

I studied Cambridge's blurred lights and wondered at its beauty, burglary and perhaps drug dealing hidden in the rain. When I read about genocide in Rwanda, I had wished to be a happy fool, chosen by grace to live a life of sunshine and beaches.

"Forget about consequences, just tell me." Ichiro grabbed him by the collars and shook him.

"He was the man who killed Sonya, my poor lovely Sonya. I didn't tell you before so you would help nab him, not for revenge, but to do right." Peter grabbed him by the collars and shook him. "And just because he's rich, just because he can afford the best lawyer. He should be in jail. He should pay for what he did. Where is justice?"

Against the lamp-stand Camellia shed a streak of tear, her shadow shivering in the full-length mirror.

"So it was her father. So be it." Ichiro released him, approached Camellia and grasped her shoulders. "You will remind me of Sonya, of love unfulfilled, of pain overflowing. But it's alright, it wasn't your fault."

"But it was my fault." She wiped away the tear and twirled the linguine.

"Don't say that. I never believe——" Ichiro glanced at Sonya's picture on the shelf.

Agent Peter followed Ichiro's gaze and said, "She paid the bartender to feed her father Screwdrivers. That's like shoving grilled salmon in front of a cat or sending naked ladies to Jim Whitfield."

"I only wanted to be free, to escape from hell, to find peace." Camellia tabbed the garlic bread with the fork. "I thought I'd be rid of them, of their silent hostility, of their cold rage. Just to get away, to live, to breathe. I didn't know he'd be driving. Why was he driving? Where was he going? I never thought... Not you, of all the people..."

"So this is it, so this is why..." Ichiro held her hand up to chest-level, lowered his eyes in thought, then lowered her hand and poured a glass of wine. "So it was to——"

"Forgive me, forgive me. Oh, forgive me." Camellia knelt before him and seized his shaking hands.

"Why? Why? Why didn't you tell me?" He drank the wine and inquired like a detective desperate for fingerprints, bloodstains and a murder weapon.

"When I found out, I was afraid, so afraid."

"Oh, Camellia." Ichiro caressed her hand, kissed her on the cheek and finished the glass of wine. He rose and walked out of the apartment, his face calm as the air before a storm.

"Ichiro... Ichiro..."

Oh, happy fool.

CHAPTER 26

AFTER HELPING RE-TICKETED PASSENGERS in the morning, whose laughter and anecdotes again had exhausted me, at noon I met Camellia at her Back Bay apartment, a studio facing the Charles River and M.I.T.'s Building 10. From her voice over the phone, I expected the tempest had intensified over Ichiro's and her path. I tried but failed to reach him and must rely on Camellia to sort through the debris. In light of their turmoil, my pain, my anger, my self-pity like gnats dispersed into the night.

On Sunday, Ichiro had drunk himself to sleep while Camellia cleaned his vomit and prepared his meals. She had gazed through the window and the drizzle to locate a crack among the nimbus.

"I felt lonely but peaceful. Wanted to come to you but knew I belonged there. All of a sudden, I realized…" She stepped out of the eat-in kitchen and marched across the stained carpet. When she handed me a cup of chamomile, I put the green-eyed teddy bear on the torn sofa and accepted it.

"Could it be?" She gazed out the window at the clouds. "I cared about Jim, but only because he loved me and took care of me when I was drifting from one dark tunnel to another abandoned barn to still another overcrowded shelter. Now, somehow, it's different."

"It's one step closer." I turned the cup in my hand.

"Your standard's too high."

"Not mine."

"When I first met him, I wanted to avoid him because his eyes were so penetrating and his lips were so determined." She dropped onto the sofa and took the teddy bear. "Do you remember the first time we had lunch, at Copley Square? He adjusted the positions of the napkin, fork and knife as if performing a religious ritual. I thought he might have obsessive-compulsive disorder. And the mumble-jumble you guys talked about only made me want to avoid him even more."

"That's not fair. Mumble-jumble yourself."

"Who said anything's fair in this world?" She rubbed her cheek against the teddy bear. "But when I learned about Sonya's tragic death and his reaction, I became attracted to him because of our shared sufferings, even though they are very different. And I thought going to the cherry blossom festival was very romantic, in a sad way. And his dedication to Sonya…" She bit her lips while the Charles' water reflected light through the window onto her face.

Throughout the week, she had stayed at his place and shopped for him, while he, as in any other day, showered, brushed his teeth, prepared and ate his meals, did the laundry and composed music. But they hadn't exchange a single word.

"He was staring at the other ring, the engagement ring, with Sonya." She pulled her legs up onto the sofa and hugged the teddy bear. "I was frightened by his calmness and preferred him yelling at me, releasing his anger and grief. Instead, everything's bottled up waiting to explode."

***

Ichiro had taken that engagement ring off his finger only recently. During previous get-togethers, he would lock his eyes onto the ring and enunciate the syllables of Sonya's name. Once, while having coffee in Copley Square, he stared at the ring for three hours, until the waitress inquired about his fiancée, at which time he burst out of the coffeehouse, leaving me to pay the bill. At another time in Mission Hill, when some paint dripped onto his ring, he spent a whole day cleaning it with turpentine.

I admired his devotion to Sonya, but feared his obsession might harm his body and mind. So I suggested that he travel to Europe for several months and studying music in Paris and Vienna. The unfamiliar faces, culture and milieu should stimulate his faculties and pull him away from reminiscence. Throughout that time, he had sent emails to describe the financial center in London, the Notre Dame Cathedral in Paris, the frescos in Rome, the beer-gardens in Munich, the castles in

Prague, and the conservatories in Vienna. He even detailed his friendship in Vienna with a Russian composer and a Hungarian mathematician. I urged him to take courses in Vienna, sample the cultures in Bucharest, Sofia, and Budapest, and take some pictures of Transylvania.

When Ichiro returned from Europe, I introduced him to Camellia, hoping an extra friend, particularly a fellow traveler through the desert, would moisten his heart's dunes. And sure enough, a wounded heart recognized the familiar scars in the other as a bloodhound could sniff out another in a sea of poodles. On Saturdays, we would have breakfast in Cambridge and serve meals in Mission Hill's soup kitchen. Whenever I volunteered at Logan Airport, they would come along to help re-ticketed passengers. In the evening, we would have dinner at Faneuil Hall, Copley Square, or Chinatown. Once in a while, we would go to Symphony Hall to listen to *The Four Seasons*, The *Emperor* Concerto, or Dvorak's Symphony No 9. Last September, at Harvard Square, we discussed the *what for*, the *so what* and the *how then* of life. No revelations except the gulfs among our views—only Camellia's obsession with happiness could match Ichiro's with perfection. And yet, we celebrated the chasms as opportunities to discover new landscapes and correct our illusions.

During one of their trips, probably fishing in Cape Cod, Ichiro shared his unfulfilled love and Camellia her desolate childhood. After that, they would have the same look toward an orphan, the same frown toward Rwanda's genocide and the same curvature of their lips toward the global economic collapse. Their pain and suffering might've squeezed bile into their hearts, but together, fellowship forging their hearts and channeling the flames, they marched into wastelands and extended scarred hands. Sharing their pains had bolstered their hearts' bond, which I had hoped could withstand any hailstorm. Now the storm had arrived…

***

After Camellia and I had tuna sandwich for lunch, we went out for a walk. Across the Harvard Bridge, the M.I.T. Civil Engineering Department's buildings confronted us as it had the first time we crossed the bridge together, but camellias no longer decorated the buildings' adjacent grounds. As in our previous walks, sedans, wagons, and sports cars passed on the left along Storrow Drive, but pain had seeped deeper into our hearts and the air felt colder, as if the onslaught of Boston's winter corresponded with our hearts' new season. She grabbed my arm and huddled close, probably less to hide from the wind than to steady the course into the future. A couple walked past also arm-in-arm, but showcasing smiles and laughter. Time had eroded our joy and deposited into our hearts grains of sadness, which only the wise could grow into a deeper peace. I caressed Camellia's hand and watched a flock of sparrows bounced back and forth in the shifting wind.

"The first time I felt loved was with Jim, so you can't blame me for caring about him. Of course, the maid, the evening gown, the diamond necklace, the Lexus, the penthouse condo weren't bad either. I admit I'm materialistic, but only a bit. It's him. He treated me like a woman, like a person, well, almost." She huddled against me. "You, you treated me like a person, without any hidden agenda. You showed me who I am. And I love you just the way you are. It's so natural."

"And Ichiro?"

"I would've given everything but could give nothing." She twitched in my arm and wrinkles collected on her forehead and down her cheeks.

Last summer, as we strolled on the same path, two boys no more than seven years old, imitating the geese overhead, flapped their arms and chased each other in circles, while the mother watched from a distance and reminded them to be careful. At that time, the breeze, soothing on my face and arms, couldn't even lift the candy wrapper on the pavement. I kept seeking Camellia's opinion of Ichiro and she kept teasing me for matchmaking. Near the Boston University Bridge, I saw a dead squirrel, peaceful under the sunlight, but, absorbed in the season's warmth, I didn't look again. But now, its image through the miracle of random events resurrected in my mind and overlapped with the sea of sand. I sifted through that day's other images to find other neglected carcasses, but could only feel the warmth of that July zephyr surrendering to the chill of today's northeaster.

"He's canceled the engagement." Camellia whispered in my ear, to prevent the driver of the sedan speeding along the road from eavesdropping on our secret.

"I'll talk to him. I know how much he loves you but the pain…" I stopped and felt his pain and her pain and the anger toward the randomness we called fate. God had given us freedom but we fumbled our responsibilities and, from limited knowledge, understanding and wisdom, toppled under free will's consequences.

"Enough, enough. I don't want to cause him anymore pain. Even if he's willing to bear…" As the wind whisked her hair into a brush, the wrinkles across her forehead and down her cheeks appeared to soak up Ichiro's pain and suffering. I held her close to shield her face from the wind and discovered in her eyes a sparkle like that of a diamond in the sand. Along the same path, she had described her birthdays without presents and her Thanksgiving dinners alone in the gymnasium-sized dining room, and told me that she knew the chandeliers' contours, the marble steps' cracks and the Monet paintings' hues better than her parents' eyebrows and earlobes. But now, amid the gust she said nothing, not that pain had evaporated, but that it had seeped into the marrow, beyond words or even sounds.

"I just wanted to be happy and to make him happy."

A streak of tear slashed through her cheek and the flesh stiffened under the salty ravine. Sunlight glistened on the drop of tear stalling at her chin. But I beheld a pair of distant eyes and listened to a distant wail. No, time hadn't washed away the memory; age hadn't smeared the scene. And even more, memory had connected the then and the now. I had often wondered how much happier I would be... I had saved Daphne a thousand times in a thousand dreams, only to see again, again her headstone towering over the earth. I grabbed Camellia's cold and trembling hand and vowed not to repeat the past.

Oh happy fool I could not be. I studied the billows crashing onto the Charles River banks and confronted the eyes of crisscrossing events, of random interactions, of purposeful calamity. Yes, I wouldn't close my eyes. I would help nab a fiend.

CHAPTER 27

Aᴀꜰᴛᴇʀ ꜰɪɴɪꜱʜɪɴɢ ᴛʜᴇ ʙᴇᴀɴ ꜱᴏᴜᴘ and the apple, I arrived half an hour early at St. Barnabas and confronted Father Jones's grin, rasp and whiskey breath, which still nauseated me.

"My dear Father Lawrence, guess what, a confession, a real confession. Yesterday, after tea time..." He adjusted his sunglasses and drew out a flash of whiskey from his robe's side pocket. "Scrumptious tea... Anyway, a young fellow, probably in the late twenties, you know, one of those yuppies, with handsome ratty jaws, green polka-dot tie and skunk-scented cologne... Don't think I'm boasting because, you know, any priest worth a cent must know his cologne, right? Well, this skunk-scented young man told me some real cool stuff. Wow, just like the tabloid, only better, and free. Just between you and me, priest to priest..." He wiggled his brows and put his index finger over his lips. "Five girlfriends, Memphis, Nashville, Atlanta, Huntsville, and New Orleans. How does this guy do it?"

"Excuse me, Father. I have to prepare—" I entered the sanctuary and walked down the aisle to the altar where the basin and chalice had disappeared.

"Runs a medical equipment scam, bills Medicare several-million dollars... oops..." Father Jones came after me but kicked the carpet and tumbled onto the floor. "Beachfront house in South Carolina..."

I again entered the confessional ten minutes earlier to wait for the scoundrel, but this time, brought a copy of Bonhoeffer's *Letters & Papers From Prison* to prevent myself from dozing into another quantum dream. Amid the musty smell, I reflected on the idea of *the coming of age of mankind* and the implication on morality, faith and religion. But images of Jim's exploits flickered in my mind and the faces of Daphne, Charlotte, Daisy and Camellia testified to their suffering. I imagined how, without Jim, the sun would warm their skins, the chrysanthemums would perfume their work, and a ham sandwich would taste of caviar.

Tunneling past reason beyond knowledge and thought and experience leaving myself into night into vacuum into unlimited unknowing discarding Maslow's Hierarchy of Needs and the Law of Large Numbers forgetting uranium's chemical symbol and Prince Andrei's last words disowning that April morning at the Tidal Basin and that September afternoon at Walden Pond. Understanding without learning or analyzing or existing into the pure perfect infinite mystery...

Father Jones came by to interrupt my meditation. He offered me whiskey, but I declined and ordered a tandoori chicken with garlic naan. When he scratched his head and swaggered down the hallway pretending to have forgotten my order, I congratulated myself on ridding of the whiskey breath that had been working its way from my skin into my marrow.

While reading one of Bonhoeffer's last letters to Eberhard, a blob reeking of whiskey slumped into the confessional's seat. At first, I thought Father Jones wanted to confess a secret, or after overindulging on whiskey he had turned the wrong corner, but I soon realized the whiskey priest couldn't find enough clothes to grow the extra sizes. The hulk pulled out a flask, swigged the whiskey and cursed at the bottle.

"Hey, here to confess. So you listen up boy, you hear me. Ain't here to play around." He gulped another draft and flaunted a tattoo on his arm. "Father, you sinned. Ha, ha, ha..." He doubled over in laughter and choked on the whiskey for half a minute before straightening up.

"I want to revisit the sins in your last confession." Though I knew Jim had disguised his voice during the previous confession, I was sure the current voice though familiar wasn't that of the last confessor.

"What in hell you mean, revisit? Hey, you but listen up, boy. Last time said um... um... um, stolen lots of goddam money... over you can count..." He downed another draft of whiskey. "Ha, what you care how much I stolen."

"Tell me about your diary." I shifted on my seat and tried to discern his face.

"Diary? What in hell you talking about, boy? Aiming to confuse me? I telling you, ain't no hobo Joe…" He coughed and cursed the seat.

"The entry on July 4, 2007."

"Hell, that be Independence Day… Hey, know what I done on that there day?"

"Actually I do."

"Hey, aiming to be funny? I said no messing with me, boy. Supposed to tell you… um, yeah, you sinned, know what I mean."

"Let's focus on your sins."

"Boy, did you sin, ha, ha, ha… firstly, you snitched to them FBI—"

"Tell me about your entry in the diary; July 4, 2007." Alarmed, I leaned forward and peeped through the partition at the leathery face. I tried to discern the tattoo on his arm, but the whiskey bottle blocked my view.

"Ain't telling you nothing about no diary. Listen boy, ain't gonna let go of Camellia, you hear. And because you snitched to them FBI, gonna be nasty, ha, ha. What you gonna do?"

I rang the bell and leaped out of the confessional into the hallway and knocking over the statuette of John, ran toward the altar. When I stepped behind the cross, a crash, as of an ox thrashing a barn, echoed throughout the sanctuary. A figure, head first, speared into the front pew, where someone had etched a broken heart on the seat. His head cracked the wood and scared off a rat. Agent Peter sprinted toward the collapsed pew, clawed the figure by the collar and smashed the head several times against the planks, until the wood shattered into splinters, some bloodied.

"Bastard." Agent Peter turned the head and boxed the face until three teeth fell from the mouth.

"Hey, that's enough. That's enough." I charged at Mad Dog Peter and yanked him away from the bloodied, naked-lady tattoo. The agent twisted around, seized my collar and was about to smash his forehead into my nose, but he stopped and squinted at me for a minute. Then he beamed and loosened the claw.

"You got guts. Not bad for a priest. Good man, worthy to be Ichiro's friend." He brushed back his hair and took out a handkerchief to wipe his hands.

"I'm a better friend to Ichiro than you are." I straightened my clothes and glanced at the figure groaning above the splinters.

Father Jones rushed down the sanctuary almost tripping over the carpet. "Hey, hey, who's going to pay for the damages? What a mess.

You know how much that pew costs? Well, actually, I don't know either, but must be expensive. And this is a church, no place for violence. I guess you agents don't have any sanctuaries. Nothing's sacred except violence and bloodshed."

"Stop the gibberish. Send me the bill and I'll take care of it. What'd you care, errand boy? It's not your pew; it's not your church. Remember, you're only a steward. So don't get carried away." Peter lifted the limp figure and shook loose the splinters.

"Hey, don't expect me to clean this mess. Violence, all you know is violence." The priest took out the whiskey bottle, swigged a quarter of a bottle and whispered to me, "Thugs, just thugs with a badge."

"He's not Jim Whitfield." I lifted the limp arm to show the naked-lady tattoo.

"Then who the hell is he?" Agent Peter spat into the man's face.

"Johnny Chandler's father."

"Bastard." Peter dumped the limp figure onto the splinters and scratched his face.

"Boy, you're violent, aren't you, FBI-man? Didn't they teach you anger management?" Father Jones took out a pad and a pen and began examining the pew, the carpet and the marble steps. "Don't you know you aren't supposed to fight in a church, you know, this being a sanctuary and all that crap? But if you're going to pay for the damages, I can give you some leeway. Then again, shouldn't waste taxpayer money. But anyway, here we go, a new cherry wood pew, a new Persian carpet, new hardwood floor…"

I stepped out into the night to escape the scent of whiskey and blood. A fog hovered ten feet about the ground and engulfed the church's upper section, including the spotlights on the wall. Only two fuzzy lights at the gate glared at the walkway and the graveyard. But a clearer darkness had already highlighted the fake penitent's contours and the color of his soul. After a dozen days adrift at sea, I met on land the cannibals' knifes and forks. As always, free choice: trot ahead or retreat into the sea. More than ever, I resolved to bring down Jim, as to topple an enemy gun-tower, and rid the world of the plague that had fed on Daphne and Daisy and Camellia and so many others along the path.

Agent Peter walked out of the church and lighted a cigarette before saying, "Do you know Edgar the mortician's dead? Shot in the head, execution style. They found him in a coffin in the funeral parlor, very convenient. Must've been trying to sell coffins, against the injunction."

He puffed on the cigarette and continued, "Maybe someone didn't like his in-your-face sales technique."

Or maybe, they found out he recycled the tombs or ripped them off with imitation smoked salmon or imitation cherry wood coffins. Or maybe someone just didn't like his face. Father Jones mentioned that someone had accused the mortician of stealing his identity. The man might be vending his anger. But would any of these justify killing him? Nip his breath, crush his heart, smother his thoughts.

As I surveyed Gilead's night scene, I mulled over how I could do the same to Jim. I must lure him out with a bait, not Camellia, but Lawrence. Yes, he would want to devour me, but the hunter would become the hunted.

CHAPTER 28

October 1, 2009, noon, Harvard Square, Boston. I stood outside the Harvard Coop facing the crosswalk and the "T" entrance under a shower of foliage and a sea of faces waiting for the green light. In the next instant, the traffic light could turn green or remain red; a herd could march out of the entrance or trample on each other; an ambulance could sing along Massachusetts Avenue or screech down Memorial Drive; I could chant Veni Creator Spiritus or renounce my vocation. At the ledge of each instant facing the chasm between one moment and the next, four billion souls awaited renewal and an infinite number of possible worlds anticipated birth. Of all the possible worlds, only one would come to be; and yet an infinite number would open up for the next instant. What world would emerge? War, famine, or global warming? What Lawrence would sprout? A priest, a physicist, or a drunken bum? How would I want to redefine and recreate myself in leaping across the chasm? Would there be a Father Lawrence in the next instant when the traffic light may be green or red, the sky azure or gray, the Charles River glistening or murky? The various Lawrences in the alternate worlds might be as different as electrons from positrons. Which Lawrence would I encounter, in five years, in ten years, in front of a mirror? Jim's face loomed above, smirking at my scattered footprints. October 1, 2009, noon plus one second, Harvard Square...

***

I sat near the cabin's windows and glanced at the diverging path in the woods. And I considered the path I should take to determine the Lawrence in the next second, the next hour, the next day. Who am I?

The boy who delighted in visiting the Lincoln Memorial just to sit on Lincoln's lap, who on receiving Jim's birthday present gobbled down the novel, and who on the frozen lake surface examined the fractal structure of a fallen but not yet distorted snowflake. Or the teenager who represented Jefferson High School's math team only to lose to those Stuyvesant High School prodigies, who stood hand-in-hand with Charlotte to admire Great Falls' white foams on many autumn afternoons, and who under Polaris's wintry light meditated on death and nonexistence. Or the adult who in a November morning grasped the Uncertainty Principle's alien world, who under the science library's dim light struggled with *Summa Theologica*'s metaphysics while preferring Reinhold Niebuhr's pragmatism, and who under maple foliages suffered the pang of severing from Charlotte. Or the mouth that had prayed for strength to hate Jim forever and sought hatred's ecstasy.

Who's this Lawrence, shadow hopping from second to second searching for the thread to connect them into a semi-lucid episode? Everyday, sniffing out more and understanding less.

In search of Lawrence. The true Lawrence, the evil waiting to shatter the façade. I stood at the desert crossroad and confronted the forking paths, rugged and winding toward destinations unknown. All roads leading to some desert; all roads creating some Lawrence.

***

I had abandoned the happy fool. I had looked at Jim's diary, refusing to blink, refusing to flinch, refusing to cower under his squinting eyes, exposed fangs and shuddering shoulders. A desert invited me for a journey, a journey under the sun, a journey through the sandstorms, perhaps a journey to end all journeys. I might plunge a knife into Jim's guts and celebrate my reconciliation with Charlotte. But I would have to abandon laud in the early Harvard mornings, the valley behind the monastery, the silence in my cell. I would have to abandon my vocation.

On the ledge, overseeing Great Falls, I had asked why and what for and found my vocation. Even with Jim's ruse I had entered the monastery to wake up early in the morning and sing Veni Creator Spiritus. Though whenever I recalled Daphne's or Charlotte's letter, I still might doubt my vocation, I had located under the heaven my song and my station. Now, as if the heavens had split to reveal a hidden truth, I discovered a new calling: to fight and outwit and crush Jim, and thus become like him. I would forsake my integrity; I would betray my soul; I would become evil to rid this demon.

***

Energized anew, I woke up at two o'clock in the morning. I washed my face and prepared for laud. I caressed my cell's walls, my bed's mahogany boards and the desk lamp's copper base. I sniffed the air and paced the floor. With my own hands, I had built the desk and chair. And I had decorated the walls with inspirations from Mohandas Gandhi and Martin Luther King, Jr. For the past seven years, in this sanctuary, I had offered my prayers to God, examined my soul, and recuperated from noise, distress and the pain of everyday life. Now, I bid adieu.

Hoarfrost had coated the bench under the maple, where I often sat to meditate the setting sun. The starlit valley, where the bare trunks extended to the horizon, slumbered in the November wind. On summer days, I would cross the stream and stroll into the middle of the woods to listen to the orioles, and in the log cabin I would read Thomas Merton's books. During sleepless nights, after helping re-ticketed passengers in Logan Airport, I would recount the day's events. I had been grateful to have the chance to talk to the travelers and understand them. Once, a Russian couple had wanted to pay Ichiro and me and ended up buying us sandwiches. After Camellia had kissed me, I stayed in the cabin for seven days fasting, meditating and examining my feelings. When Ichiro visited the abbey, everyday we would trot into the woods and sit on the bench beside the pond. We would discuss Zen, musical scales, and Quantum Chromo-Dynamics and share our Logan Airport adventures. Communion. The past seven years' memories converged on me in the stillness of the early November hour.

Soon, I would have a new home, but not a new sanctuary where fear, joy, and memories might settle. In these grounds, among the maples and birches dwelled my memories and roots. And yet, there's a time for everything under the sun. A time to tolerate Jim and a time to crush him.

Sun Tzu in *The Art of War* said, know thyself and thy enemies, and hundred victories in hundred battles. Jim's Achilles' heel is his believing himself more artful and venal than anyone else. And so, I would be preparing my arrow and practicing my aim.

Father Theodore came up to me and said, "Don't be a stranger. Let's have tea sometime, if not here, then Harvard Square, if not there, then in heaven." He stroked his beard and gazed into the valley.

"What if we arrive at different destinations?" I said.

"Then pray for me. I hate the heat. Can you believe it, a Ghanaian afraid of the heat? The wonders of creation."

And so, he reminded me why he was my spiritual director. I would miss him. But a child must learn to walk and a skier must learn to fall.

The bell rang and footsteps converged toward the chapel. Under the starry sky, the valley to the right, I followed Father Theodore into the building. Along the hallway, beside the pillars, the walls and the icons, the air chilled my skin but I looked forward to chanting Veni Creator Spiritus.

After leaving the monastery, I would marry Camellia.

CHAPTER 29

My knee ached, while I drove down Route 2 toward Cambridge. And glares from the oncoming cars hurt my eyes. Once upon a time, I could drive from Boston to Washington D.C. without my knees or my eyes complaining. I had exercised to strengthen my body and read to gain knowledge and meditated to gain understanding and fasted to strengthen my will, but entropy worked harder and revealed a new wisdom, under which all mortals, all living things and all matter must bow. Ichiro had hiked up and down the Franconia Ridge Trail like a kid skipping down the sidewalk, while I had burnt every ounce of precious fat to catch up. But now his body was rebelling. Giving up health, memory, reasoning, possession, loved ones, and finally life. I had learned from the saints that detachment would disperse pain and suffering and sprout sanctification and enlightenment. And yet… and yet… I wanted to stand on a peak and gaze down upon autumn foliage red, orange and yellow, waves upon waves surfing in the crisp wind. I wanted to understand the duality of particle-wave and space-time and the fundamental laws of nature. I wanted to share in Camellia's and Ichiro's laughter on a newborn day. I wanted to fight a Jim Whitfield, to know that I can hate. To rub this aching knee, to search this fading memory, to shed tears for Charlotte and Camellia and Ichiro, and through all these to purify the heart and encounter Lawrence. And yet… and yet… enlightenment from a precipice, freedom from the Dow Jones, from the debate on health care reform, from the genocide in Darfur, from Jim Whitfield's plots.

I stopped by Walden Pond and glanced into the water's reflected surface, where a maple leave ascended from the bottomless sky about to plunge out of the lake. In the fallen blade's jitterbug, a smile, a song, the fragrance of morning daylily. In the whisper of silence, stocks surged, engines roared, particles collided. The sound of white noise. The throbbing of the foliage, the wind, and the waves resonated in my cells, as a C note would vibrate a tuning fork. My mind wandered across the Milky Way, through the heartbeats of asteroids, pulsars, and white dwarfs, into my soul's alcove. In the instant between being and nothingness, I perceived the dynamics between fear of and desire for intimacy, the pain and suffering of the Rwandans, the balance between fiscal and monetary policies, and DNA's dice play to rejuvenate the species. Alone, under the heavens, paths divergent, the foundation of my being. I am because I AM.

I stopped by Concord for breakfast and paid $3.37 for muffin and coffee. As I handed the five-dollar bill to the cashier, I recalled how much I had hated paying bills. Even though I had been here before, the muffin and coffee tasted different and the chatter and laughter also sounded different. I examined the tabletop, swirled the saltshaker, and listened to the town's morning chitchat. In the next booth, an aged couple discussed Thanksgiving dinner's menu, which would include the favorite dishes of their children and grandchildren. At the abbey, we would have a special mass and a dinner with visitors. After early morning mass, I would stroll down the valley to the woods, and in the cabin meditate for an hour. Then I would help prepare the mash potato. Last year, I invited Camellia and Ichiro for the celebration. Ichiro discussed Meister Eckhart and St. John of the Cross with Father Theodore from noon to sundown, until Camellia yanked him away to bobsled down the valley. She threw snowballs at every approaching monk, and I spent about an hour stopping her. Only when she grabbed Ichiro to bobsled, did I have some time to prepare the potato. After dinner, I taught Camellia and Ichiro to chant Veni Creator Spiritus and she complained about not understanding the *gibberish* while he studied the lyric like a Latin scholar. Afterwards, I returned to my cell and read *Moral Man and Immoral Society*. This year, I would look forward to Thanksgiving with Camellia and Ichiro, but without the abbey, without the cabin, without the cell. Part of me had disappeared. Giving up. One day, I would give up my health, my reason, my friends and my memories and be ready to return to dust. But today, I would enjoy the setting sun, the autumn foliage, and the twilight culture. And I would recall the cherry blossoms showering over the Tidal Basin.

In the game of life, victory means defeat. I must not seek to win or lose… perhaps not even to play the game…

***

When I stepped into Camellia's apartment, I grabbed her hand and slipped the ring onto her finger. "Like it? It cost me $1.99."

"I'm not laughing. Try again." She twisted the ring on her finger. "But it fits nicely."

"And I'm not joking."

"But you're a priest."

"Not anymore." After refusing Charlotte, after years along the desired path, to destroy Jim and save Camellia, I had abandoned my vocation, my calling, my true north; I had abandoned Lawrence. I had renounced my priesthood. And, sacrificing my integrity, I had donated to agent Peter, Jim's diary detailing embezzlements and money laundering, but not the sections flaunting the scoundrel's affairs with Camellia and Daisy. Had I not risen to the occasion, some knight would've grasped Jim's neck and another would've guided Camellia out of the desert. But I must act according to my character. Loving Camellia and detesting Jim, I wouldn't hesitate to crush his hissing head with a rock and, failing that, to perish under his venom. After thanking me, Agent Peter had begun sifting through the autobiography to target specific credits and debits and build a case against the enterprising preacher.

"Why should I?" Camellia said.

"Ichiro—"

"But you aren't Ichiro."

"Then convince him—"

"He's gone."

Though an ache descended from my throat through my chest and stomach into my abdomen, I had expected my friend, like I, to seek solitude in some mountain or desert, to sort out the thoughts and emotions whirling into a tornado.

"Yes, yes, yes." Camellia showered my face with kisses. "Like I said on Valentine's Day—"

"We must find him."

"Don't worry. I won't substitute you—"

"He needs us."

"He doesn't want to be found. Respect his desire."

I feared that he might perish in the gusts and not emerge from the storm to greet a waiting friend. And I couldn't stand by while he struggled with the puzzle's pieces and tried to fit them into a picture. Perhaps the only picture might have snowflakes under the sky or drizzles in a fog or grains of sands among the dunes.

"I'm sure you want me to—" She tried to pull out the ring but in the end just twisted it around her finger.

"It would be ours."

"Aha, I knew there was a catch." She grabbed the teddy bear and huddled it.

"If you believe I don't care—"

"Did I say you don't? When I'm with you, I can truly be myself, be the person I didn't know existed because you poured out a part of yourself. You're like a mirror. Before meeting you, I hadn't thought about leaving Jim even though being a mistress... You made all the difference. You're like... But Jim used Ichiro and me."

"It has nothing to do with Jim. Jim's Jim and—"

"And you want me to do it for you?"

"You would've done it for Ichiro."

"Are you jealous? Yes, I believe you are." She clapped her hands and pinched the teddy bear's nose. "I never thought you'd be jealous."

"I hope he'd be jealous of me enough to..." I put my hand close to her abdomen but stopped about one inch in front, and without ESP couldn't sense the fetus's movements.

Without the abbey to care for my needs, I would have to worry about food, clothing, bills and taxes and perhaps even forsake prayer and meditation. Action against contemplation. I must reconcile and integrate these two colliding worlds, similar to unifying the strong, gravitational and electro-weak forces. I must choose the food to eat, the clothes to wear and the services to solicit, against cost, health, preference, fear and my false self-image. And so, I began to appreciate Ichiro's frustration in deciding between beige and turquoise for a raincoat. Camellia, who reluctantly acquired her worldly savvy, would hold my hand and lead me through the darkness, while I treaded through the taste of salsa, curry and Marinara sauce and the sound of pennies, dimes and quarters against the register. I would learn to equate a dollar with a cheeseburger, two rolls of toilet paper, and a fiftieth of a monthly electric bill. Then, I would find out inflation has revised these truths just as new leaders would political realities, economic laws and religious truths. I would learn to count my pennies and invest my quarters with another Donald Larsen and end up in the Bowery next to Whiskey-Breath. But if I stayed close to Camellia, I would survive. I would miss the abbey but not regret marrying her.

"When the time comes, I'll make amends to Ichiro." She tightened her lips, walked over to the mantel and grabbed the picture of Ichiro and her under a shower of cherry blossoms. Through the taut face and pressed lips Ichiro's eyes radiated hope into the future. Camellia, both arms embracing him, smiled through her eyes. Behind them, the Tidal Basin's ripples twinkled under the sunlight while mandarin ducks waded through the water. In her hands the picture quivered, and she turned to the window and glanced out at the water. The light drizzle had continued into the afternoon and a fog had descended on M.I.T.'s buildings.

"He wouldn't blame you. I know it." I walked to the mantel and examined the other pictures of them in Sturbridge, Mystic and Cape Cod. On the coffee table lay a copy of Ichiro's dissertation: *A Study in Infinity: Fundamental Properties of the Aleph Set.* Although these ideas had become coffeehouse gossips, at the time Ichiro completed the thesis, his idea had stimulated astrophysicist to apply them to the Big Bang Theory, near space-time singularities, to explain the infinite number of galaxies in the universe.

"Let's do it soon." She walked over to the coffee table and grasped the dissertation. "I'm happy. You make me happy."

I would've wanted to wait for Ichiro to return and tried to salvage his and her love, but Jim should be monitoring us and must learn of our marriage as soon as possible. I would advertise the news in the local newspaper and on the Internet and send an email to invite him to our wedding. The jealousy and anger and shock would propel him here to stop us, to crush me, and to surrender himself to Peter and the other FBI agents, who would be craving to nab him for embezzlement and money laundering. After he has taken his abode in a jail, I would visit him once a month to flaunt my smiles and show him pictures of our— Camellia's and my—child. He would have enough time in prison to reflect on his failure and defeat.

"Oh, they've arrested Johnny for killing Edgar the mortician." Camellia inserted the dissertation into her backpack.

CHAPTER 30

ON THE WAY TO THE LARSEN MANSION in Memphis, I stopped by a Virginia gun show, where men and women were trying out pistols, revolvers, rifles and machine guns, and bought an Intratec TEC-9 semi-automatic handgun. Camellia frowned, but didn't question me.

Afterward, as we drove along Route 40, she glanced at the birches yellowing along the road as if searching for a birthday present among the ovate leaves. "You know," she said, "if my father's really dead, I actually would feel relieved, knowing I'll never have to see him again, knowing those eyes will never see me again. Like not having to eat spinach or liver anymore. Do you think I'm coldhearted? Please don't."

I didn't comment. As I drove into Memphis, I planned my destruction.

When we arrived at the Larsen estate, where ten acres of oaks and birches inside a ten-foot fence surrounded an elongated marble mansion, Mrs. Larsen in satin dress and cashmere scarf strolled through two columns of servants to greet us. But Camellia, whose face stiffened upon seeing her mother, only stepped into her childhood home through my appeal.

"Apologize for the mess." Mrs. Larsen requested a manservant in tuxedo to bring three chairs from the kitchen while workmen removed sofas, TVs, chandeliers, china, paintings and statues.

"Hey, I thought you can't sell the stuff once the government seized your house." Camellia strutted into the living room. She grabbed a cushion and, huddling it, dropped onto a chair. "Where're my stuffs? Better not have sold them."

"They're taking them to a government auction. I saved your things. They're in the basement." Mrs. Larsen opened the cherry-wooded cabinet beside the fireplace and poured a glass of zinfandel. "I'm so afraid of not seeing him again, not having the chance to apologize —"

"Well, don't worry about that. I'm sure he'd known it all along. And to even out the score, he probably had several mistresses. Maybe he's hiding in one of their bosoms now." Camellia threw the cushion at a workman who was carrying a vase to the foyer. "Let's get my stuff from the basement and have a bonfire tonight. Out with the old and in with the new. No more baggage from the past."

"How could you say such a thing? You heartless…" Mrs. Larsen choked and doubled over, and a maid brought over a napkin while another a glass of water.

Camellia poured a glass of zinfandel and requested some Swiss cheese from the maid. Before I had a chance to open my mouth, the doorbell, as if unable to brave the showdown, hummed a melody and interrupted the silence. As the echoes ricocheted into the hallway, a workman carried into the living room a case of gold coins and requested Mrs. Larsen sign a receipt.

When the butler opened the front door, Sylvia's crimson lips thrust into the foyer and her perfume seized the living room. From her eyes, I anticipated a storm over the squall. The air hampered my breathing and I had to gulp down the tea to moisten my throat. The butler gaped at the intruder and held the doorknob for a minute before shutting the door and adjusting his bow tie.

"Hey, there's no life insurance policy here for you. Buzz off. Hire a hit-man to knock off your husband if you want the money." Camellia popped out of her chair and under the ceiling's dangling wires blocked Sylvia in the middle of the room. The servants remained in two rows and looked past the two women while two workmen hauled a sofa into the living room.

"Ah, the mother and daughter slut team, shoulder to shoulder. Good, make it more fun." Sylvia flung the mink coat over a maid's outstretched hand as if it were a hook. Then rubbed her hands as Felix Grandet would in front of gold nuggets.

"Please watch your words." I stood up and confronted the crimson lips and acidic perfume.

"Oh, Father, didn't know you in here whorehouse. Excuse me. But they don't have no decency or shame so nothing's below them. And I suggest you stay a ways from them and this here whorehouse fore they corrupt you." She took off the gloves and flung them into the maid's face. "Reckon you're a decent man and a devout man-of-God, but they... well, they know how to use—"

"Hey, bitch, shut up. I know what you did." Camellia lunged at the crimson lips, but I rushed forward and stopped her.

"Ha, so does I, so does I. Want to trade dark secrets? I bet mines juicer than yours. When I was coming over here and imagining your expression... " Sylvia raised both arms as if in prayer. "I begun singing hallelujah."

"Mrs. Pastor, what'd you want?" Patricia paled and collapsed onto the oak chair that a workman had moved next to the marble staircase.

"You a nitwit? Or just playing games with me?" Sylvia stepped into the kitchen, opened the refrigerator and took out a slice of raspberry cheesecake. "Ain't but one reason I'm here. Show time." She grabbed a bottle of whip-cream from the cabinet and splashed a streak on top of the cheesecake. "Hell, it's the day of reckoning."

"For you, maybe. You're in the wrong place. The insane asylum's one mile down the road to the right and your friends are waiting for you there. Better hurry and not disappoint them with your standup comedy." Camellia freed herself from me. She threw the mink coat onto the floor and wiped her soles with it before giving it back to the maid.

"Wouldn't it be interesting if I open your there bedroom door and find my husband in your bed?" Sylvia, not aware her mink coat had wiped Camellia's shoes, grabbed a fork, scooped a piece of cheesecake, shoveled it between her crimson lips and reentered the living room.

"Oh, so you lost your husband and have to go knocking on every bedroom door in town to find him. Well, should start with those inno-cent young girls in your church, the pretty ones of course." Camellia walked up to her and snatched the plate and dumped it into the trash-can.

The muscles beneath Sylvia's eye twitched twice before she turned to Patricia. "Don't think I don't know about your affair with him."

Patricia cringed on the chair and tucked her knees toward herself to block Sylvia's whipping breath. But Camellia said, "Come on, you call that juicy? That's as old as those wrinkles around the corners of your eyes. You're probably the last person in town to know about it. Don't you know they've been gossiping about it in the diner, the Town Hall, and even after Sunday services while you were busy putting on layers of powders to cover those ancient wrinkles. Here, I'll do you a favor and let you know some of his more recent flings."

I pulled Camellia by the arm and held her cold hand. "That's enough. Let it go; let it go."

"Ha, go ahead and laugh." A grin sprouted onto Sylvia's red face and blossomed into a guffaw as she reached into her alligator-skin handbag and yanked out a batch of pictures.

"What'd… what'd you have there?" Patricia leaned forward and raised her hand, but tumbled sideways and rolled onto the floor. Camellia glanced down and smirked while I helped the fallen lady onto the sofa that the workmen had left in the center of the room.

"Don't worry. It ain't you. You too ugly for show and tell." Sylvia slapped onto the table the batch of pictures. "But need some pictures for the pony show and naturally to give credit to your husband's PI." The pictures showed Jim and Daisy on a cruise to Jamaica—kissing on deck, frolicking in the beach and making love in the cabin.

"Donald had no qualms with Jim." Patricia almost fell out of the sofa again.

"Of course not," Sylvia said. "Why else would he allow Jim to sleep with his wife?" She walked to the cabinet and took out a bottle of merlot. Patricia convulsed and curled up like a dying worm.

Camellia sipped the wine and pushed aside the pictures. "So? You enjoy looking at pictures of your husband making love to his mistresses. So what? What'd I care? You're wasting my time. If I wanted to see porno—"

I squeezed her hand and turned over the pictures.

"Oh Father, I see you her new beau. You poor pitiful man." Sylvia sighed and shook her head. "If it ain't too late, I'd like to give my humble two cents: dump her like a piece of shit."

"I'm going to marry her."

Sylvia covered her heart with her hand and sniggered as tears squeezed out of her eyelids. She took out a tissue to tap her lashes. "Oh, dear, dear, I'm so, so sorry. Such a pity. My sincere condolences. My poor, poor Father. If I known, I'd bring a wreath and prepare one of them eulogy."

"We're not interested in buying those pictures so you can go pitch somewhere else," Camellia said. "There're probably enough dirty old men and of course dirty young men in town for you to make decent money. So buzz off and don't waste my time. I know you're bored because your husband, with so many mistresses, can't spend any time with you, but I'm busy." She shoved the pictures onto the floor.

"Ha, ha, but just the appetizer. You be patient. Here come the main dish. Won't be disappointed, I promise." Sylvia thrust her hand into the handbag.

"This is enough, Sylvia. Please leave. I have pictures also, but won't show them. Let bygones——" I gathered the pictures and handed them back to her.

"But Father, you'd be interested in this. I'm sure, especially since you're gonna marry her. Don't you want——" Sylvia accepted the pictures but yanked out another one.

"No." I recalled dinner at Ichiro's place and the resulting enlightenment. Sensing knowledge would ruin my bliss, I decided to be a happy fool. But Sylvia had already slapped the picture onto the table.

Jim was kissing Camellia in front of the Eiffel Tower.

"Like I said, no." I held Camellia's hand and kissed her on the cheek and she smiled like a little girl with a Siamese kitten for Christmas.

"And like I said, we're not interested in the picture. Go peddle somewhere else. But I think even a dirty old man wouldn't want it. Good luck." Camellia finished the glass of wine.

Patricia moaned and twitched. She rolled over and fell onto the floor. I rushed over and found her fainted and cold, but her breathing steady.

"Ha, before you but reject it, you should might ask her. I'm sure she be very interested in it." Sylvia shifted her eyes and laughed like a hyena. "Tell you what, since I'm feeling generous, I'll give you the picture for free. That's right, free. Ha, ha, ha, for your enjoyment. You know, you must entice the customer with some free samples." She doubled over and guffawed.

"Your tactic has failed. I'm not stupid like her. You've called your buff and lost. You hear, you lost." Camellia raised her hand as if to slap Sylvia, but only grabbed the glass from her. "But I've something for you. Interested in pictures of you and your lover Peter? Nice quality photos, taken with a thousand-dollar lens."

A maid wetted a towel with cold water and brought it over. I put it on Patricia's forehead but she didn't wake up and her face remained pale.

"How dare…" Sylvia twitched her face for several seconds, then grinned and took out a pistol from the handbag. "Know how to use this here gun? Well, very easy, any old fool can learn. Don't need to be no rocket scientist. You just squeeze this here trigger. Heh, heh…"

"You can't scare me." Camellia handed the glass to the maid, straightened up and marched toward the crimson lips.

"That's enough. That's enough." I left Patricia and rushed toward them.

"Ain't gonna scare you." Sylvia smirked and put the pistol on the table. "Just wanted to give you this, a gift for sleeping with my husband." She grabbed Patricia's handbag, yanked the gloves and mink coat from the pale-faced maid and marched through the front door.

Camellia and I looked at the pistol and at each other. I held and kissed her hand. "Never mind her. She's probably gone nuts."

"But something's wrong. I can sense it, from her eyes, from her lips, from her laugh, from her tone." She held my hand as if it were a plank in the stormy sea. I wanted to comfort her but also sensed the venom from Sylvia's breath.

While a workman was pushing the refrigerator through the doorway, Patricia moaned and woke up. Before sitting up she cried, "Is it true? Is it true? Tell me it's not true."

"What'd you care? Did you care when I didn't get presents on my birthdays and for Christmas? Or when he wouldn't allow me to go out with my friends? Or when he barged into my room and … and…It's too late to pretend now, when you lost him and all the money… Don't expect me to pity you. No one pitied me."

I put my finger over her lips and wiped away her tears on both cheeks. She kissed my fingers. Her face pristine as a rainbow after the rainstorm.

"Is it true? Is it true? You must tell me. Oh, God… no…" After struggling for a minute, Patricia sat up on the sofa and convulsed. I thought she was having an epileptic fit. I was so shocked by her distorted cheeks and dilated pupils that I forgot to help her.

"Forget it. It's none of your business. What're you going to do if it's true? Take this pistol and shoot him? Say how sorry you're? Or maybe shoot me? Ha, at least he was nice to me." Camellia bit her lips, but tears continued to flow down her cheeks.

"That baby—" Patricia raised her hand toward Camellia as if trying to grab a plank to stay afloat.

"That's none of your business either." Camellia pushed her hand away. "Go and enjoy your blood-drenched retirement with the money you stashed away in the Swiss banks."

"You must tell me. I beg you, I beg you." Patricia rose from the sofa but collapsed back onto it after wobbling for three seconds.

"Let's go." Camellia grabbed my hand.

"She looks pretty distraught." I hesitated, glancing at Patricia's twitching cheeks and quivering lips.

"Father, please... do you know... is it..." Patricia raised her hand toward me as if requesting benediction.

"Yes."

"No."

"Yes."

Patricia trembled for a minute before grabbing a tissue from the maid. She wiped her tears, while down the hallway a workman dropped some china and outside the bay window a sparrow tumbled down into the bush. "You're his daughter."

CHAPTER 31

I ARRIVED AT DAISY'S CONDO and parked my car in the visitor's area. When I saw Father Jones entering his car in the residents' outdoor garage, I called out to him, but he appeared not to have heard me. He sped out of the garage and onto the street, honking at an old lady in his path. I ran over to check on her. After confirming she was unharmed, I strolled along the flagstone walkway to the condo's front entrance. I entered the lobby, woke the concierge and requested to see Daisy Walker. He yawned and rubbed his eyes and studied me for a minute before calling her and informing me to proceed along the arcade and up the stairs to unit 207. I thanked him and strolled on the walkway next to the six-lane swimming pool, where two men were racing down two lanes and, near one corner, a young couple was splashing water. I admired the competitors' stamina and shivered just watching them in the water. Heavy clouds had gathered even before I'd entered Memphis and now the nimbus seemed about to shed tears.

After yesterday's revelation, Camellia had disappeared and, knowing she would look for Jim, I came to extract from Daisy the lecher's latitude and longitude. I vowed to free Camellia from that demon forever and wouldn't hesitate to stab, to shoot, to strangle or to exorcise. But Father Jones's presence troubled me. He was unlikely to be visiting a parishioner, who, if twenty-percent wise, would flee a mile away from his whiskey breath. He might've been visiting a friend, a mistress or a business partner. Or, he might've been contacting Jim through Daisy.

At the end of the arcade, I walked up two flights of stairs to the second floor and searched for unit 207. The young couple had disappeared from the pool, but the two swimmers under the drizzle continued to race each other. A sparrow, escaping from the rain and indicating my destination, landed on the balustrade in front of unit 207. I saluted the bird and rang the bell.

Footsteps approached the doorway, the door jerked open and Daisy's rosy but emaciated chin and light-blue dress greeted me. Her eyes had lost luster, probably from yearning for Jim.

"Oh, Father Lawrence, I didn't... didn't expected... oh, come in, please come in." Her harp-like voice against the drizzle's moan almost hypnotized me, but I returned from alpha-state and treaded on the carpet into the foyer, where a coat rack and two shoe cabinets greeted me. I took off my shoes, walked up a four-step stairs into the living room. Between matching recliners, the brown velvet sofa, which confronted the coffee table in the middle and the plasma TV on the left wall, saddened me. However, vases of daffodils, daisies, and orchids decorating the coffee table, the side tables next to the recliners and the TV stand's left and right ledges cheered my heart.

"You came in the nick of time, I mean I need your help. I did notice the poor thing but directly he... eh, my friend did get." She guided me toward the balcony and slid open the door to reveal a blood-soaked sparrow missing a wing. "I was watching, eh, my friend there quit the building and did see it. The wing sure look broken, ain't it? Might could you help it?"

"Looks like some teeth bit off its wing. It'll need a vet, but let me take it in." But before I could reach it, the bird hopped off the balcony's edge and tried to fly, but somersaulted in the air and dived into the pool.

Daisy shrieked and grabbed my arm. "What ought we to do?"

I went downstairs to the edge of the pool, where raindrops excited circular ripples that clashed into one another. The sparrow was floating toward the center lane. I went to the lobby to inform the concierge of the dead bird, but without opening his eyes, the leathery face only yawned, as acknowledgement, and reentered dreamland.

I flipped through the sign-in sheets to identify Daisy's visitors the past two weeks. I returned to her unit, where outside the front door, she rushed forward to inquire about the bird. After learning of its death, she walked through the doorway and said, "Sometimes sure feels helpless. Could might not even help no bird." I agreed, unable to help not only the bird, but also Camellia and Ichiro and Charlotte. But I refused to throw up my hands, to retreat to the rabbit hole and to suffer Jim's smirks.

"Father, you have a seat. You want coffee, tea, or sparkling water? We got mocha, Java, and French roast. And chamomile, oolong, Earl Grey, green tea and iced tea." In the living room, Daisy's voice rose and fell while her eyes locked onto my loafers as if admiring the worn leather. I asked for green tea and flipped through the floral arrangement book on the coffee table. I matched a photo with the pot of orchid at the bay window, where the drizzle had sprayed a layer of gray mist to shield this dwelling from the approaching darkness.

She brought the green tea in an ivory cup carved with morning glories, the color of which matched that of her dress. While sipping the hot liquid, I pointed at the gray dress socks, one lolling on the recliner and the other sneaking halfway into the bedroom. "Looks like Father Jones left his socks here. Guess he'll have an excuse to return."

"Oh, he must've..." She blushed, walked to the sofa and the doorway to pick up the socks and put them into the bathroom's laundry basket.

"I thought you love Jim."

"Over anyone else in the world, over myself. Oh, Father Jones..." She sat on the recliner, put both hands on her laps, dropped the rosy chin onto the collarbone and stared at her pink slippers. "It... it ain't what you think if you think... there be a reason... he came..."

"You don't have to explain. I didn't come to talk about Father Jones, not that he's not interesting. But there's something more serious and urgent." I put the cup on the coffee table while she fiddled with her fingers.

"Nothing I wouldn't do for him. Ain't always sure about everything, but this I'm sure."

"If you really care about him, then you must help me."

"Please you help Johnny, he be innocent. I heard he gone to jail, couldn't reckon it be true. You but know him, then you know it be a mistake for sure, for sure." She glanced at me and dropped her eyes while the tremolo echoed between the walls. But her fingers continued to knead one another. I began to understand why Jim was attracted to her, and thus hated the serpent even more for deceiving and seducing this child, this lamb. Who instead of wasting away her youth in this jewel-encrusted coop, could've loved a man more worthy of her gentleness and strolled down city hall or the town square with her soulmate.

"But he confessed. I'm not a crime scene investigator. I couldn't analyze the evidences, but could only trust his words. Perhaps he despised the mortician for ripping him off, charging an outrageous fee for the funeral service. I'm sure you could empathize with him, knowing the mortician used fake smoked salmon." Her concern for Johnny instilled in me a seed of hope, that she still loved him, in spite of her devotion to Jim.

"No, no, he couldn't of killed no crooked banker. He ain't violent; he ain't a killer." She wrung her hands and put them flat on her laps.

"On the other hand, Jim had embezzled money from his church and laundered money through his missionary organization—"

"No, no, I don't want to hear no more. I love him, I love him, I love him over anything in the world, over myself." As tears rolled down her cheeks, she put both hands to her ears and tried to scream, but only whimpered.

"If you love him, help me find him. You know the FBI is after him and if he runs he'd get hurt." I felt sorry for her and hated myself for knowing Jim's deception and trickery, as if participating in them.

"He but a good man is what he is."

"Do you still care about Johnny?"

"Help him. He didn't kill no greedy banker."

"Of course, he didn't. He confessed to killing Edgar the mortician."

"I'm but speaking the truth."

"Were you speaking the truth before?"

"You don't got to believe me nothing." Her rosy chin paled against the darkening bay window and her lips trembled.

"I want to believe you if you'll help me do so." In my mind, a spark, from dendrites relaying impulses, ignited an idea, fleeting yet poignant enough to leave a bitter aftertaste. "Are you saying what I think you're saying? Or am I hallucinating that you're saying something? Or are you tricking me into believing you're saying something?"

"Like I said, I'm but speaking the truth, I'm saying something or I ain't saying nothing." On top of the blue dress, her fingers couldn't grab onto one another but her hands refused to leave her laps.

"If the something you're not saying is true, then he's a clever rascal, as clever a rascal as Jim."

"Oh, please you don't slander him. Like I said—"

"I know, I know. He's a good man. We're all good men or good women. That was why Edgar the mortician ripped you off and that was also why Johnny killed him. Or is it Donald the greedy Larsen?"

"He didn't kill nobody. I done told you that. Don't you but believe me? Oh, Father Lawrence, believe me, believe me."

"You keep saying that, as if you know who killed him."

"You sure must think I ain't a decent girl, but I ain't no liar."

"I don't think you aren't a decent girl. But I know you're protecting Jim. You said you'd do anything for him. So why not lie?"

"Oh, that Johnny sure a fool, an honest fool."

"If he didn't kill the greedy banker, who did? Tell me, I'm listening and I'll believe you. But if you don't tell me, how can I believe you?"

She tried but couldn't knead her fingers. She sobbed and wiped her tears. "Might could I have some chamomile, or but anything hot? Sure getting cold."

I entered the kitchen and treaded on the marble floor. In the pantry I searched through a sea of tea bags for chamomile and at the cabinet I sifted through several sets of ivory china to locate a cup engraved with lilies. While I was pouring hot water from a Chinese teapot, she entered the kitchen with my cup. She pulled out two armchairs and invited me to sit next to her. I gave her the chamomile and I watched her sip the tea and waited for her to speak. Against the windowpane, the rain tapped out a melody, while in the kitchen her breathing modulated the tune.

"Much obliged." She regained her rosy hue but her hands continued to tremble.

"Do you need all these things?" I looked around and asked, only because I knew she didn't cared for the cherry-wooded table, custom-made silverware, jade saltshaker, and the thousand teabags.

"They be gifts and it's the thought counts."

"From a good man."

"Oh, Father, please you don't tease me. I know you don't like him. But you sure wouldn't understand. Sometimes I sure don't understand, why of all the people, a married man."

"You're not the first person to tell me that I know nothing about love."

"You sure a man of ideals. I respect though sure don't understand none of it."

"I hope not, I really hope not. If those are only ideals and not the norms…"

"I got a confession."

"Oh no, no, no, I'm the wrong person." I waved my hands as a drowning duck would flap its wings. "Should've confessed to Father Jones when he was here. He would've stayed any number of hours to hear it. Just make sure he doesn't record it and enjoy it in the stillness of night."

"Sure would of been silly to confess to him."

"I haven't thought of that, but come to think of it, you're right. Very silly, not to mention awkward."

"I can trust you, can I?"

"I've encountered enough dark secrets and would prefer not to know more but if it'll help you—"

"Jim did tell me, as you repent, God forgive you."

"I'll have to agree, even though it's out of his deceptive mouth."

"But then he preached about—"

"Forget about his preaching."

"But I still scared of the fire from God. Jim did say so long as he being with me, I be alright. But mayhaps in the future, as they catch him… oh, what I gonna do?"

"It's not him, it has nothing to do with him. Don't you see he has nothing to do with God? You can repent without him."

"I did killed the caretaker."

"For ripping off your father and driving him to suicide?"

"He going to go to the FBI and help them to corner Jim, for a lighter sentence. He be an evil man, already gypped Jim out of millions of dollars and would of destroyed him. How could might I let that happen? I did tell you, I would might do anything for him, even kill."

"But there's one problem: you couldn't have known Edgar the mortician was Donald Larsen in disguise, not from here in your casta-way island." I scrutinized her whisper and examined her downcast eyes, trembling lips and clinched hands, convinced she had killed Donald the mortician. But I sensed Jim manipulating her index finger, and thus wanted her to implicate the three-handed puppeteer.

"But I knowed it. I sneaking into the funeral parlor's back room. I heard him talking over the phone to his wife, told her never be looking for him. He ended the call, I shot him and he fell into the coffin. Don't you not see?"

"Not everything, I still don't know what kind of gun Jim gave you. Can you show it to me?"

"Didn't you not hear me? I shot him. I killed him. It have nothing to do with Jim."

"Of course it has everything to do with him. But there's still something I'm not sure. When he visited you last Monday to inform you that Edgar is Donald Larsen, did he buy you that dress? It matches you well, simple and pristine. But couldn't be Jim, he's showy, vulgar, and worldly." Although the sign-in showed Edgar visiting her last Monday, I could hear Jim's snicker echoing through the forgery.

"You stop it. Of course he given this to me last Monday. No, no, I mean… he never been here last week… no, never… oh, how might could you know it being Monday." The cup shook and hot tea spilled over her hand but she gaped at me, unaware of the liquid scorching her skin. I grabbed a towel and wiped the liquid from her hand, now as rosy as her cheek.

"And Johnny will be paying for it."

"Father, please you go with me to that there police station. I too scared to go alone. You know everything, you can tell them how I but killed the fiend. But please you leave Jim out of this. He but given me the gun for my protection." She drank the tea and stood up, waiting for me to take her to jail.

"It appears all the evidences point to Johnny: his fingerprints, his footprints, Donald's blood on his jacket."

"That couldn't be. I killed him. I must of left some fingerprints. Maybe they be blood on my clothes." She pulled out a tissue and wiped her tears. "But, oh, he, I mean Jim, never asked me to kill him, never. He but told me how evil that banker-caretaker, after cheating him of all his money, now helping the FBI to corner him."

"Of course he didn't. Why should he? Now that you killed Donald Larsen, he had nothing to do with it. Innocent as a rotten mushroom." I seated her down and checked her hand but it had only slightly reddened.

"But he hasn't nothing to do with none of it. I killed that there fiend on my own."

"Do you want to save Jim?"

"I know what you want from me and you ain't gonna get it."

"Agent Peter put Mr. Chandler in the hospital for a week, mistaking him for Jim." I described how the agent boxed Johnny's father until the latter's teeth fell off.

"I don't want to hear no more. You trying to trick me." She put her hands over her ears, but I knew she still could hear.

"If I could reach him first—"

"No, he sure too smart. He been gone. They can't catch him." She waved her arms and fidgeted in the chair, then stood up, pulled at the skirt and walked to the window.

"Do you love him?"

When she turned her head, tears were rolling down her cheeks. She lowered her eyes to the carpet and paced between the window and the bedroom doorway and she returned to the kitchen and poured a cup of coffee.

I stood up and glanced at the drizzle outside the window. I put on my raincoat and, hoping she would reveal Jim's rendezvous with Camellia, walked to the front door. No doubt she loved Jim, and loved him more than anything else in the world, otherwise she wouldn't kill Donald Larsen, but her devoting to and worshipping him would only destroy them both. I pitied her for her misplaced love, so unreserved, so naïve, so attractive to a villain covering an irrepressible snigger. Johnny, much more than Jim, would've been worthy of her love, but a fiend's intrigue changed their path, as Donald Larsen's drunk driving that of Ichiro and Sonya. As I turned the doorknob, the forces of free-will, creating random events, were shoving me into one of the multiple futures beyond this instant's ledge. At the next instant, all other futures collapsed saved the one I entered.

"He be going to Whitfield Park tonight."

CHAPTER 32

Before going to Whitfield Park, I visited Johnny, not in the urine-scented jailhouse but on the town hall terrace, which observed the hotels, the restaurants and the foreclosure signs. After discovering Edgar the mortician was Donald Larsen, the mayor, the sheriff and the entire police force consoled and praised Johnny. They treated him like a VIP. When I requested a visit, the sheriff told me to meet Johnny and his chaperon on the terrace, where the inmate could enjoy the fresh air and grab a burger at the local diner. They were eating, chatting and laughing as I approached, but the rotund-faced officer, on seeing me, excused himself and went into the waiting room to admire the mayor's Washingtonian pictures around the walls.

"Ain't no idea they treat felons like big bosses." Johnny shrugged his shoulders while relishing the afternoon air, though the wind slapped his face.

"They want to give you a chance to escape and enjoy Thanksgiving at home." I leaned over the bench and whispered, "That'll make them very happy."

"But killed that there funeral man. Ought to pay for it, like Pastor Jim did say, an eye for an eye. Ain't it the way?" After glancing at the officer eat donut and drink coffee, he thrust an index finger into his right ear and swiveled several times.

"Tell me, why'd you kill Donald Larsen?"

"You trying to frame me, Father? Ain't kill no Donald Larsen. He escape town long ago." His trout eyes almost popped out and his warrior face frosted, but the boyish voice betrayed his hesitation.

"I see. Taking the fall for someone else's crime is noble but foolish, just like a foolish lover." I pulled my collars together to shield the gust, admiring the lover's desire to sacrifice for the girl, whose heart had merged with Jim's soul.

"Don't get none of your crap." He curved his lips and caught a soggy leaf falling from the birch tree. "What you here for, Father? Ain't got no time for you, so you speak and leave me be."

"There's no need to hurry. You have plenty of time. Unless, you want to return to the precious solitude, which like the dinosaurs soon would become extinct. I empathize completely, knowing how difficult it's to find solitude in the age of Facebook."

"Don't care nothing about no dinosaurs nor no Facebook. And don't need no priest for no confession neither." He bit into the cheeseburger, threw the onion over the terrace and wiped his hand on the mayor's gilded statue, which stood akimbo on the terrace and surveyed the town.

"Don't worry. I'm not here to hear your confession, but to tell you something, you'd probably be interested to know." Two sparrows landed on the statue's head and began chatting.

"Ain't nothing worth a damn I'm interested now, but my three meals." He shook the cup and slurped the soda.

"Not even Daisy?"

He stopped slurping, the straw still in his mouth, and, cheeks sucked-in, raised his eyes. I waited while a wet leaf landed beside him on the bench and flattened in the puddle.

"Hey, Johnny, you wants some of them ice-cream? And you, Father." The officer, having finished his donut and coffee, walked into the terrace and leaned on the statue. Johnny nodded, straw in his mouth, but I declined and the man wiped his hands on the statue and disappeared behind a door.

"That's your cue, to escape. If you go downstairs and exit through the backdoor, there might be an abandoned car with keys inside."

"Ought to knock you over then." After pulling the straw out of his mouth, he flexed his muscles. But afterward he only thrust his finger into the ear for a few swivels and continued to eat the cheeseburger.

"No need for that, I won't hold you back. But before you escape, give me a few minutes. I'm sure the nice man won't be back for a while since the ice-cream shop is several blocks down the road."

"Ain't going nowhere, but back to my cell I belong."

"That's very noble. But what if she doesn't want you to?"

"Knows something I don't?"

"Worse, I know something you know. I know Daisy killed the mortician. She confessed, not that I wanted to hear her confession."

"Father, you gone ding-a-ling? Daisy ain't kill no mortician, so you don't never accuse her again." He dropped the cheeseburger and leaped over, and his hands grabbed my raincoat's lapels and clamped my neck.

"There's something I don't understand. The sheriff said all the evidences pointed to you."

"You prefers them pointing to you?" He shook me a few times to fling the rain from my jacket, then released me and, like gelatin, collapsed onto the bench.

"I understand why you're doing it."

"That whore monger did rip me off."

"If Daisy confesses to murdering him—"

"Like you did say, all them evidences points to me." The Mad Lion thrust his nose at me, and opened his mouth to pant, but didn't charge.

"Of course, you tampered with the evidences before the police arrived. Were you following her?"

"Oh, you couldn't hardly know how much I loves her."

"She asked me to help you."

"No, Father, you help her, so you listen to me confess."

"I heard her confession already."

"Then I'd say you bounded by your oath. Pastor Jim come back, he help her then. You tell him, much obliged. He be a good man." He thrust his head over the balustrade to soak his head in the rain. "Damnedest thing, how come she to do it? Reckoned him did rip her off for the funeral service. Doesn't hardly matter no more. That there whore monger did deserve it. But got to save her, that's all. Good thing Father Jones but let me know her going there. What you do, as you be me?"

"I can tell you who put marijuana in your backpack and framed you." Though I regarded my oath sacred and even now as a layman wouldn't divulge any confidence, I wanted to make another exception, for the lover and fool.

"Don't matter no more, long as Daisy taken care of. You make sure tell Pastor Jim take care of her." He finished the cheeseburger and threw the wrapper over the balustrade.

"Let me tell you what a scoundrel your Pastor Jim is."

"Hey, you don't say nothing bad about him, you hear. He a holy and godly man. But wished to follow and serve him. How come anyone but want to frame me?" After finishing the drink, he threw the cup over the balustrade, and growled at me while raindrops drummed the terrace.

Unable to release my malice, I pulled out Jan Moscowitz's business card. "Here, take this. He's the best."

"Might could you pay this here parking ticket for me? Much obliged." He grabbed the card and gave me the parking ticket, fifty-dollars and a tract on *The Gospel According to Jim*.

Before I left, he asked me to persuade his father not to stand in for Jim anymore. I agreed and left him on the terrace to await the officer and the ice-cream.

When I arrived at his father's house, only the sheepdog responded to my knocks. At the driveway, the next door neighbor, Mr. Jackson, told me Mr. Chandler hadn't been at home for more than a week.

CHAPTER 33

Dᴇᴀʀ Lᴀᴡʀᴇɴᴄᴇ,

I'm going after Jim Whitfield, not to save the world from this devil nor to seek justice for his victims, but to fulfill my promise to Peter and rid you and Camellia of the cloud lingering over your paths. Maybe my last journey, toward the setting sun, the waning moon, the last maple foliage. Whether I stand or fall, I delighted, as I had your friendship, in the wintry sunlight on the frozen Charles River, the summer breeze gliding over the surface of Lake Louise and the autumn redness sliding down the maple slope of Mount Lafayette. Though I wished for a third path, I would gladly accept the shame of falling under the bullet or the vice of snuffing out Jim's breath, to secure your and Camellia's future. In all our decisions, in all our actions, in all our ventures, the risk of failure, of a false step would flutter like the wind varying in strength and direction and hurdle us to a mount or a ditch slightly north or east of our Shangri-La. But we adjust and readjust, not waiting for the wind to cease, for it may never, or before it does that elusive paradise may have disappeared or we returned to earth's bosom.

I suspect Father Jones, for whiskey or women or prearranged confessions, had been hiding Jim, maybe in the church cellar, and channeling his messages to you. But the villain—Jim, not Father Jones—wouldn't be able to resist checking his emails and exposing his tracks and lair. His Achilles' heels: his inflated ego and his delusion of grandeur, one inviting an arrow and the other a bullet to end the reverie. I will examine his emails from noon to midnight to noon and examine his emails from noon to midnight to noon and sniff out his tracks and lair and nab the fiend or pierce his fungal heart.

Your friend,
Ichiro

CHAPTER 34

I DROVE TO WHITFIELD PARK in the evening and parked my car at the visitor's lot. As I strolled along the foggy path looking for Jim, I feared becoming him. By confronting and destroying him, I wanted to purge within myself the greed and lust and deceit that had polluted the air, the water and every speck of dust on the ground. But by decapitating the serpent's head and saving others, I would doom myself. And by embracing hatred and shunning love, I would replace him.

Under the mist, I rubbed the cold handgun and aimed it at a distant boulder. Though reluctant to discard my integrity and my soul, by granting Jim a bullet, I would save Camellia and confiscate Ichiro's chance to plunge into the abyss. Better that I enter hell than Ichiro. I paced along the ravine, its cliffs darkened under the drizzle, hoping to meet the preacher and fulfill my mission, before strolling to the electric chair. I took another step into the darkness and listened for silence— the familiar silence of the trees, the grass, the air and the cosmos. After tonight, I would relinquish silence and, without my integrity and soul, enter hell.

Nearby, a gunshot echoed through the night.

The streetlights cast shimmers in the drizzle and soggy pigeons waded under hawthorn bushes. I gripped the handgun and, heart throbbing against chest and eyes glancing at the reflecting ground, listened for another sound in the white noise of rain against branches and pavements. The lone call, like a horde's vanguard, foretold the final battle, to raze the last bastions. But the night, like history's current after another holocaust, returned to stoic calm. For a minute, I stood pondering a baby's birth, a young man's burial, and in between, the sandwiches, the books, the exams, the medicine, and the violets, like DNA, identifying and summarizing that line segment in time. Handgun in pocket, I marched over a raccoon's carcass toward the gunshot, hoping not to meet Camellia or Ichiro, whom more than any others I wanted to save from those fangs. I passed a bench dripping of rain and a few birches losing their leaves, toward the gurgles, but the fog hid my view. Some ten yards ahead, footsteps marched, probably also toward the gunshot. Below the fog, about ten feet in front, a pair of suede boots stomped forward and disappeared into the rain screen.

Jim. It must be him.

I grasped the handgun and jogged toward the boots but lost the footsteps while catching my breath under a leafless birch. Yet, the hope of finding the serpent drove me deeper into the drizzle and fog. The path winded to the right toward the riverbank, beyond which rushed the current, its grumble overpowering the whisper of rain and wind.

Steps on the wet pavement. Rapid, unsteady, uncoordinated… Not the steps of a hunter, not the steps of a hound, but the steps of a prey.

In the middle of the path, I stopped, raised my head to soak in the rain, pulled out the handgun and released the lock. I worked my fingers to warm up and waited for Jim, the prey. Camellia probably had shot him. Now, I must finish the job before she could shoot again. Among disheveled footsteps, calmness. I wouldn't hesitate.

Out of the drizzle, a potato sack toppled into a puddle. And moaned. The bundle twisted on the ground to reveal a red blotch, diluted by the rain, and a head of disheveled blonde hair, which at first looked like cat's fur. The bloodshot eyes darted from left to right; the mousy lips twitched as if feeling the rain; the wrinkled cheek dripping like wet leather.

I approached, pondering on those familiar eyes, and lifted up Father Jones and, under his groans, checked the bullet wound in his left arm.

"Ouch, help me… help me…" He drooled and grabbed me by the arm. "Father… Father Lawrence… oh, I'm so… so glad to see you… ouch…"

"Did he shoot you?"

"Some son-of-a-bitch shot me… wants to kill me… help me… protect me…" In the rain, he waved his arms and swung his mop-like hair.

"Did you see him, with suede boots?"

"I ran… I ran… from that abandoned shack…save me… he's got a gun…"

"Let me bandage your wound."

"No, no… got to run… he may be here soon…but I found out… Jim Whitfield…"

"Is he coming after you?"

"Agent Peter's actually him, the bastard." He twisted away and staggered in the rain toward the riverbank.

"Stay here and I'll call the police." I listened for another set of footsteps. The intimacy between Sylvia and Agent Peter would support Father Jones's claim. But Jim's diary entries… Was that a ruse for his escape? Not with Sylvia, though. His love for, or rather obsession with, Camellia compelled him to abandon everything for her. But if he had abandoned Sylvia, she would snitch on him.

"Got to… got to go…" The priest leaned against a tree trunk for a few seconds, but continued toward the riverbank.

"Be careful. Don't tumble into the water." I hesitated, but walked toward the drunken priest to help him, rather than going after Jim the FBI agent. Before I could reach the riverbank, the priest pointed his gun at me.

I stared into the gun barrel and thought the whiskey priest was toying with me or succumbing to alcohol, which, diluted by sweat, had been pouring down his forehead. But his dancing brows alerted me that he might've envied my hearing the preacher's confession, the details of money laundering and statutory rape, anecdotes that the good father must've lusted after since taking the vow.

"Adios, amigo."

Great Falls and Arlington Central Library with Charlotte, Symphony Hall and Harvard Square with Camellia and Ichiro, Walden Pond and Mount Lafayette in solitude, and images of Daphne, Jim, and Sylvia flashed through my mind. Death, like a thief, had tiptoed behind me to plunge its dagger and finish a day's work. What sunshine, what lilies, what quarks, what sonata, this life. A point in space and time, life began, traversed a line, an arc, or a loop, perhaps through discontinuities, and at another point along the same fabric, it would cease. At each instant, all the steps, all the moments along the trajectory would disappear, leaving the colors, the contours and the shades ever fading like exposed paintings. Along with images of dreams and fantasies etched in my memory, until one instant death decides to confiscate these relics. Though I sought to detach from the world, I treasured those images, those melodies, those smells, and wished to see Charlotte, Camellia and Ichiro and hold their hands before departing from this sky, this earth and this air.

The barrel stared at me. The finger pulled. But the trigger refused to click. The gun had jammed.

"Damn it, what's this bullshit." Father Jones fumbled with the uncooperative weapon, pulling and pushing the lock to release the trigger, while whiskey-sweat poured down his forehead and mixed with the rain.

As death rolled the dice and thumbed its nose at me, I wiped the rain from my face and ran toward the whiskey priest, hoping to grab the gun before it could release a bullet into my heart. But as I approached the riverbank, Father Jones wiggled his brows and again pointed the barrel at me.

Three shots saluted the night and suppressed the murmur of stream and rain. I stood and waited for the pain. I waited to collapse. I meditated on the topology of a black hole. An elongated moan answered the shots, but I felt no pain and I saw no blood dripping out of my chest. Water leaped up and danced in the air as Father Jones, arms flapping through the mist, dived sideways into the stream.

Perhaps, the preacher, alias the agent, had arrived in time to save his old friend, or only to silence the priest for sniffing out his secret. Or perhaps Father Jones offended some believer during mass, confession, or counseling sections. Or perhaps, before becoming a priest, he had impregnated a teenage girl.

I ran toward the water. The current was carrying the still body down the stream into the fog. I raced along the riverbank through the rain screens, but past a reef gathering withered leaves, I couldn't see the drifting body. The wet soil hindered my pace and at one point a boulder forced me to detour. The fog descended with the downpour and my raincoat began to drip, but I followed the river until it swirled to the left and a hill blocked my path.

Lost among the shower and birches, the murmurs and whispers, I glanced at the walls of rain and still wanted to seek out the preacher, but couldn't abandon the whiskey priest to a river burial. Without a mobile phone, I had to search for a payphone and call the police to rescue Father Jones. I left the riverbank and, through the fog and through the rain, reentered the paved walkway, but without a GPS, I searched for a map. About fifty feet into the path, a homeless man lay beneath a birch, neither shivering from the cold nor blinking from the raindrops into his eyes. I hesitated for a second, then lurched forward to find some insomniac, mobile phone in hand, loitering in this night.

In the distance sirens like a homing whistle beckoned me. I raced beside birches and benches, witnesses to my staggering trot, toward the high-pitched sound hoping to find help for the floating priest. The rain had returned to drizzle when I approached the blinking red and blue.

Two police cruisers parked at right angles on the grass and four policemen surrounded Patricia Larsen and the rain shelter. I approached the policemen and described Father Jones's getting shot and flowing down the stream but not his trying to shoot me, and two of them ran into the woods. The other two said they were taking Patricia to the police station. They suspected she had shot someone, probably Father Jones, because blood spotted her overcoat.

"I didn't shoot anyone, you hear me, I didn't." She tried to leave the shelter but the policemen blocked her path. "Father, tell them. I didn't."

I sat beside her in the shelter and, though angry at her neglecting and abandoning Camellia, tried to comfort her, but ended up staring at the blood patches on her overcoat and rejoicing in a new reality: she had shot Jim, not Camellia. In this future, Jim would die, Patricia would be executed and Camellia would soar in the sky. But if Patricia had only shot Father Jones…

I sensed, from her stammer and her tears, that she still loved the serpent, even after more than twenty years and even though he had abandoned her for younger and prettier women, including her daughter.

"Hey, lady, you be in deep shit as he die." The equine-faced officer rubbed the stubble on his cheek and hollered through the drizzle.

"No, he can't die; he can't abandon me… he must live… he must take me away…" Her face turned as pale as the fog and her neck and fingers twitched its anapestic beat.

"Was Jim wearing suede boots?" Perhaps after splattering on Jim's clothes, Father Jones's blood stained Patricia's overcoat. But more likely, Camellia shot Jim, either before or after he shot Father Jones.

"Agent Peter…" She dropped her head but her fingers continued to twitch.

"He was wearing suede boots? Or he shot Jim?" I thought she was trying to confuse me when her pupils dilated, but the babble, pitch rising and falling, revealed fright more than cunning.

"I followed him but with the rain, I lost him in the park. He was quick, knew his way around, seemed to be following someone."

"Father Jones was shot."

"I didn't shoot him. After I lost him, I wandered through the park... It was dark... I was getting wet—"

"Lady, I don't give a hoot you gotten wet." The other policeman, beardless and chubby, strolled forward and spat onto the ground.

"Officer, please let her continue." I tried to hide my annoyance, but my voice sounded like Agent Peter's.

"I heard the shot—"

"I'd say you heard it. You did shoot him." The policeman took out a cigarette and put it in his mouth and chatted with his partner about Donald Larsen's murder. They seemed to celebrate the Ponzi schemer's dying an unnatural death.

"I didn't shoot him... I was running and panicking ... blood, there was blood... I bummed into him..."

"Agent Peter?"

"Jim."

"Did he say who shot him?"

"I took out my gun and pointed it at him." She must've shot him while panicking and babbling her love for him. Camellia probably didn't even meet Jim.

"Look like a confession to me." The policeman threw away the cigarette and took out a pad and a pencil.

"I took Donald's gun when I followed Agent Peter because I wanted to shoot Jim. I hated him for... for..."

"Go on, you did shoot him, ain't it so?" the chubby policeman said.

I searched her face for a look, a twitch or a wrinkle to confirm his words and to end my worry and suffering. Like the chubby policeman, I delighted in that evil thought but unlike him, for Camellia's sake.

"No, no... no, I couldn't shoot him. How could I? I pointed the gun at him, but when I saw his face... though a different face, he probably had plastic surgery. I still love him, love him like the first time..." She scrutinized the mud and leaves on the ground, probably recalling and perhaps savoring her fling with Jim. I wanted to inquire about Jim's most attractive feature but refrained myself. Like Camellia, she probably only wanted someone to care about her and to take care of her.

"Ain't that romantic?" The policeman tapped the pad with the pencil.

"Not as romantic as on a rainy night in the park looking for an injured priest in the water." I refused to believe her words and I grabbed her arm as a chill zigzagged through my nerves. "Did you see Camellia?" My mind's eyes beheld Camellia pointing the gun at Jim and pulling the trigger. But not Camellia, only Patricia.

"When he hugged me, I thought he was going to run away with me, but… but…" She sobbed and said, "He knock me out cold… he… how could he…"

Even now, she couldn't believe Jim could prefer Camellia. If she'd known he was running away with her daughter, she wouldn't hesitate to shoot him, then herself.

"When I woke up, I tried to find him."

"Where's your gun?"

"I lost it."

"Ain't that convenient?" The policeman sneered and spat. "Bet we'll find it in there water… one shot fired… and we'll match it to the bullet in that there dead priest…"

"Not the priest, Jim." Annoyed at the cloudy mind smoking a cigarette, I stood up, turning my back on him, and pondered the direction to look for Jim and Camellia. But the uniform drizzle hid grass, trees, benches, scoundrels and desperate souls. After deciding to head toward the abandoned shack, I asked the other policeman for direction.

"Someone shot him in the arm, but not me." She grabbed my sleeve and shook it.

"Are you talking about Jim or Father Jones?"

"What'd you mean? Father Jones is Jim."

CHAPTER 35

I SPRINTED DOWN THE CORRIDOR between sycamores that displayed racial slurs, sexist insults and artworks of copulating males and females, toward the abandoned shack. Crushed stones, plastic cups and paper wrappers guided me along the path. The drizzle began to lessen as I approached an abandoned white high-heel, but the sky refused to brighten and enlighten a monk pondering the preacher's deception. To the right, a rocky-trailed foothill rose to hide my destination, but I knew the abandoned shack lay beyond this obstacle, a surprise ready to challenge my resilience and perhaps an answer to ravage my mind and heart. The whiskey priest or the violent agent? The shack, its paint shedding like unwanted skin and the planks rain-soaked and moldy, surfaced behind the hill as I turned right on the path. To the left, a breeze stirred the leafless branches, to warn me not to proceed one more yard. But I marched past another white high-heel toward the shack ready to confront my foe—my fear, my hatred and my ignorance.

But in the shack, a smile greeted me—a smile the colors of a spring meadow's rainbow, the smell of a summer garden's jasmine, the taste of Thanksgiving night's fresh baked bread.

"Lawrence, Lawrence, I knew you'd be here. I was hoping I wouldn't see you here but I knew... I just knew..." Camellia, in sneakers, burst out of the shack and embraced and kissed me.

"Same here, same here. But just as you had come, I also came." Even through my joy, I wished she had been home in bed dreaming of an apple orchard's new sunshine. But tonight, only drizzle, blood, gunshot, police, whiskey priest, and the eel-like Jim Whitfield. "Forget about Jim." I pulled her back into the shack away from the drizzle.

"But you couldn't, or else you wouldn't be here." She pulled out a handkerchief and dried my hair. I toppled the dusty table to hide the blood streaks on its surface and pulled up two creaking chairs.

"He was still dreaming of a new life with me somewhere far, far away. Like another galaxy." She looked through the cracked window into the wet darkness.

"He'd never let you go as long as he's alive. So I came to solve the problem." I touched the handgun in my pocket and still wouldn't hesitate to put a hole through Jim's forehead and spend the rest of my days in jail. Having considered the pros and cons and the costs and benefits, I would profit by this chore.

"I came to confront him. I wanted to kill him, to rid him from my life and to rid him from your life, so we'd be free to live, without looking over our shoulders."

"But he might not have known you were …probably fell into Sylvia's trap without a clue…mesmerized by you…" I tracked the rat scurrying from the window toward the fallen cabinet.

"But you saw the pictures of Agent Peter and Sylvia. Shouldn't that—"

"Jealousy is very motivating, and stimulates creativity. Jim showed me that… very creative, even ingenious…" Just as jealousy had inspired him to trick Charlotte into writing that letter, it also had counseled Sylvia into orchestrating his tumble into the abyss.

"He said he loved me and wanted me to run away with him. Didn't care I was—" She waved a plane ticket in front of me.

"He was probably sincere about that, at least as much as he could love anyone. He'd give away his precious fortune, might even stop womanizing just for you. But did you—"

"I was angry with him but also with myself. I was so desperate for love." She collapsed onto the chair.

"Did you shoot Jim?"

"Should I have? And would you turn me in to the police? No, I wouldn't torture you like that." Her lips curved up, a lily blooming under the clouds, but her hands as if searching for a plank among the waves struggled on her laps.

"We can get out of the US. Maybe Canada."

"A monk, helping a killer escape. How romantic. You're so unpredictable, and attractive." She ripped the ticket into several pieces and tossed them into the air.

"I'm no longer a monk."

"I looked forward so much to marrying you." She leaned over, hugged and kissed me.

"We'll have to do that in Mexico."

"I love you too much to marry you."

In the drizzle and fog, a new melody seemed to spring from the night but dawn tarried beyond the horizon. Beneath the cobwebs, I held her hands and studied her soft but sad eyes and prayed for a night without clouds, a world without Donald Larsen and a universe without Jim Whitfield. A breeze whispered through the broken window, but I couldn't isolate the adages from the whines.

"Check it if you want to know." She drew out her gun and handed me it.

"Do I want to know?"

"Funny, I thought you always want to know the truth. The truth will set you free and all that."

"I know we're friends." Relieved by her voice and gaze, I embraced this lost child, but a shock zapped through my spine as another dread raced through my mind.

"What is it?" She seemed to have felt my shudder.

"Could it be? But no…" I jumped up and gazed through the broken glass into the swinging branches beyond the path.

"If you say it couldn't be, then it wouldn't, whatever it is. I trust you."

"But I don't trust myself." I sat down on the broken-backed chair and felt its legs shaking under my weight. "You and Ichiro are so dear to me. For that very reason, you two can cause me so much pain and worry."

"You don't believe me? But I didn't kill him. He was good to me, better than Donald and Patricia."

"I'm so glad you're here." I caressed her face. "Where's Ichiro?"

"He's helping the FBI go after Jim, trying to find his identity, which I just discovered. Very clever."

"Then, could it…could it be possible…"

"Could what be…" She froze and gazed into space, "no… no… it couldn't be…"

"If you say so."

194

"No, but you said so… you said so…"

"But like I said—"

"He wouldn't…" She bit her trembling lips. "No, he didn't shoot Jim." But I knew from the fear shining through her eyes that she didn't believe those words. If I were Ichiro, with nothing to lose, I wouldn't hesitate to go after Jim, to stop him from harassing Camellia and Lawrence, to remove this fiend from the world and fulfill the promise to Sonya and Peter. And afterward…

"Yes, he would. Of course, he would." Camellia walked to the doorway. "For Sonya… for you… for me… Of course he would." She opened the door. "I must find him. I must be with him."

"Your baby. You should rest. Let me find him. I would do everything possible."

She turned and wiped the rain from her face. "How could I keep it, knowing its father is my father? How could I?" She left the shack and walked down the path between the trees.

A thunder resounded in my head and I felt dizzy and leaned on the door, only to break a hinge and almost fell onto the ground. I had failed to save the fetus. I clutched my fist before the whispering wind, helpless under the drizzle. I wanted to punch Jim's snout and twist Sylvia's beak. But life: the process of releasing, giving up, letting go… And yet, I refused to fold my hands, to play the victim, or the bystander. No, I'd find Ichiro. And if Jim was still alive, then…

I charged out of the shack and raced down the path, but through the fog couldn't see Camellia. As in a dream, I felt the natural laws crumbling before me and must reinvent a new logic to survive in the inferno. But my mind refused to give up reason's biases and adopt the reality of chance and chaos and other stochastic processes. The rain on my face only heightened my reasoning and consolidated my determination to nail Jim. Like Ichiro, I had nothing to lose and wouldn't hesitate.

"Ah, Father Lawrence, just the man I'm looking for. Have you seen Camellia?" A giant stepped out of the fog, his hair dangling over his forehead like cooked spaghettis.

CHAPTER 36

"Don't take another step forward, Jim." I pulled out the gun and pointed it at Peter's nose.

"Father, I believe you need a pair of glasses, mistaking me for that bastard. Or are you just trying to insult me? Of course, this fog messes with one's eyes and mind. But if you didn't recognize my voice, at least you must've recognized my shoulders. Who else would have such shoulders, right? If that didn't convince you, here's my knuckles."

"Pretending to be an FBI agent is a clever disguise."

"Ah, but shooting like a real agent, now that's another story." Peter flicked away the rain dripping down his hair. "Let's do a shootout. If I drop, you've got your man, but if you drop, oops...I'm very confident I'll be having French toast and black coffee for breakfast in a few hours. What about you?"

"You don't have to be an FBI agent to shoot me down."

"Then you're in a loss-loss situation. Better pray to your God that I'm not that bastard." He combed his hair with his hand and, with his oxford, kicked the dirt. "I guess you're in God's hands."

"Maybe it's my time, but Jim's not getting away from my bullet." I searched his eyes for deception but only found mockery.

"Are you trying to steal my job? Now, that'd tick me off."

"Do you think I'd be concerned about ticking people off?"

"Ha, gutsy, not bad for a priest. Okay, I forgive you."

"It's nice of you to forgive me. But you haven't convinced me you're not Jim Whitfield."

"What? Are you a detective or something? You want evidence, proof and all that crap? And stop insulting me." He tapped his foot and shoved his right hand into the coat pocket while the wind whistled behind him.

I tightened my grip on the handgun as my dorsal and abdominal muscles tensed up. I twitched and my pulses drummed against my ears. But unsure of his identity, I didn't squeeze the trigger to unload a bullet into the broad shoulder.

"Ha, you hesitated. I wouldn't. Like they say: he who hesitates is lost. Father, you're not much of a gambler, much less a vigilante." He pulled out a piece of folded paper and threw it at my feet. "Here's the evidence you wanted."

I glanced at the note soaking mud water and gazed at his grin taunting this cornered mouse. From the road's left side, as if matching my agitation, murmurs of wind and leaves rose and fell. Camellia's lips and Ichiro's eyes flickered on my mental screen and with my free hand I steadied the gun.

"You know, I can shoot while you're picking up the note. But hey, can't play it safe all the time. No risk, no gain."

"I expect nothing less from Jim Whitfield."

"Ha, but that mousy priest's the bastard."

"And he said you are. Isn't that convenient?"

"Hey, I thought he's just another whiskey priest but Ichiro told me he's the bastard and I trust him. Even if you don't believe me, you can believe Ichiro." He shoved both hands into the coat pockets and winked at me. "Didn't you know him? Why can't you recognize him?"

"Have you seen Ichiro?" I picked up the note and read Ichiro's handwriting: *Father Jones is Jim Whitfield in disguise. He told Daisy Walker that he would be at Whitfield Park tonight to meet someone.*

"Ha, don't you know he likes to send the old man for dirty jobs?" Peter grinned from cheek to cheek and flung the water beads from his hair. "Wouldn't want him to be in danger."

"Are you saying you care about him? Or only trying to preserve him." To ensure success, Ichiro wouldn't have told Peter about coming to kill Jim. The FBI agent, for all his roughness, would've tried to prevent his could-have-been son-in-law from dumping his life into the ditch. And Ichiro had a pair of suede boots.

"He had a right to know the truth and you know it. I talked to him about getting back with Camellia, but you just can't force things. You got to give them some time."

"Camellia had an abortion."

"I heard it's the bastard's bastard."

"I know compassion's not your forte, but please keep your mouth clean when you talk about Camellia." I lunged forward and stepped into the puddles, splashing mud onto his trouser legs.

"Well, you're quite sentimental for a monk. So you care about Ichiro and Camellia, right? And probably want to mince Jim Whitfield into Salisbury steak. Then know I'm on your side. I want to help these two young people and destroy that Antichrist, not that I believe in your religion. No offence, to each man his own belief." Peter glanced at the muddy trouser and tried to fling away the mud. "The bastard disguising as a whiskey priest. Quite clever. Should've seen through it though. But lucky I got Ichiro the brain. Ha, got to admit, he's quite clever, breaking into the fiend's email account. Must've drunk a lot of coffee at that Internet café."

"You were looking for Camellia."

"Don't worry. She's alright. Jim's the guy in deep shit."

"Someone shot him."

"Ha, you think it's her?"

"Not anymore. But if it's—"

"I used to think all monks are pretty dull, but you're a character, not quite as interesting as the bastard, but not bad. So, you want to find out who shot Jim Whitfield? Okay, Sherlock Holmes, tell me who you suspect?"

"The police think Mrs. Larsen did it."

"Well, old flames are usually on the top of the list of suspects. Crimes of passion are very common. But you think she's got the guts to pull the trigger?"

"If I've to guess—"

"You suspect me, don't you?" Peter lifted his raincoat to reveal a gun.

"Ichiro has a pair of suede boots."

"My gift to him for helping to bust Donald the greedy Larsen's Ponzi scheme. You like it? Sorry, we're not close enough for me to give you a pair. But Ichiro might, so go ask him for a Christmas present."

"But what if Ichiro shot Jim?"

"Then I would have to tamper with the evidences and frame someone else, maybe you." He winked and wiggled his brows.

"That's a decent plan. I can't argue. Better me than him. But you seemed so sure he's not here."

"What'd you think I am, your two-cent copper arresting that Mrs. Larsen without any evidences? I am FBI." He yanked out his badge and waved it in the rain. "This means credential, years of training and hard work."

"While you were not getting drunk."

"Everyone needs a break. Do you know how many loved ones I've lost? Before Sonya, there was my wife… and before her…" He thrust the badge back into the pocket and, body shaking, spun around and wiped his face, then standing akimbo, gazed at the bare trunks on the hill. "What would you know?"

"I'm sorry. I take that back." Though ignorant of the agent's suffering minutes before Sonya's death, I began to understand why Ichiro consoled the brute, whose fist with an engraved ring could break any nose.

"Don't worry about Ichiro. He didn't shoot the bastard."

"If you say so."

"I shot him. He was talking to Camellia in that shack and I shot him." He giggled like a boy skipping classes to go to the beach.

"But you aren't wearing suede boots."

"That son-of-a-bitch thought he was using me to seduce Sylvia, but he didn't know I had my eyes on her since high school and wanted to marry her. So he gave her to me and I got the chance to close in and grab him by his neck. But I took my time, to wait for something I could put him away for life and throw him with Tim the Switch-blade, or Conan the Barbarian, or Malcolm the Mobster so he can make the most of his jailbird experience." Peter smashed his fist into the tree trunk and cut his knuckles. I stared at his bloodied fist while a squirrel squealed and climbed the branches, slipping on an elbow but then accelerating toward the top.

"It's all right. It's all right." Peter waved his other hand but accepted the bandage that I offered. "Thank you." He bandaged the back of his hand. "Of course, Sylvia wanted to get his money and focused on the life insurance after we found out Donald the greedy banker had conned Jim the greedy preacher of his embezzled fortune. Well, not exactly, because the sneaky preacher stashed some money in his Swiss bank account but Sylvia couldn't access it. I didn't care about the money, just wanted to marry her, nab the fiend, and watch his flesh rot in jail. You may think I'm heartless. Well, maybe I'm, but almost all my sympathy had gone to my sister, my wife and my daughter. There's only a few drops left and those are reserved for Ichiro."

"I wish you have more joy in your life. But we have to journey through our lonely path to heaven or hell." I sympathized with him. But I couldn't condone his violence toward Mr. Chandler.

"From what I heard through Ichiro, I thought you don't believe in happiness. But in my case, it doesn't matter. Maybe, once upon a time, I wanted to be happy but now, I could care less. Without them, what does it matter? When you've lost a diamond, no, three diamonds, what good's a crystal or even a pearl? Yes, Sylvia's just a pearl."

"In the end, you let Jim drown in the stream. Why?"

"What're you babbling about? If I saw him drowning, I'd yank him out of the river...Then I'll castrate him and let him bleed to death. Unless there's a more delicious way."

I turned my eyes from the beast five feet away, but sensed in my guts another euphoria. The anger and hatred seemed to resonate with his words and rejoice in camaraderie between savages.

"Don't look at me like a monster. You need monsters like me to stop monsters like him."

"What does that make our world? A jungle, a wilderness, a wasteland, an Armageddon?"

"If I have the chance, I'd do it, but he ran away from the shack and I lost him."

"Someone finished your dirty job near the stream, but not exactly as you'd like it."

"I thought he shot someone, like one of those donut-eating coppers. Who had the nerve to seize my trophy?"

"Ichiro."

"No."

"Can you be sure? You gave him the suede boots."

He hesitated, lifted his eyelids above the irises for five seconds, then pulled out his gun and ran down the path probably toward the stream. I followed and called after him, but in the fog lost him. His footsteps lingered for a while before disappearing in the wind. I trotted on twigs, leaves, puddles, foam cups and paper bags along the walkway, trying to retrace my path to the stream. The image of Ichiro shooting Jim haunted me. To help him, Peter would mangle and reshape the evidences, but Ichiro's action would forever define him, a killer willing to bend justice and arrest another's heartbeat. I had reserved that abyss for myself. How could Ichiro, as a friend, seize it from me and amble into hell?

CHAPTER 37

DEAR LAWRENCE,

As you may have guessed by now, Peter's hatred toward Jim Whitfield goes beyond that of an agent toward a criminal. When Peter was in college, Jim got his sister pregnant and she committed suicide. Though without proof, he suspected Jim from the very beginning and since then had been consumed by such hatred that he had to take sleeping pills. Sonya told me that it might be the main reason that he had entered the FBI. He has been researching on how to torture Jim ever since I knew him. You can imagine how that destroyed his peace of mind and in some sense his health (his liver is deteriorating). But this very hatred drove him to distinguish himself among his peers. When he asked me to help nab Jim, I sensed a man about to collapse or go mad. I feared for his health and sanity. Sonya's death only fueled that determination to torment Jim. When Daphne's letter confirmed his suspicion, he got drunk for a week. For sure, he would've taken justice into his own hands. I'm glad that he would no longer have the chance.

I have continued to love Camellia even after the news, partly because Peter's obsession warned me against that passion call hatred, but her eyes and her smiles would remind me of her role in Sonya's death. Can I bear the pain of loving her while knowing she had a hand in that death? Is it fair to Sonya? At every glimpse of Camellia's face, I would taste the short but memorable times with Sonya. I even pretended that she was Sonya during our last few days together, when I struggled not to blame her. Is it fair to her? I am an imperfect man living in an imperfect world, trying to weave through the chaotic interactions of semi-causal events with linear logic, contradictory emotions, dialectic wisdom, and mortal integrity. On a dark night, I would search Polaris to guide me, but on life's journey only the internal North Star could lead to that instant when eternity freezes time.

Since Jim has perished, I will commit seppuku. Not because I could not bear the pain any longer, not because I hate Camellia, and not because I want to escape from life. No, I seek the same immortality that Sonya has achieved through her death. In the evening before the sun sets, in the cherry blossoms' bloom before the petals wither and shrivel, in the epitome before the shivering tune decays, I shall capture eternity in an instant, immortalize it in the space-time fabric, slow down the clock by approaching the speed of light. Eternal glory. The myopic, deaf, wrinkled, grumpy, senile, incontinent and impotent Ichiro shall not exist, only shall live the youthful and triumphant and glorious Ichiro.

I would've sacrificed all these for Camellia and it wouldn't be sacrifice but selfishness. But we, like two porcupines, would only poke our quills at each other, not intentionally, but unavoidably. And she has enough pain and suffering for a lifetime. She only wanted to be happy but I couldn't even offer that. Someone else, maybe you, would bring her happiness. Please take care of her.

I look forward to sitting at a precipice facing the canyon, the opposing peak, the azure sky, and the scattered clouds and savoring the breeze and the cherry blossoms against my face. The blade would be sharp; the blow would be swift; the pain would be short and sweet. I would live an eternity in that moment before entering eternity.

Farewell my friend and take care. Wish you a fulfilling and meaningful life.

Your friend,
Ichiro

CHAPTER 38

Before returning to Boston, I asked Agent Peter to check Ichiro's credit card transactions and find out whether he had bought a bus, train, or plane ticket. Two days after Camellia and I returned to Boston, the agent informed me that Ichiro had bought a ticket to Seattle. Camellia decided to fly there to meet him, perhaps for the last time. On the day of her flight, we met at Harvard Square for lunch.

"When I first came to Boston, I was so happy, to be free of Jim, to smell the unfettered air." Camellia sipped her coffee and glanced down Mount Auburn Avenue where students were strolling to classes. "Oh, it isn't that he abused me, he treated me as well as he could. But I wanted to soar through the clouds to a bluer sky and a lighter air, to survey the distant land, to use my wings as they are meant to. I tasted that when I left home, for a few mornings, before cold and hunger…"

At the piano, a young lady was playing the Adagio sostenuto of Rachmaninoff's Piano Concerto No 2, the melody a fabric of the Siberian steppe wringing my heart. I wished Ichiro were drumming the keys. "Is that why you like sunbathing at Walden Pond?" I said. In the summer, when we picnicked at my favorite location, she would change to her bikini and ask Ichiro to rub on the sunscreen. She would spread the beach towel and lie on her back. I would unpack the food and chat with Ichiro about the Central Limit Theorem's philosophical implications or the mathematical structures pervading Bach's music.

"Thank you for helping me find myself, my true self." Camellia reached across the table and touched my hand. "My experiences here have been so memorable, mostly because of you."

"Only the beginning of the journey." I pressed her cold hand.

"One day at a time and one thing at a time. Now, I must find Ichiro."

"You may be the only person who could prevent him from suicide."

"Why should I?" Camellia's eyes tracked a sparrow's path down the street.

"You love him. I know you do even if you deny it."

"I love him more than I can understand and it scares me."

"But not scare enough to stop him?"

"I love him so much that I want the best for him. The best, do you understand? Even if—" She banged her fist on the table and shook the spoon on her plate.

"What's more valuable than life?" I waved my hand and dropped the spoon onto the table.

"What's more important than happiness and fulfillment?"

"Life's a gift."

"Some gift. I wouldn't mind giving it back in exchange for a refund." She took out the engagement ring and held it up to her eyes. "I understand Ichiro so much better than you do. Oh, Lawrence, your antiquate ideas, so romantic yet so impractical. You're such a Victorian. But we're in the twenty-first century; we've passed through Auschwitz, Hiroshima, Sarajevo and Darfur. We can never go back after our eyes have been opened, after we've tasted the fruit of good and evil. We can never erase our memories after we've known."

"Life isn't an antiquate idea, neither is gratitude for life. They transcend space and time, memory and history."

"When pain exceeds pleasure, when suffering exceeds happiness, when cruelty exceeds intimacy…well, why bother?" She held the ring above the cup of coffee as if about to drop it into the liquid.

"We're more than our senses, more than our thoughts, more than our feelings—" I put my palm under the ring while the steam simmered my skin.

"Yes, yes, yes, eternity, immortality, yes, Ichiro's seeking that and will achieve it by giving up his life. In the peek of life—" She withdrew the ring and pushed my hand away.

"How can we ever be sure? Even if—" I couldn't forsake life's sanctity, a last lily in the expanding wasteland. But could life only be a multifunctional system where electromagnetic energy from oxidizing carbon molecules fuels mitosis until, through the years, entropy overwhelms the organic structures?

"Well, neither you nor I can be sure and no one can guide us. So, don't impose your philosophy on him. I'll help him in whatever way I can even if I don't understand him." She dropped the ring into her handbag.

Camellia held the cup in midair and listened to the Rachmaninoff piece and finished the coffee only when the tune ended. "Let's have dinner. My treat. After all, I'm eight-million dollars richer, you know, beside the four-million Sylvia donated." She took out her credit card and waved it, but patted the back of my hand. "Just kidding. Yes, I enjoyed the evening gown, the diamond necklace, the limousine, the penthouse condo, and why not. But now I'm certain it wasn't what I really wanted. I'm not Sylvia and would never want to be. I want to give my part of the money from Jim's life insurance to Daisy. She's so... so naïve... so dear... I just feel sorry for her. She can get away from here and start a new life. She deserves it. Anyway, I'm glad Sylvia wouldn't get any."

"Of all the time we went out for lunch, dinner, or only a cup of coffee or tea, how often had I paid? I think it's about time."

"How could I allow a monk to buy me meals, it'd be like stealing from a homeless man."

"That bad?"

***

After dinner, I drove Camellia to the airport as the sleet began to fall. She gazed at the Boston skyline as the car sped through the Mass Pike. We didn't talk. We relished the silence that was nurturing our hearts. I hoped she would convince Ichiro to treasure his life, but didn't mention my desire again. At the terminal, she kissed me and I waited for her flight to leave. At the parking lot, while I was relishing the gust from Camellia's departing flight, the Gilead police phoned and informed me that Arthur, who had been arrested for killing Father Jones a.k.a. Jim Whitfield, wanted to see me.

CHAPTER 39

UNDER LIGHT SLEET, the Gilead jailhouse between the bar and the casino flaunted its graffiti as if sneering at the passersby. As I approached the jailhouse, from the bar, a drunkard staggered past me and grabbed the seven-foot iron-gate for support, but the guard swung the club and chased away the young man. A showgirl grabbed my arm and invited me to *have some fun* in the casino, but I thanked her and freed myself. I showed my ID to the guard and passed the spiked gate into the jailhouse courtyard, where two policemen were playing poker, probably five-card stud. Soggy cigarette buds and dog dung lined the steps into the redbrick building and random scratches and cracks decorated the door. Inside, two old men on the bench played backgammon while an officer leaned against the wall and chatted with a young lady in lingerie. Above the bench, coupons and menus from sandwich shops, pizza parlors, Chinese restaurants, and roadside diners covered the bulletin board. The officer behind the counter was chatting on the phone about Sunday night's football game. Near the window, a teenage girl, chestnut hair and fair skin, was eating cheeseburger and French fries and, with every bite, slurped some soda. Behind them, bangs and cusses, sometimes alternating and sometimes simultaneous, echoed through a locked gate into the waiting room. I sat on a chair and watched the sleet for twenty-eight minutes before the officer finished the phone call and asked me for my favorite football team. After signing in, I sat down and watched the sleet for seventeen minutes before the officer, complaining about the local football team's disastrous season, led me into a reception room that reeked of sweat and mushroom. Flaking walls, two barred windows, a low ceiling-fan, a scarred table and two slanted chairs in the middle of the room.

When the slender young man in prison uniform walked in, I wanted to shake his hand for killing Jim Whitfield and preventing Ichiro from doing so. But before I could greet him, he lifted his handcuffed wrists and said, "How could a con man thrive among people come of age?" The blank-faced prison guard accompanying him stepped forward, so Arthur shrugged and while the handcuffs jingled, lowered his hands and sat in a chair.

"Perhaps we're compelled to worship con men to avoid the responsibilities of adulthood. Freedom can be frightening." I pulled a chair, sat down, and confront his penetrating eyes. I had wanted to meet Arthur ever since reading the young man's words and deeds in Jim's diary. I admired his thinking for himself and expressing his thoughts before a Jim Whitfield.

"More so than slavery?"

"Not having to overwork those gray cells and evaluate every morsel of belief can be quite relaxing and comforting."

"So is hibernating in the summer."

"And once in a century you might hit on something true."

"What if I'm not a gambler? What if I don't want to live till a hundred?"

"You're courageous and courageous people have to suffer the consequences. Remember, causality and the natural laws."

"So you think I'm in jail because of causality? Because of the conservation of good and evil in the universe?" He shook his handcuffs. "Now I know you're not a priest, just like the fake Father Jones."

"I've found out that an ex-priest can be quite thoughtful, having stepped across the boundary from the Sahara Desert into South Bronx. Of course, a fake priest can be quite charming." I took out Jan Moscowitz's business card and told Arthur to contact him for his defense.

"I didn't ask you here for a lawyer." He took the business card and examined it. "No, I'll plead guilty and accept the appropriate punishment for my action."

"For saving me." I pondered the *appropriate punishment* for murder and recalled my plan to kill Jim. Had Arthur not shot him that night, I might've fulfilled my destiny and taken the young man's place in the cell. I should scold him for hijacking my mission but also should thank him for preempting Ichiro's attempt on the priest cum preacher, whose plastic surgeon probably could turn water into wine.

"For delaying your return to God. But you can do one thing for me." He tapped the business card on the table. "I misspelled Niebuhr on my blog, please help me correct it. My password is 'demythologization.' Thank you. By the way, how's Johnny?"

"Sentenced to death."

"Didn't your super-lawyer help him?"

"Like you, he had another plan." I didn't tell him that Johnny was covering for Daisy and that love might overwhelm justice.

"After I shot Jim Whitfield and saw him fall into the stream, I wanted to turn myself in but was as tired as having written a novel, having developed a recursive estimation software, or having finalized negotiation for a merger. So I slumbered in a shack nearby and slept until the next afternoon. Do you know how that feels like?"

"I would've, but no, I lost my chance. I should say: SOMEONE stole my chance. So don't rub it in."

"I hadn't had such a deep sleep since a child. When I woke up I was delirious with fever not knowing if I'd die in the shack. I lay on the hay between consciousness and delusion waiting for death to take me to heaven or hell. I hadn't confessed to God but was too tired to."

"You could've confessed to Father Jones before shooting him. He would've loved to hear it, of course until he finds out what you've planned."

"Ah, that would have been poetical, hadn't thought about it. But, I'm not a Catholic so I don't need a priest to confess. Direct access. Anyway, when I recovered from my fever three days later, I woke up to the morning sun a new man in a new world. The evil stench of Jim Whitfield had left the world and me. I sang hallelujah and praised God. I didn't even want to turn myself in. The sparrows and crickets were calling out to me to celebrate a new day. But in the end I accepted my responsibility and entered the police station to greet the officers in the name of God." He lifted his cuffed hands and the chains jingled to match the silent melody. "When I followed Mrs. Larsen into the park, I was ready to kill the fiend. There's a time to kill and a time to heal, a time for—"

"I didn't come here to hear your confession or your exegesis. I was forced to hear Jim's sick confession but had enough already."

"And I didn't ask you here to hear my confession or exegesis either. I just want to let you know—"

"That you're a martyr?"

"That I'm not a slave."

"But perhaps a superman."

"Would I be here if I were a superman? No, only psychotics would dream of being a superman and only the greatest of them would write about them. But I couldn't be a guilty bystander—"

"Then call Jan and show—"

"I believe you're jealous."

"That you're in jail? Perhaps you should come see my cell, that is, my former cell."

"That I was one step ahead of you. But that's life. Father, you got a lot to learn about this world. A horse may win by only a nose but first prize will always be leaps and bounds more than second. And Jim had always taken first prize."

"What about the seven thousand seven hundred seventy-seven losers for every winner?"

"Rest assure, the winner's usually worse off than the losers." He patted my forearm, but when the guard grunted, he pulled back his hand.

"Very comforting."

"When George Jackson killed twenty-eight students and seven teachers with his father's 12 gauge double-barreled shotgun, Johnny saved me by taking a bullet in the arm. I wish I could do something for him but I'm not a lawyer and I don't have any money. Now, I couldn't even help comfort Daisy."

"If Daisy has a gun, she'd shoot you without blinking."

"And I'm sure Jan is a good lawyer."

"The best. But only for those humble enough not to select their own punishment." I picked up the business card, which he had dropped onto the table, and gave it to him again.

"I have nothing to prove." He took the card and scraped his chin with it.

"Except that you're just and fair, even toward yourself."

"Is that such a bad thing when we have Jim Whitfields at every corner of every street in every city winking and smirking at us?" He bent his thin lips, like a sage losing faith in his confidants, his beliefs and above all himself. "To observe robbery, rape, and murder with folded hands and crossed legs is to participate in them in spirit and action, or should I say, inaction. Any conscientious man, or woman, would rise to defend the weak and oppose the strong, and to the extend his cowardliness impeded his action, so much less is he conscientious, so much less is he a man, or she a woman. If I truly believe in life rather than death, how could I not stop a butcher from extinguishing a life?" He leaned forward as if emphasizing his point. "No, Father, I couldn't subscribe to your philosophy of detaching from the world, of permitting evil to destroy truth, goodness and beauty, while I save my soul from damnation and washed my hands of the blood of the world. No, my conscience wouldn't allow that. And you might object that my desire for good might perpetrate evil. I might but I would take responsibility for that evil and accept the punishment."

"I don't doubt your sincerity. You seek to be righteous through a fallen body, in a broken world. I've contemplated—"

"Don't implicate yourself. Save it for another time and another place and another Jim Whitfield."

"But what if you were wrong? How can we always be so sure of the boundary between right and wrong, between good and evil? And what if you're only justifying murder? How much evil has been perpetrated in the name of love, justice, decency and humanity, in the name of God? Even if not, now, Jim wouldn't have a chance to repent. He's well defined and all other possibilities for him has ceased."

"Yes, an imperfect solution for a fallen humanity in a broken world. And I'm sure you'd understand: a society of moral men would still be less than moral. So we can't hesitate. We can only accept the responsibility. Of course, no man can do that, only God can. I know. So now I'm at God's mercy as I always have been and should." His sad eyes matched his pale lips. "But by choosing my action, I chose the man I want to be. Just as I am. Better than pretending to be someone else."

"But since we're not omniscient, or even well-informed, our decisions are correct only about fifty-percent of the time. So that's as if we're rolling a dice, gambling with our as well as others' lives."

"Ha, so I'm fifty-percent decent, not too bad. Do you seek a hundred percent, Father? Do you want to load the dice?"

"If I try, I'd end up with zero-percent. Like you, I would decide and I would act, not allowing evil to breed through inaction, but I had seen enough destruction from good intentions to be skeptical. Too many decent people with good intentions ended up..." I leaned forward and stared him into his pupils. "Do you fight from becoming another Jim Whitfield?" I sensed that he would understand my fear, my struggle, and my dilemma. To fight a battle where victory would mean defeat and defeat would mean a hell on earth.

He folded his hands and closed his eyes as if in prayer. "Everyday, every second. But in a world come of age, we must not pretend to be infants and use God to legitimize our fear, cowardice and inadequacy, but carry our crosses and walk the narrow path." The tone of a warrior, more intimate with blood and scar than with milk and bread, who must battle enemies across the Gobi Dessert where sandstorms would be more lethal than bayonets.

As I was about to leave, the warden rushed in to inform us that someone had rescued Father Jones from the stream two days ago. But the DNA results arrived only a few minutes ago to confirm that he is Jim Whitfield.

CHAPTER 40

O N SATURDAY MORNING, I drove from Gilead, through Kentucky to
Charleston and arrived at the maximum-security prison beside the se-
cluded woods to visit Jim Whitfield. The West Virginian zephyr accompanied me to the barbwire fence, which in front of the guard station soared thirty feet. At the foot of the fence, near the entrance, several rust-red blotches decorated the concrete pavement. Behind the
front gate, four SG-550 rifles, two sticking out of each guarded tower,
tracked me along the cigarette-budded path. After an iron-gate and a
security scan, I entered the visitor's lobby, where pictures of the FBI's
most wanted criminals decorated the walls. I paced between window
and wall while waiting for the guard to process the previous visitor.

At the front desk, the campus map showed the inmates' cells, the
caféteria, the courtyard, and the solitary confinement chambers. After
years in his mansion and his mistresses' condos, Jim should find his
new home and neighbors stimulating, but would miss the afternoon
naps or the midnight swims or filet mignon breakfasts or cruises with
his mistresses. A more gracious man would thank Mr. Jackson for
scooping him from the stream and exchanging him for the $20,000 re-
ward. But he was probably cursing the man for neither sharing the reward nor hiring him a New York lawyer.

After learning that the preacher cum priest had taken abode in the
maximum-security facilities I slept dreamlessly until seven o'clock in
the morning, missing my personal prayer time. Arthur would receive a
lighter sentence and only have to breathe the jailhouse air for about

two years, before returning to the wasteland to hunt another Jim Whitfield or Donald Larsen or Father Jones or Edgar the mortician, in the local bank, church, school, diner or funeral home. And Ichiro, unable to slay Jim, couldn't enter hell. But having fulfilled his promise and completed his mission, he would still depart from us and enter into eternal glory. I had tried to persuade him to travel a different path, but my words before Sonya's spirit dispersed like the cherry blossoms under the wind.

Before leaving for Charleston, I phoned Camellia and urged her to seek happiness with Ichiro. To find him and prevent him from committing seppuku. But each day, Sonya's spirit seemed to tighten more and more around Camellia's emotions and Ichiro's thoughts. And selfishly, I lamented my friend's departing to an oasis.

***

The leathery-faced chubby-cheeked receptionist, having finished with the previous visitor, scanned me and said the prisoners here were as unredeemable as Hitler had been. He believed I could profit more by praying to my nonexistent God. I thanked him for the wisdom and requested to see Jim. He fumbled through the prisoner list for three minutes before disappearing through an iron-gate. Leaving me alone with the criminals' photos.

Outside the window, a guard rushed across the courtyard and spoke to his comrades in the guard station before returning to the gray building and barred windows. A legion, guards in green berets and camouflage uniforms, marched in formation to the building and aimed rifles at the front door and the windows. I hummed Veni Creator Spiritus and studied the gray path before me. In my pocket, thirty-one dollar and thirty-six cents, enough to live a month, excluding rent. Though research funding during the past decade had been drying up and this recession had choked the last morsels, I would apply for a position at Brookhaven National Lab. Still, whether working in the lab or the kitchen, the new experience, ruffling my status quo, would mold my thoughts and emotions and perhaps knead out more wisdom and compassion.

The receptionist strolled through the iron-gate and told me Jim had died. I searched his eyes and nose and lips for a twitch and waited for him to wink or wiggle his brows, but his face remained as stiff as the iron-gate behind him. I waited for the punch line and he said Jim's been murdered last night. I requested to see the body. After hesitating for a moment, he whispered through his teeth, "Castrated, bled to death."

I thought I misheard. But he repeated the words. The guards had caught a psycho-sadistic killer for murdering Jim. Though the preacher's enemies numbered more than his wine collection's labels or Donald Larsen's Ponzi scheme victims, I spotted the signature of the steel-fisted agent bent on avenging his sister. But I had expected the Simon, a.k.a. Peter, to sneak into the prison after midnight and vanquish his archenemy.

CHAPTER 41

Before leaving the maximum-security prison, I visited the carcass and discovered on its right arm a tattoo of a naked lady. As I expected, Mr. Chandler had accepted Jim's money for a final role-play and agreed to spend his remaining years with Mad-Dog Clint. Jim's ten-thousand dollars together with the twenty-thousand dollars reward would pay for an LA lawyer to defend Johnny and reward the judge for his leniency. I wanted to report the bribe but decided to give Johnny, through this imperfect solution, another chance to breathe the Gilead air.

After I found out Daisy had called in the morning and learned of the murder, I phoned her from the prison. When she didn't pick up her phone, I called Mr. Jackson to relay the news. Though he sobbed like a hungry baby, I interrupted him and requested that he visit Daisy and inform her of the dead man's real identity.

I had planned to go to Memphis the next morning to update Daisy on Jim and Johnny and to hand over the document granting her all the insurance money. But after the revelation, I left the prison in the early afternoon and sped toward Tennessee. I worried that grief might drive her over the edge. Through the light snow, over the gray landscape, my solitary car passed signs, exits, wheel covers and paper cups. Ahead, more signs, more exits, more wheel cover, more paper cups, more snow, more gray landscapes.

By evening, I arrived at the condo community and parked my car in a visitor's space. Light snow had continued to fall through the afternoon and a white carpet led me to the front entrance, where snores shook the windowpanes and front door. Through the snow curtain, as if in a dream, I saw yellow tapes sealing her condo's front door. Against the balustrade, a rotund police officer was eating donut and drinking coffee.

A chill slithered through my spine and, after recovering from the shock, I marched toward her unit hoping my intuition had deceived me. But along the arcade, beside the outdoor pool, where snowflakes were triggering ripples on its surface, Mr. Jackson stepped out of an alcove, rushed to my side and handed me an orchid-stamped yellow note. The twitches beneath his eye alarmed me as much as his dilated pupils. I hesitated for half a minute before accepting the decree from the trembling hand.

Daisy was dead.

I studied his lips and tried to understand his words, but gazed at the strange light snow, foreign outdoor pool and alien marble balconies, unsure of the street, the city or the country, or the day, the year or the century. Mr. Jackson continued to ramble but I could hear only a constant ringing, from some motor spinning in my head.

Daisy had committed suicide.

I must've stepped into the wrong universe when waking up or exiting from the car. The police officer was probably eating a muffin and drinking hot tea. But I could no longer escape from this universe, this reality, this world, where previous choices and decisions had paved the way for the light snow, the yellow tape, the police office and Mr. Jackson and his note.

I read the note from Daisy, as snowflakes splattered on the yellow paper. After she had learned of Jim's death in the morning, she cried until noon. She had a tuna sandwich and a cup of cappuccino while reviewing the past three and a half years' photos, the affair showering her with sunshine and blossoms. She remembered the first bracelet and earrings. She remembered the first time he counseled her after Johnny was expelled from the church. She remembered the first time they kissed and made love. She remembered their first cruise, to the Caribbean, frolicking on Jamaica's beaches and from the deck watching the sunset. Without him, she couldn't continue to live, the pain too great to bear even for a day. She learned true love from him and loved him enough to die for him, but since that wasn't possible, she would die with him. She thanked me for caring about her and asked me not to tell Johnny about her death. She had signed a document giving all Jim's life insurance to Camellia and wished her a happy life. She had transferred her condo and savings to my name and asked me to pay the sanatorium fees and during holidays visit her mom. She also gave detailed instructions to take care of the orchids, especially during the winter.

Under the steady snow the letters faded into blotches and the note soaked until it split in two.

I cursed Jim Whitfield.

CHAPTER 42

HEY CAPEK,

May you live a millennium, and suffer every second. May you be damned for all eternity. Your life mission is to destroy me, but you failed, letting me escape in front of your nose. Could've shot me in the face, but you just let someone else shoot me in the back.

When I woke up in the hospital, I lamented at not having killed you. Should've gotten a shotgun at the Virginia gun show. At first, thought you shot me, three times. But I remembered the shots came from the side and you were running toward me, your arms flopping in the air. Didn't know who shot me but for sure something bad was waiting for me in jail. So, I called Chandler and asked him to impersonate me one last time. Turned out really to be his last time, that poor man. This time, I asked the good plastic surgeon to help fix up Chandler a bit, so he looked more like me. I mean Father Jones, of course. Didn't care too much for that face. Anyway, a few thousand dollars was enough to have the doctors and nurses and officers look the other way. I didn't expect that Simon, a.k.a. Agent Peter, to be such a sadist. When I heard what had happened to Chandler, I swore to destroy that savage. You live in another world, a world within your head where the lion and the lamb coexist. Well, in the real world, one of them always eats the other for lunch.

You should've been contended to serve and worship me like everyone else. Didn't I give you a book for your birthday? Didn't I allow you to tie my shoes when everyone else turned their butts on you? Didn't I allow you to participate in my project and let you be the bait?

I love Charlotte and I love Camellia, more than you could ever feel in your cold heart, always thinking about enlightenment, sanctification and transcendence. Well, there's nothing except the wine, steaks, women, mansions, limousines, Mediterranean Cruises and whatever else you can enjoy now, so like some sage once said, "Eat, drink and be merry, for tomorrow, we die." You've wasted your life. But I had Camellia and I'll always have Daisy.

The first day I arrived here in Las Vegas, I got drunk and woke up in a hotel room with a prostitute. Went to a steak restaurant and ordered filet mignon and cabernet. But the steak tasted like rubber and the wine like vinegar. Well, I may be drunk in the hotel instead of sleeping with my mistresses, but not because of you. You can do nothing to me. I'll rot in these hotel rooms, near these luckless gamblers, beside these flashy neon signs, but not because of you, or Simon.

Come to Las Vegas for a duel; show that you're a man rather than a roach. Prove me wrong. Look for me in the Caesar's Presidential Suite. Here's your chance to go to hell. Probably think you'd meet me there and finish the duel. Well, I won't be there. I want to say it doesn't exist, but my hell is you. So if you kill me, you'll go there, but you'll release me from hell. How's that for irony? But come soon, before you miss your chance to live in the inferno.

Simon's here in Las Vegas, with Sylvia. And they did the drive-through marriage thing today—well, they must still think I'm dead. Even though that son-of-a-bitch tampered with my brakes and hired a thug in Moscow to try to kill me, he won't bother me after tomorrow. He may even ask you to kill him if you're kind enough to do the favor. Of course, I'm mean, so I won't help him. Anyway, the newlyweds must be celebrating old Jim's castration—would've joined them if they'd invited me—but they don't know that Sylvia will have an accident tomorrow. Some drunkard will slam his sports car into her when she goes to pick up her wedding gift. A diamond necklace from her former husband. If she's lucky, she'll be in a coma. And Simon would naturally be devastated, losing his second wife through another tragedy, having already lost his sister, his wife, and his daughter. But that's payback, things come around, not that I believe in karma. Don't bother calling the police. No need to be a nosy Samaritan. By the time you receive this letter, you'll hear it in the news while enjoying your coffee. Go to the Internet and check the local news in Las Vegas.

Simon may need your service. So come, like they say, two birds with one stone, and make the best of your trip and your gun—make sure your gun won't jam. But like I said, time's not on your side. So better seize my invitation, chance of a lifetime. Of course, you always miss your chances.

Even though Camellia and Daisy will miss me, the money they got will be enough to give them a nice life. What more could you ask for in life? I worked so hard for the past twelve years just for a decent life. But of course, I enjoyed my work too, unlike ninety-eight percent of the population.

You may have married Camellia, but I love her more than your stoic mind could ever imagine. You may have stolen her from me, but she had her best years with me. You can't make anyone happy; you just don't have it in you. Search your soul and admit it. You know it's true. You belong in the desert. You love the sand dunes more than Camellia. She could've been so much happier with me but you ruined her life, just like you ruined Charlotte's.

Take care of Daisy before she finds a good man. That fool Johnny would've been fine. But he's a fool. Still, he did the right thing. Better him than you know who. But Arthur, never. And I don't want any jocks near her. If you see someone like me coming near her, kill him and kill him quickly. I worry about her and, with a dunce like you protecting her, worry even more. I should hire a bodyguard, but I don't trust any of them.

If, big if, if you're able to kill me, take care of my dog, Mini. She eats chicken, no pork, no beef, not ever. She needs a walk in the morning and another in the late afternoon, not late morning, not noon, and not evening. She likes a lot of sun but not rain or fog, so don't take her to Seattle, or worse, London.

Look forward to seeing you, my hell, and your gun's barrel and helping you enter your hell, which is just in your mind and would vanish as soon as your weak heart stops.

Your eternal foe,
You Know Who

CHAPTER 43

Jᴵᴹ ʜᴀᴅ ʟᴜʀᴇᴅ ᴍʀ. ᴄʜᴀɴᴅʟᴇʀ ɪɴᴛᴏ ꜱɪᴍᴏɴ ᴋᴇʟʟᴇʀ'ꜱ ᴛᴏʀᴛᴜʀᴇ ᴄʜᴀᴍʙᴇʀ and deceived the insurance company. He had ridded himself of Sylvia and crushed his nemesis Simon. But the letter's tone and content revealed his total defeat and showcased a man at hope's edge, a man yearning to plunge into the abyss rather than confront defeat's looming clouds. I thought I knew the curvature and thickness and sharpness of the blade that had sliced into his flesh and the contours and lengths and roughness of the fingers that had grasped the handle. But another dagger, whose shape and size and weight I knew nothing of, had plunged through his heart. As I read the letter in my Cambridge apartment, the snowflakes outside reminded me of nobler sentiments than bitterness and hatred, of loftier ambitions than revenge and conquest. And yet, like most mortals, I savored the lingering venom between my teeth, more delicious but also more harmful than dark fudge New York cheesecake.

After reading his letter, I called the Las Vegas police department. Sylvia was in a coma after a hit-and-run. And her husband, after smashing his head through a glass door in the hospital, had been admitted into a sanitarium.

Two days later, through dancing snowflakes, I returned to Edison and found Charlotte lunching with Mr. and Mrs. Singh. The front yard's pear tree had shed its fruits and leaves, and the squirrels had disappeared from their playground. In the driveway next door, four chil-

221

dren tried to make snowballs with the scant powders. Snow had covered Perfecto Lane, but my presence had left two tracks tailing my car.

I joined Charlotte and her neighbors for lunch: curry chickpea and garlic naan. After a discussion on the health care reform, the young couple went to their front yard and played with the children.

I was cleaning the dishes and watching the snowflakes melt on the windowpane when Charlotte came beside me and blurted out the Ponzi schemer's name, which always seemed linked to some grief or misery. I rinsed the forks, the spoons and the plates, and shut the faucet.

"He cheated people of millions of dollars," she said.

"More like billions."

"I had an affair with him."

"Forget about him. He's just another con man trying to wring out as much money as possible from anyone, anywhere, anytime, anyway he can, in this modern, or rather postmodern, jungle. Survival of the fitness, nowadays not measured by physical strength, but by mental agility."

"I want you to know everything. It gives me peace and a sense of closure. He knew that his wife had an affair, actually, with Jim. What a small world. But he didn't confront her, just tried to get back at Jim by conning him of all his money. Well, he was somewhat successful and would've been more so, if the FBI hadn't uncovered his scheme. Okay, from now on, he doesn't exist."

"Now, let's talk about something I actually care about. Let's go back to Virginia for Christmas, to reminisce the good old times, as old people do." I put her arm through the bend of my elbow.

"I have a Christmas present for you," she said.

"You think we don't have Christmas presents in the monastery? Last year, I made some bookmarks—"

"And I thought you would've given your fellow monks *Beyond Good and Evil* or *Why I Am Not a Christian*, to nourish their souls."

"Actually, Father Theodore suggested studying *Being and Nothingness*."

"I'm certain you'd like this present, not everyday you could get something so special." She led me into the living room and sat on the sofa.

"I believe we already have our Christmas present." I remembered Jim's letter, the content and the tone, and couldn't refrain from smiling, as if the last snow had melted and the orioles were beginning to sing a new song.

"What are you hiding?" After studying me for a moment, she waved her hand and said, "Never mind, my present to you is better than anything you can imagine. Oh, how happy I am. You'll thank me, you'll hug me, you'll kiss me."

"Okay, I will."

"Guess what it is."

"Last time you had me guessing that birthday present from morning until evening, I ended up missing dinner and almost had to go to bed hungry, on my birthday. Talk about phobia."

"Oh, that was entirely your fault. How could you not have guessed what I was giving you? Oh, Lawrence, I should've been mad at you but I wasn't."

"For one thing, I'm not a mind reader; for another, I don't know what girls think. It's beyond me."

"Yes, that is your problem." She grabbed the picture of us at Great Falls—we were smiling into the camera while foams rumbled in the background. "Theology is not beyond you; quantum physics is not beyond you; but understanding a girl's heart is beyond you."

"That's why Jim got the girls."

"You guessed it."

"I've always known it."

"Not that, the present, I mean the present."

"Did you know? But how could you? He only wrote to me. Oh, did he write to you?"

"What're you talking about?" she said. "Who? Wrote what?"

"Jim, a letter."

"Of course not, he wouldn't dare write to me, especially after what I said to him."

"Then how did you know?"

"Know what?"

"Do you get the feeling we're doing some comedy routine that's not funny? Should I start asking 'who's on first'?"

"But we're talking about the present, not the fat and skinny comedians."

"Perhaps a redhead." I took the picture from her and lamented distant faces that had vanished through the dust of time.

"My present to you."

"I mean Jim's crushed. He's lost the will to fight."

"That's my present to you."

"But you said he didn't write to you."

"He didn't. I spat in his face."

"Are we talking about the same face?"

"The same despicable face, the face of a hyena, except with a rat's eyes and a pig's snout. He came here about two weeks ago. Guess he was on the run."

Enlightenment. I realized that in his letter, Jim didn't disclose his visit here, just as Napoleon wouldn't mention Waterloo. Only two people could defeat him, not me, not Simon, not Sylvia, but Camellia and Charlotte. I studied her sparkling eyes to search the jab through Jim's heart and discovered Waterloo.

"He wanted to see me once more before fleeing, probably to the West Coast. That was his mistake because he didn't realize I had been waiting for him, had been preparing for the ultimate blow, had been aiming at his heart, just waiting for the chance, to banish him into hell." In her excitement, she wheezed and leaned on the sofa's handle, and sweat beaded on her forehead. I sat on the sofa and held her hands and I asked her to inhale and exhale until she calmed down. I went to the kitchen and got her a glass of warm water, and after drinking several drafts, she pulled my sleeve and said, "Do you know what I did? That's my present to you. Can you guess? Oh, come on. Try it, try it. Oh, okay, I guess it's not easy for you, but it's actually very obvious."

"Thank you for your present. I don't know what you did, but it's the present my evil heart desires."

"Don't tell me you're going to repent; but it's so enjoyable. And you're not a priest anymore."

"I don't have to be a priest to repent."

"Oh, but there's no priest around."

"I don't need a priest to repent."

"But you must know what I did before you repent. Yes, you must enjoy it for a while. No, a long while, before you repent."

"You mean like enjoying adultery before facing the music?"

"Now, you're getting the point," she said. "Oh, I'm sorry. I just got carried away. I'm so happy. Yes, we must repent together even though I don't believe in your God. You wouldn't mind, would you?"

I watched her eyes shine and prayed for a few more smiles, a few more dinners, a few more moonlit nights on snowy riverbanks and a few more trips, to Times Square, Flushing Meadow Park, Mystic Seaport or Cape Cod. Afterward, the daily routines at my desk or in the laboratory would contrast with these scenes—scenes sealed into my neural network until my final departure—and elevate them into Arcadian dreams, which would drift between consciousness and unconsciousness and evade id and superego.

"We'll go to Great Falls, Bull Run, and all the places we used to go." I drained my glass and, feeling her cold hands, put a log in the fireplace and lit a flame. Maple scent, sweet but not heavy, filled the living room and reminded me of the monastery and the woods, deep in which I had marked a spot, seven feet by four feet, for my final abode. Camellia, during the candlelight dinner on Valentine's Day, had promised to write the epitaph, but not having read much poetry, suggested a haiku, one of Basho's, from a book on Ichiro's bookshelf. But he suggested a poem from Tu Fu, a sober and meticulous poet.

"I told Jim that we'd made up and that we had an affair and it was the jewel of my life, something I'd treasure forever." Charlotte finished the glass of warm water and blinked before the fireplace. "You know what, I would."

Before her face, angelic and jubilant under the dancing flame, I rubbed my face and forehead and tried to focus on the glass, unsure whether to get a hearing aid or a lemon tea or both. But she repeated her invention as if it were the second law of thermodynamics.

"Oh, you look so scared. Is it so bad to have an affair with me? It would have been nice."

"But it isn't true."

"But he believed it. You should have seen his face, that smug face crumbling like a blown bridge. Those beady eyes draining of life and vitality. I wish you could have been there to enjoy it. All the suffering would have been worth it."

The words, the sentences, the desperation, the agony, the despair from Jim's letter fitted into the jigsaw puzzle, which depicted the last thrust, the last bite, the last hiss of a pierced viper. Just as Julius Caesar had his Brutus and Napoleon his Wellington, so Simon Keller had his Jim Whitfield, and Jim Whitfield his Charlotte Gibson.

***

We drove to Virginia and visited the graves of Daphne, Charlotte's parents, and my uncle and aunt. We visited her old home but the area had been converted into a community of multilevel staggered townhouses, each unit, even during this recession, selling for close to a million dollars. Next to the community, Lee Jackson Memorial Highway rumbled with traffic and showcased a new era, where the greenback, sweeping up the coast and across the land, had redirected families, schools and churches. But Great Falls had defied history's current and, indifferent to bank bailouts, cash for clunkers, and health care reform down the river, continued to tumble on the Potomac.

"These places are only as good as the memories they invoke, but by themselves mean nothing. All we have are each other and our memories, of the laughter, of the pain, of the love, of the jealousy, of our foolish youthfulness. Not the house, not the tree, not even Great Falls." Charlotte leaned on me as the wind surfed upon the current and cut across our faces. "If we're in the Sahara, if we're in the Outback, I'd be just as happy, as long as you're by my side."

Like Daisy, she poured every ounce of laughter and tear onto her loved one, not expecting to receive a whisper in the wind; and I, like Jim, worshipping the Pareto Principle, would give twenty percent of song and lament, twenty percent of embrace and caress.

After the snowstorm, we returned to Edison for Christmas with her neighbors, and in the middle of laughter and songs, Charlotte's health deteriorated, until she was confined to the bed. Mr. Singh suggested going to the hospital, but she refused and preferred to die at home, next to the fireplace, the lone chair in the kitchen, and the pictures, of me and of the children.

***

On New Year's Day, while lying in bed, she grabbed my hand and said, "Do you think of yourself as Pilgrim in *Pilgrim's Progress*? If so, what character would I be?"

I described the loneliness after my parents had died in a car accident, and the anger toward the drunk driver who had survived with only an injured knee and a bruised forehead. Ever since, I had struggled with causality and free will and searched for immutable laws in chaotic events and for freedom in the human network.

"When I read *Narcissus and Goldmund*, I kept thinking that you are the perfect Narcissus. If I hadn't known you, I would never have believed such a person could exist."

"I wonder whether Narcissus would shoot Jim."

"I wonder whether you ever felt as Santiago did, giving all you've got to catch that marlin, only to helplessly watch it being taken from you piece by piece."

"When I renounced the priesthood, I lost my marlin, not piece by piece, but in a single swoop. Poof. But losing the goalpost, stepping into mud, passing through a rainstorm, and trying to cross a chasm, they are parts of the journey, a journey from birth to death."

I held her hand. She closed her eyes. The wind knocked on the windows but I tried to focus my attention on her features as the light cast my shadow onto her.

On Sunday, she groaned through the night, as mankind had through the rise and fall of the Roman Empire, through the Dark Ages and the Renaissance and Enlightenment past the World Wars, to the age beyond Nietzsche and Sartre. She groaned through the next day, while the sun shone on the snow, while the clouds drifted across the sky and while the earth rotated on its axis. I stayed with her, through the day and through the night, sat on that chair, poured water with that pot and ate with that fork, that spoon and that bowl. Soon, these would be my companions, as they had been hers. I gave her the drugs and she took them. I gave her the painkillers and she took them. I cooked for her and she ate her meals. I helped her to the bathroom and she urinated. I did the laundry and she wore the clean clothes. I saw her skin paled by the day. I wouldn't leave her for a moment. Even when I dozed off, I could hear her groan. I wanted to experience every moment, even though each bored into my heart. It was my obligation; it was my privilege; it was my life, someday becoming my memory. I examined all the details and etched them into my mind, so my memory would remain distinct even when my mind had clouded.

***

"What day is it?"

"Tuesday."

"I'm scared."

"I'm here."

"I'm scared I would become so delirious that I won't recognize you."

"I will be here and I will recognize you. I'll hold your hand and you'll know it's me."

"I made two cheesecakes. One is for you, I hope you'll like it. The other is for Shakti. Please don't forget to give it to Mrs. Singh."

At her request, I read Henri Nouwen's *A Letter of Consolation*. She had borscht. I ate bread. Later, I held her hand as she groaned in pain. "I'm okay." She held the picture of us at Great Falls. "Why couldn't we have known better then?"

"We were not wise enough. We couldn't think far ahead enough. Sometimes we were too focused on next month to treasure the seconds and the minutes. And sometimes we were too preoccupied with the hours and the days to see into the years and the decades. We were too preoccupied by the colors, the sounds, the smells and the sensations around us, by our feelings, moods and fantasies within us."

"This pain is real." She touched her upper abdomen.

"And yet, I could only feel a different pain, not yours. Even as I hold your hand, we're separated."

"But you share my pain, I know it because I could see it on your face. What you feel is a reflection of my pain. We're not separated."

She groaned herself to sleep and I sat by the bed and listened to her breathing, trying to feel her pain. At around midnight, I walked out of the bedroom and followed my shadow through the living room into the kitchen and made a chamomile tea, staring at the solitary chair while the minutes passed. When I returned to the bedroom, I sat on the chair and turned on my laptop. Outside, under the streetlights the snow glimmered and the reflected light, a lone beacon in the fog, cast a slender shadow onto the drape. I ignored the claw-like shadow and sipped some chamomile tea.

To prevent Ichiro from entering into his eternal glory and joining his beloved Sonya, I emailed him and informed him that, even after absorbing three bullets and soaking in the stream through the rainy night, Jim continued to pollute the air and trample on snails. I couldn't allow another heart to cease its throb, another consciousness to extinguish into darkness, another set of memories to pass into oblivion. No, I wanted to see him marry Camellia under April cherry blossoms that showered into the turquoise lake. I wanted to see their smiles against Walden Pond reflecting orange-yellow foliages. I wanted to see their children chase after yellow swallowtails among rosebushes and chrysanthemums. And they, yes, even Ichiro, would grow old, their sights diminishing, their hearings fading, their hairs graying, their fleshes emaciating, their minds dwindling. Selfish, indeed; mortal, for sure. But my search, my journey would continue in the presence of God, until the last breath.

Woe and joy to mortals who have tasted heaven, who have seen the dark night, who have encountered THOU. No eyes could gaze the midday sun; no ears could listen to the Siren's songs; no hands could touch the stove flame. But the brilliance, the sweetness, the warmth.

When I gave up all my belongings and entered the monastery, I drifted nauseous upon the sea, clouds looming overhead and waves crashing left and right, front and back. In the seven feet by five feet cell, beside the hardwood bed, I paced on the linoleum floor, a thousand *ifs* fluttering through my mind. On moonless nights, I would count the shadows of yellow birch and white oak branches shivering under starlight until a shifting fog hindered my solitary game. On October mornings, under red maple foliages, I would meditate on my heartbeats against the wind's random tunes, a chord enriching the solitary melody. I was used to buying my bread, paying my phone bills, and organizing my daily schedules but had to learn to wake up at two o'clock in the morning for laud. Not worrying about grocery, payment or other daily chores, only worrying about not buying, not paying, not organizing, not living. I went to seek meaning but lost it; I went to seek myself but lost it.

Only after four months of counting branches, of contemplating my soul, and of lusting to buy, to pay, to organize did peace greet me like a forgotten old friend. I woke up at two o'clock chanting Veni Creator Spiritus, the same yellow birch and white oak branches outside the window, the snowflakes drifting under the starlight, but a new mood, of a stranger coming home, or rather of a wanderer realizing he was at home and had been all along. Wherever I stood, I would be at the center of my home, a home without boundaries.

Only then did the pain of losing Charlotte, instead of sapping my energy, motivation and aspiration propelled me to count the rainbow's colors, to distinguish the oriole's cadence, to isolate the maple-sweet air and to filter my heart's kaleidoscopic moods. From lava's ashes, the buds of fir and spruce would drip of morning dew and thrust toward the new sun and the young sky.

When I strolled down Memorial Drive beside the Charles River, while Back Bay's evening lights reflected red, yellow and green on the watery mirror, the full moon rising behind Prudential Center would escort me past Harvard Bridge toward Longfellow Bridge. When I strolled through Haymarket pretending to buy fruits and vegetables, the same moon would trail me through the stalls of tomatoes, apples and honeydews. The pain lingered. The pain permeated my flesh, fat, and marrow. The pain flaunted bravery never sought. But now, I could love her more than ever. I held Charlotte's hand and savored an eternal moment.

I felt sad but not lonely, a new pain settling into my marrow. She was journeying to death alone as one day I must, but reconciliation bound us beyond death. A light snow outside the window danced across the courtyard and descended upon the barks, the benches and the trashcans. Celebration. As Sonya had continued to live in Ichiro, so Charlotte would in me, through memories of the mornings at Arlington Central Library, the afternoons at Washington Memorial and the moonlit nights in front of Healy Hall.

I caressed her cold hand and leaned against the side table. The picture there revived memories of our outing at Great Falls Park. We had lain on the grass. Pretending to be children, we studied the drifting clouds and looked upon the sky for a horse, a daffodil or a castle. As the clouds hovered overhead, I felt the earth moving, rotating, revolving and the false security of home, family and knowledge fled from my reveries. We discussed our fears, our hopes and our yearning for a better tomorrow. All her words, all her laughter, and all the tenderness of the tuna sandwiches returned through the picture and guarded against cliffs further down my path.

While the clock chimed in the living room, I folded her hands and pulled the blanket up to her shoulders. The snowflakes again knocked on the windowpane an anapestic beat. The wind whistled a D major tune. In the kitchen, I warmed my hands against the stove flame and chanted Veni Creator Spiritus. Next to that fork, that spoon and that bowl, and on that chair, I checked my emails.

***

Dear Lawrence,

Camellia is with me. What a joy to see her. We climbed Mount Rainier this afternoon, and on a ledge overlooking the misty chasm and the cloud-capped peaks, discussed love and lost, life and death, happiness and meaning, not that we understand any of them. The perfect spot to enter into everlasting glory, the eternal nanosecond demarcating life and death, where awaited Sonya. The ledge, the expanse and the wind were as I had imagined them; the snowflakes would substitute for the cherry blossoms, the gray heaven for the blue sky. Camellia, pristine under drifting snowflakes, did not persuade me to abandon my plan, as you probably would have, because she loves me and wants me to be happy. Not that I doubt your love for this odd fellow. The color of her eyes, the contour of her nose and the curvature of her lips again reminded me of Sonya's tragic death and incited in my stomach the familiar turbulence. But pain can deepen character, as you often said, for the man, or woman, who can direct its path. I only regret not being able to stop her from having an abortion, not allowing the baby to mature into its potential before drifting away from this world. The only question: would I sacrifice? Sacrifice immortality, eternal glory, and the beauty of not withering into a dilapidated, senile and maybe lewd but certainly grumpy old man. For her happiness. But not only hers, mine also. To accept decay, decline and decomposition. To give up immortality, eternal glory, as you would obscure knowledge and dark night. To be or not to be?

My friend, take care of yourself. And if I choose one way, take care of Camellia and allow her to take care of you. I am mailing you a reference for employment that would especially be useful if you are to apply to Brookhaven National Laboratory. May you blossom into the Lawrence of your potential.

Your friend,
Ichiro

***

I sent Ichiro the contact information of three Seattle colon-cancer specialists from Mr. Singh, and went to bed with Charlotte's photo on the nightstand. When the phone rang, I suspected Jim was calling to talk to her for the last time.

I had always feared walking into the desert, not because of its desolation but because of its dunes repetitive and endless to the horizon. Wandering through the same yellow sand, under the same burning sun, through the same sandstorms. Having abandoned my sanctuary, I would enter the desert alone, to leave in the sand endless footprints only to be obliterated by the wind, to walk the same path each day expecting the same path tomorrow, and perhaps to cease wondering at the bloom and wither of lilies only to linger for death. But no, even in the desert, I would seek a new sanctuary, to contemplate a grain of sand in a sea of dryness, and to find the man Lawrence among shadows, illusions and false lights.

Bright night surfing upon the crest of a probability wave by a Fourier transform reached Hilbert space the wilderness beyond existence the phantom space of mathematics the mirror world where a kick there would cause a jerk here through sinusoidal ripples in the uncertainty between yes and no space-time emerged from nothing to exist for a million years before returning to the void for another eternity. In the horizon of the next galaxy a positron and an electron mated and gave birth in annihilation to twin photons streaking at the speed of light toward opposite infinities to reencounter at the other pole of the space-time hydrosphere birth life decay death the cosmic cycle beyond space-time beyond matter-energy beyond I-thou beyond Alpha and Omega.

###

ABOUT THE AUTHOR

While working overseas as Project Director for a consumer electronics company, Leonard Seet came upon a parchment, which he had drafted in college after booing a novel's ending. The chicken-scratches had begun to fade, but he succeeded in deciphering the text. The writing was amateurish, but the plot had potential. So, to relieve work stress, he began rewriting the story, along the way learning the art of the trade. Several years later, he resigned from the company to write short stories and literary novels.

During the fall of 2011, Leonard enrolled in the Jennie McKean Moore Fiction Workshop at George Washington University to learn from author Tim Johnston, *Art of the Story*.

Leonard Seet is the author of *The Spiritual Life*. He writes articles for Blogging Authors. Through his writings, he probes the dynamics of existence, including human consciousness, good and evil, and rationality and spirituality.

Visit the author's blog:

http://leonardseet.blogspot.com

www.ingramcontent.com/pod-product-compliance
Lightning Source LLC
Chambersburg PA
CBHW070103260626
47160CB00004B/1291